T0171700

OF MY BLOOD

a novel by

ELLEN S. WILDS

authorHOUSE®

AuthorHouse™
1663 Liberty Drive
Bloomington, IN 47403
www.authorhouse.com
Phone: 1 (800) 839-8640

This is a work of fiction. All of the characters, names, incidents, organizations, and dialogue in this novel are either the products of the author's imagination or are used fictitiously.

Published by AuthorHouse 02/15/2016

ISBN: 978-1-5049-6169-1 (sc)
ISBN: 978-1-5049-6168-4 (e)

Library of Congress Control Number: 2015918812

Print information available on the last page.

This book is printed on acid-free paper.

Lovingly dedicated to the members of the Markland Medieval Mercenary Militia, without whose support, suggestions and low life this book would neither have been possible nor necessary.

CONTENTS

PROLOGUE

He Is Dead and Gone, Lady

He is dead and gone, lady,
He is dead and gone;
At his head a grass-green turf,
and at his heels a stone. Hamlet, Act 4 Scene 4

October 1692

The news of his death had shaken the sleepy villagers and sent curious rumors flying throughout Devon and down into Cornwall. Mad Jack Hawkwood, dead in Jamaica.

Aye, dead and gone, thought Simon as he pulled his cloak closer about him against the cooling autumn air that smelled of the sea and the wet rocks below. Simon absentmindedly stroked the neck of his horse as he stood in the lonely copse beside the small chapel. The road along the cliff stretched long and empty in both directions. There was no sound except the wind and the roar of wave against rock in the Atlantic's unwearied battle with the craggy Devonshire coast.

Simon Hawkwood was very much his father's son. He was tall with a long angled face and deep set eyes. His curled hair and trim beard were as black as the elegant velvet suit, his gaze as keen as the fine sword gleaming at his side. Every inch of Simon revealed his father's moody looks and impeccable taste.

If there was a trace of Simon's mother, no one knew it. She had vanished during Simon's early childhood, and in nearly thirty years of life Simon had never heard his father speak of her nor brook any mention of her. Simon still carried the bitter memory of lashing he had suffered when as a boy he had pressed his father too closely on the subject.

And now that same father lay dead of fever, and buried beneath the earthquake rubble of Port Royal. Simon felt no sorrow, only an unashamed curiosity about Mad Jack's legacy. So he waited on the cliffs near Hartland Point in lonely vigil.

From the road to the south came the clatter of hooves and Simon's attention focused on the three approaching riders, his fingers tightening around one pistol. The riders reined to a halt beside the chapel and a smooth low voice called, "Hallo, brother, are you there?"

Simon relaxed and led his horse from the trees. "Greetings, dearest Anne. Ready for this night's business?"

"Aye," the beautiful dark woman laughed, "ready enough."

Simon cautiously eyed her two companions, wrapped in cloaks, their faces masked by the shadows from their hats. "Your escort?"

"No risk to you, Simon," growled the big man on Anne's right. He chuckled deeply and doffed his hat in a courtly bow. He was a bearded, burly man, his dark hair and thick beard flecked with grey.

"John Ward, as I live and breathe?" Simon exclaimed. "When did you make port?"

"More than a fortnight ago," Ward replied. "'Twas I that brought the news of your poor father's death."

Simon sniffed sarcastically, "Poor father."

"Now, brother, do not talk so," Anne reproved. "He was ever fond of you."

"I will believe that when I know that I am his heir," Simon answered sourly. He turned his attention to the swarthy, mud spattered young man on the third horse.

"Eben Carr, of course," Anne said.

"I expected O'Flynn," Simon muttered.

"Aye, but I am quartermaster now," Carr replied crossly.

"Easy, Eben lad," Anne said soothingly. "No one doubts your authority." She laid a gentle hand on the young man's shoulder, a hand that he lifted to his lips with roguish gallantry. "Besides," Anne continued, "Father has left something to Eben. Or so says Lawyer Stone."

"Aye, there's a fine one to trust," Simon replied. "But let us be off then. I hope to have my fortune before the night is out." He swung into the saddle and followed his companions at a brisk trot down the long road to Bideford.

They pushed their way through the Red Cock's common room, crowded as it was with rum soaked sailors and their jaded tallywives. The ceiling was low and the room dimly lit by the lanterns that hung from the blackened beams. Everywhere was the smell of spilt liquor and sweat.

"I still don't see why we are reading the will in a tavern," Eben protested, as they climbed the narrow stairs to the quieter second floor.

"Some trick of Stone's, I'll wager," Simon replied under his breath.

"No trick at all," Anne said. "He would not risk all of us in his own home, and thought neutral ground to be safer until the will's contents be known."

"Surely he cannot think that you and I will argue over Father's property, no matter how divided," Simon replied, astonished as they crowded onto the tiny landing in front of a closed door under which shone a light.

"No, indeed not," Anne laughed. "There could be naught for us to argue. Belike, 'tis some other concern, but I could not persuade Hugo to speak of it."

As she reached for the door knob Simon pushed away her hand and paused to check his pistols' priming. He eased the door open. "You are too cautious, brother," Anne said, boldly walking past him. He stepped after her, leaving John Ward and Eben Carr to follow. The four stopped just inside the door, staring at the small group waiting within.

The room was furnished with a long oak table and several chairs whose velvet cushions were frayed and worn. The windows were covered with oiled paper and an old rag rug lay on the wooden floor. A cheery fire burned on the small hearth and candles in pewter lamps added a little light to the table.

Seated at the head of the table was a small, white wigged gentleman with the face of a kingfisher. His spectacles were carefully balanced on his beakish nose and through them he peered sharply at several papers before him. He looked up at the newcomers, a crinkled smile slowly stretching his small mouth.

To the right of Hugo Stone sat an elegant lady of indeterminate years, her maternal features and blue eyes framed by soft fair curls and a black silk veil. The unrelieved black of her mourning attire accentuated her delicate build and pallor.

Beside her sat a boy of perhaps fifteen years, his black velvet suit in stark contrast to the stiff white collar of his shirt. He, too, was pale, fair haired and blue eyed, his face betraying his age with its smooth skin broken by a few small pimples. He was not a particularly attractive boy, his expression a mixture of disinterest and disdain, his nose turned up as though there were a bad smell.

Across from him sat another youth, a year or so older. He wore a kilt of Scots tartan, the plaid swept up from behind and pinned to the shoulder of his dark woolen jacket. He was less pale than the other boy, his hair auburn and his cheeks ruddier. Along his chin was the slight beginning of a beard. His cap lay on the table in front of him, one small white feather and a sprig of heather adorning its band.

Hugo Stone arose and walked swiftly to greet the new arrivals. "Dear Anne, how lovely you look!" he said as she submitted her cheek to his avuncular kiss. "Simon, I was hoping you would not be detained," the lawyer said as he grasped Simon's hand in an oily handshake.

"If it would serve you better to see me so, then I am certain I should not be here tonight," Simon answered coldly, pushing past the lawyer. "Let us sit, sister."

Unperturbed, Lawyer Stone extended his hand to John Ward who responded warmly. Eben gave only a curt nod as he passed by on his way to the table. Anne had taken a seat beside the pale youth, Simon took his beside the Scot. John Ward and Eben Carr sat together further down to the left. Eben immediately sank low in his chair, pulling his hat down over his eyes, thus gaining a most disapproving stare from the strangers at the table.

"I believe we are all here now," Stone said briskly.

"Indeed, Hugo," Simon remarked, "there seem to be a good deal more of us than I expected." Anne nodded in silent agreement, the glow of the braziers catching the sheen of her ebony hair coiling down over her black bodice.

"Ah, yes," Stone said slowly. "I suppose some introductions are in order." He coughed nervously, shifting his weight. "Your dear late father was somewhat less than thorough in that regard." Uneasy glances passed between the two groups of strangers. "Starting then with those who have just arrived, may I present Mistress Anne Hawkwood, the late captain's daughter." The young woman nodded at the strangers, her jet eyes studying each reaction. "And across from her we have Master Simon Hawkwood, the captain's eldest son." Simon gave a quick tilt of his head, his lips pressed firmly. "Next to Master Simon is Captain John Ward, the deceased's business associate of many years." Ward gave a small salute. "And lastly may I present Mister Eben Carr, quartermaster aboard the Chanticleer, another long time associate of the departed Captain Hawkwood." The shaggy haired, lanky youth gave no sign of greeting, but merely shifted in his chair and propped a muddy boot on the table.

Stone paused hesitantly, his fingers slipping inside his black coat. "If you have need of a pistol, Hugo," Simon said, "let me assure you that I carry a brace of them with me." Hugo's hands jerked away from his coat, his smile broadening.

"No need at all, Simon. No need at all." Again the lawyer paused, then turned to the black veiled lady. "May I present to you Mistress Margaret MacDonald Hawkwood, your late father's widow."

A sudden stiffening shuddered through Simon and Anne. Eben shifted his boot along the table to clear his view of the veiled lady. "Father never mentioned another wife," Anne challenged quietly.

"Nevertheless, 'tis true," the lady replied briskly in a thick Scots accent. "I have been wife to him for nigh sixteen years now." She patted the hand of the pale youth. "This is my son by him, Jamie Maclain Hawkwood." Simon's face darkened, his scowling eyes boring deep into the boy. Jamie, for his part, stared back resolutely, his expression indignant.

Anne directed her attention to the other Scot. "Knowing my father's propensities in the joys of the flesh, am I to assume that this is yet another of my brothers?"

The young man blushed and shook his head. "Nay, lady. I am no son of the late captain, but a nephew of Margaret MacDonald here. I came here to live with her and my cousin Jamie."

"I trust that someone in your past has seen fit to give you a name," Anne said lightly. "To call you nephew of my late father's widow seems impersonal to say the least."

"I am called Tristan," the youth replied with a shy smile. Then he added, "Tristan MacDonald of Glencoe." The name brought a trace of bitterness to his voice and an awkward silence followed.

Simon continued to stare at his newly acquired younger brother. "There always seems to be more kin to acknowledge when the will of a rich man is read," he said acidly.

"Are you challenging my birthright?" Jamie demanded.

"No more than you would challenge mine," Simon replied.

"Brother, I pray you," protested Anne. "I do well recall our father's sense of humor and it may well be that he had nurtured this final jest, lo, these sixteen years just so that he might be amused at the gates of Heaven." She smiled with supernal impishness.

"Heaven my arse," Eben muttered, flinching as Ward jabbed him hard in the ribs.

"So," Anne continued, "before we start challenging one another, let us have Hugo read the will and see if there is aught to challenge."

"Well spoken, Mistress Anne," Stone said with relief. He drew from a sheaf of papers a single yellow parchment covered with fine black lettering and signed with an elaborate flourish. Adjusting his hinged spectacles, Hugo Stone squinted at the writing and then read slowly the last will and testament of the late Captain John Hawkwood.

CHAPTER ONE

The Famous Flower of Serving Men

My father built me a shady bower
and he covered it over with primrose flowers;
The finest bower I ever did see,
My aged father he built for me. folksong

"Father must have been a very strange man indeed," Jamie remarked as he, his mother and cousin jounced along in the hired carriage bound for the Hawkwood estate. The morning sun shone brightly on the rough road and the air was cool with the waning of the year. They had left the seeming comfort of Bideford's narrow streets for the wild empty land along the rocky shore.

"Aye," agreed Tristan. "Imagine, leaving all the money to Simon, a ship to Anne, another ship to his partner, a sword and coin to that odd quartermaster, then making you heir to all the house and land. I'd say you did well enough."

Jamie gave a sour laugh. "And I canna sell it in any part. I must suffer my kin and any they desire for company to be quartered there -- all to maintain the family trade."

"And dinna forget that you must keep the 'family retainer' till he drops," Tristan chuckled. "What was his name?"

"Diggory Larsen," Margaret said. "And Lawyer Stone has told me that the old man is in fine health and has served the family faithfully for many years, so dinna be making fun of him."

"Mother, did you know of these other Hawkwoods?"

"I surely would have told you, Jamie, if I had known." Margaret sighed, then said, "I was only once at the Rookery, and that after your father had stolen me from the clutches of his patron, Lord Golding." She daintily pressed a lace edged handkerchief to her cheek. "We were at the Rookery for but a few days, then he bundled me into a ship and took me back to Scotland where we were married. He charged me no to return here until I was sent for and that time was no to come until his death." She paused thoughtfully. "I do remember a little girl on the estate. All black eyes and hair she was, and pawky for her four years. I suppose that must have been Anne."

"She has grown into a fine and gentle lady," Tristan said with a wistful smile.

"She has a good dowry now," Margaret added. "A ship such as the Chanticleer will no doubt draw a host of suitors."

"And will it no matter that her mother was some dockside tart?" Jamie asked crossly, staring out of the carriage window.

Margaret frowned. "Anne is no bastard, no matter her mother. Your father was always careful with his children. True, he preferred his legitimate progeny, but you may find, my son, that he was nigh as fond of his bastards. Lawyer Stone said that the captain searched for them in all the ports, gave them education or decent work. You, with Anne and Simon, are the legitimate inheritors, and 'tis your good fortune that you were preferred o'er your elder brother."

"He could contest the will," Tristan ventured.

"I think not," Margaret said. "Lawyer Stone assured me that neither Simon nor Anne would deviate from the terms of the will, if we will but keep to the conditions and no interfere with their commerce. He also hinted that there would be grave consequences should we tamper with that commerce. 'Tis after all the source of our fortune and 'twould be foolish to put an end to that."

"But now I have a house and land that I canna sell and can ill afford to keep," Jamie answered, turning back to her. "Am I to be dependant on such as Simon for my livelihood and leisure?"

"You really dinna like your brother, eh?" Margaret said.

"My brother doesna like me."

"Indeed," Tristan observed, "I dinna think your brother has much liking for anyone. Never have I seen a man with such a black look o'er his good humor."

"'Tis like their father, the pair of them," Margaret remarked. "Anne and Simon have the black looks outside and in from the Captain. It has always been a great blessing to me that you, Jamie, took none of that from him." She put a gentle hand on her son's shoulder. "'Twould be best to learn to live with your kin in peace."

"'Twas no in my plans to have more kin than I have now," Jamie muttered.

"Then your plans must alter to accommodate them," his mother answered firmly. "'Tis their good trade that will keep us all, and for them we will keep the house in good order."

Jamie again looked out at the Devonshire countryside. "I canna wait to see it," he said gloomily.

In the great house on the cliff Anne paced the thick carpet angrily. "Damn that Hugo for a rogue!" Anne said wrathfully. "No warning at all. This situation changes everything."

She sat with her brother, John Ward and Eben Carr in the Rookery's great hall. Ward and Carr were wrapped in their cloaks, ready to depart.

"How much do you think they know?" Ward asked, pulling on his hat.

"Simon and I discussed that last night. There is no way to know until they get here and we can sound them out." Anne drank deeply from the beaker in her hand. "God's truth, I would not trust that cherubic widow for all the chocolate in New Spain. And as for that pasty faced puppy of a son -- well, I have yet to see any sign of my father there."

"Aye, he has none of the coloring nor the temperament," Ward agreed.

"You and Eben had best return to the ships. We will send word when it is safe to unlade *The Bold Cockerel.* As for the Chanticleer, dock her in Bideford and keep quiet. It may take a day or two before we can be sure of the cove." Anne settled back in her chair.

"And how shall we be sure?" Simon asked tensely. "After all, that puppy as you call him, is now heir and owner."

Anne smiled disarmingly. "Simon, you know as well as I that there is a great difference between ownership and possession."

Jamie was not sure what he had expected of his newly inherited property. It certainly was not what he found upon his arrival at the Rookery. "Mother," he whispered in awe as they drove through the tangled jungle of a garden and got their first glimpse of the house, "that is without doubt the ugliest house I have ever seen."

"Well," Tristan said, "it certainly is -- defensible."

Jamie merely nodded as he stared at his inheritance. The house was a large structure best described as an architectural monstrosity, combining all the worst identifying features of its history and previous owners. The original edifice was early fifteenth century, built upon ruins of unknown function. To the small square keep had been added another taller tower and two Tudor wings, with further modifications made by a defense-minded Hawkwood during the civil war a generation ago. The ruined outbuildings, like the high stone parapets and gunports, served as the charred and tumbled reminders of those Hawkwoods who had loyally supported the ill-starred Charles the First.

Everywhere there was wild growth and disarray. Masses of ivy reigned supreme and no effort had been made to control the weeds and thick undergrowth. What few tools there were lay scattered and rusting against crumbled walls and toppled statuary.

"If Father was such a gentleman, how could he allow his home to fall into such a sorry state?" Jamie asked.

Margaret shook her head in bewilderment. "'Tis no as I remember it. When he did come to Oban he was always finely clad and mannerly, such as any man you might meet at Court. Perhaps being at sea so much in his last years he had no time to care for his property here."

"Well, I shall have a word with the servant man about this," Jamie announced as their coach drew to a stop on the cracked cobblestones before the wide front door. The three Scots alighted. The hired driver handed down their chest and then drove away down the long tree-arched lane.

Within the large door was another smaller door and it was the smaller door that opened as they approached it. Through it stepped a bald, wrinkled little man with a toothless jaw and a hideous scar that ran from his left temple down to his neck. From his right ear dangled a gold ring that he fingered itchily. His shabby woolen trousers and frayed shirt were much spotted and streaked. Around his waist he wore a red sash with a tattered gold fringe and in his right boot could be seen the hilt of a dagger.

"A fine day to ye all," he said in a thin cracked voice.

"Who are you?" Jamie asked bluntly.

"Diggory Larsen, young master."

"You are Diggory Larsen! The -- the servant?"

"Aye, young master. Welcome to the Rookery." Larsen gave a crooked smile and stepped back inside the door. "Come in and bring your fine family with ye."

Jamie entered first, his hand protectively on his sword hilt. Margaret followed, shivering slightly in the dark interior. Tristan came last, dragging the chest through the door where Diggory took it from him. "Master Simon and Mistress Anne are waiting for ye in 'ere," the servant said, pushing open the door on the left. "I can shift the chest alone."

The door opened into a large dark foyer. On the right a wide wooden staircase curved up to the upper floors. On the left the double doors opened into the great hall, a room which was in sharp contrast to the house's exterior. The warm light of the fire and the two braziers danced on the rich surfaces of polished wood and heavy velvet hangings. Magnificent tapestries covered the walls and gilt carvings shone from the ceiling beams. Over the mantel hung the family device of a black kestrel, the motto below, *Of My Blood, For My Blood*. On the far left was a cabinet filled with fine glassware and above it the wall was adorned with all manner of weapons -- swords, daggers, muskets, pistols -- some old and rare, others exotic. Treasures glittered from every corner. There were carved ivory and jade pieces, huge silver bowls and gold salvers. Jamie's eyes opened wide at the vision of wealth that was now his.

Anne sat in a huge carved chair by the wide hearth, the silver beaker in her hand throwing gleaming lights around her. She had doffed her mourning attire and now wore a splendid dress of rose velvet and gold lace, the full spreading petticoats brushing over the thick Persian carpet beneath her feet. Across from her stood Simon, leaning against the great stone mantel, his black suit accentuating the tired lines of his gaunt face. He puffed his pipe, studiously ignoring the three who stood by the door.

"Welcome," Anne said, rising regally. "Welcome to your new home."

"You'd almost think it had been left to her," Jamie whispered to his cousin as Margaret moved forward to accept the chair offered to her by Anne.

"I hope you will all be very happy here," Anne said, handing Margaret a goblet of wine.

"Indeed, you seem to be quite at home," Jamie remarked.

"We grew up here, Simon and I," Anne answered. "'Tis here that we come between our travels and 'tis here that our many business associates come when there are matters of trade to discuss. Father was, as you know, heavily involved with shipping -- foreign and domestic goods, their transfer and delivery. We also play at the Bourse, gambling with stocks. These activities require many contacts as you can well understand."

Jamie strode across the room and said flatly, "Trade doesna interest me." Anne and Simon exchanged a subtle smile. "If you travel so much, am I to take it then that you will no be staying?" Jamie asked boldly, his eyes on Simon.

Simon slowly tilted his beaker, watching the dark red wine flood against the shine of the silver. "I have no idea. I shall be here for a time while Hugo Stone sorts Father's papers and arranges the payment of my allotted portion."

"Tristan, do come in and have a glass with us," Anne invited, extending a cordial hand to the youth who remained by the door. "How careless of us to forget you!"

"Aye, indeed, lad," Margaret said, turning to him.

"I had thought you Hawkwoods would rather I leave you to get better acquainted," Tristan answered shyly, but he joined them by the fire, accepting wine from Anne and giving her a grateful smile.

"To our good King William, long may he reign," toasted Anne.

"To the King," answered Simon. That not one of the Scots raised a glass nor drank the toast was not mentioned by the elder Hawkwoods, but neither was it overlooked.

"Have our rooms been prepared?" Margaret asked, breaking the tense silence. "The ride from Bideford has tired me."

"We took the liberty of selecting your rooms last night," Anne answered. "If you find that you desire some other, arrangements can be made after supper. Margaret, I have given you Father's apartments."

"'Tis most thoughtful of you, my dear," the older woman replied. "I hope that they are not too far off should I need to call a servant."

"Those rooms adjoin mine," Anne answered, "so if there is aught you need, I will be within easy calling distance. It will, of course, be necessary for you to pass through my rooms to reach yours, but I do not mind."

"You are most kind," Margaret said.

"As for Jamie and Tristan, I believe the quarters in the east wing will be to their liking," Anne continued. "'Tis more private, that wing -- better for lads with the passions of youth, if you do understand me."

Margaret's light laughter brought a blush to her son's pale cheek. "I do well understand," she giggled. "Like his father he'll be, no doubt."

"Where is Simon staying?" Jamie asked curtly.

Simon slowly turned at the mention of his name and fixed the boy with a cold stare. "My rooms are in the west wing," he answered dryly, "overlooking the cliff."

"Is that old man the only servant?" Tristan asked.

"Certainly not," Anne said with surprise. "Poor old Diggory would be hard pressed to manage a large estate such as this by himself."

"As the grounds well demonstrate?" Jamie suggested.

Anne nodded. "I fear Diggory was a far better sailor than he is a groundskeeper. Father could not bear to set him on the streets when his day at sea was done and so let him stay on here. He manages well enough for our needs. We also have a cook and a scullery slut who have their rooms above the pantry, and there is a serving girl named Angharad who will see to the chambers. And you lads are not to tamper with her," Anne cautioned sternly, turning to Jamie and Tristan. "She is just fifteen years old and we had trouble enough finding such as she. You can spend your lusts elsewhere."

"Good cousin," Tristan cooed, "how could you be suspecting lads such as our good selves?" He traded a merry grin with Jamie.

"Perhaps I have been too long in the company of men," Anne answered, "and spent too much effort to be accepted as a lady. I can't say there's a one outside my kin that I respect o'er much when it comes to his regard for women."

"You were with Father much?" Jamie asked, leaning forward and staring at her earnestly.

"Aye," she nodded. "I sailed with him from childhood."

"A strange life for a little girl," Margaret commented, "and surely it wouldna be the most healthy for a lass of fortune and marriageable years."

"I've managed well enough and none would dare cross Father." Anne stared into the fire. "He took me all over the world and showed me everything that is in it ... India, the Indies, the Orient, the Barbary Coast, the Americas. Rare and wonderful places."

"But was there no danger in all this?" Tristan asked.

"Of course," Anne said, "but there is danger on land as well. Oh, I have been in battles -- with the Spaniards, the French, with savages and blackamoors. I learned to fight and," she looked at the two younger men as she anticipated the next question, "I have killed one or two who tried to do me harm. It was exciting and the risks are no greater than those of being robbed and murdered by some nefarious highwayman on any English country road."

Simon laughed uncomfortably. "Aye, the country abounds with the blackguards since our victories against the French."

"What will you do with the ship Father left you?" Jamie asked, his casual tone belied by the gleam in his eyes.

"Why, the same as before," Anne answered, puzzled. "I have had charge of the Chanticleer for over three years now."

"'Tis too great a responsibility for a woman," Jamie chided.

"Aye, but I have been elected and have good officers that are respected by the crew."

"Is the Chanticleer large? Is she armed?" Tristan asked.

Anne looked at him in surprise, then laughed. "No, not large. She's a Dutch built merchant ship of some two hundred tons. She carries ten six pounders on her lower deck and two swivel guns above."

"And what do you use her for?" Tristan asked.

Anne traded a quick glance with Simon, then said, "Why, to take merchandise to neighboring ports. the Bold Cockerel is a huge frigate and takes time to unlade, so it is often more expedient to let the smaller vessel manage the short trips to Bristol, Holland and the like."

"And does Simon go with you?" Jamie asked pointedly.

"I detest travel by water," Simon answered acidly. "My greatest fear is that when I die I will find myself on the banks of the river Styx and must cross water to exchange one miserable world for another."

Anne settled back comfortably into the cushions on her chair. "Simon is a great asset to our trade despite his dislike for the sea. He was Hugo Stone's clerk for many years and from him learned about contracts and transactions, and playing the stock market."

"So you like to gamble?" Margaret asked with a delighted smile.

"Aye," Simon answered, his voice warming. "I gamble with most anything and anyone, but I seem to have better luck with stocks than with cards or dice."

Jamie frowned. "Let us leave this topic. As I said, trade doesna interest me."

"And what does interest you, Jamie?" Anne asked, her eyes narrowing.

"I find philosophical pursuits of more value," Jamie answered, wrinkling his short nose haughtily. "Philosophy, religion, politics -- those be meaty topics worthy of a gentleman's conversation."

"Aye," Simon sniffed, "and like to end you in a duel over some trivial matter that no man can know the truth of in this life."

Margaret sighed daintily. "Jamie has the finest education and has shown a keen grasp of debate, often bettering his tutors."

Anne smiled slyly. "Well, I think we can all be proud of Jamie's fine intellect, but 'tis also true that all he has had over the years has been in some measure paid for by the less refined matter of trade. 'Tis our trade, sweet Jamie, that gives you the leisure for your educated pursuits."

To this Jamie could merely nod uncomfortably.

That evening, after the new master and his family were settled into their rooms and had enjoyed a splendid meal, Jamie and Tristan wrapped their cloaks around them and went for a stroll along the cliff's edge beyond the house. Below them, barely visible in the waning light, was fine stretch of smooth sand bordering a little cove. The cliff face was pocked with crevices and small caves, dotted with scrubby vegetation clinging tenaciously to the rocky wall.

"Do you think there is a path down?" Tristan asked, leaning giddily over the edge. "'Tis a long fall should one miss his hold."

"Aye, there must be a path," Jamie answered. "Mother said she and Father departed on his ship and 'twas from this cove they sailed." They walked further along the cliff, looking for a path. "You were over much interested in that ship of my sister's," he chided.

"Aye, that may be," Tristan replied, "but it wouldna harm us to keep such a vessel in mind should something go awry."

"Nothing will go awry," Jamie said. "And I doubt if my sister would interrupt her schedule for such a venture as ours."

"She is no of the faith?"

Jamie shook his head. "If she and Simon have any faith at all, 'tis no ours. Soon enough they'll see that Mother is a Catholic. She ne'er could keep it to herself. How we'll manage then is up to God."

"God and your lawyer," Tristan added with a grin. The light was fading fast. The house was little more than a great grim shadow behind them. "Will Lionel come soon, do you think?"

"I canna tell," Jamie answered. "The Navy patrols are thick since the French defeat at La Hogue. He may not be able to get through." He stopped and looked out over the ocean, then turned back toward Tristan. "We'll no find the path in the dark. We'll have another look in the morning."

They started to walk further along the cliff, but skidded to a halt as a figure leapt up in front of them. "Evening to ye, young master," Diggory's cracked voice said. "Mistress Anne sent me to look for ye."

"Oh?" was all Jamie could say.

Diggory came forward and seized each boy by the arm in a grip that was a painful surprise from a man so small and old. "She bid me warn ye not to be out along the cliff after dark."

"We can well take care of ourselves," Tristan said.

"Oh, surely ye can," the servant creaked, his scarred smile hideous in the failing light, "but these rocks be treacherous footing when night comes. Not safe for unwary lads. Best to stay in after dark." He pulled his charges toward the house, his grip never slackening.

"If 'tis so dangerous then what may I ask are you doing out here?" Jamie demanded pertly.

"Why, I be looking after ye, young master." Diggory's toothless gums twisted into a leer and the last of the light made an evil gleam along his scarred face.

Another thing that Jamie learned on that first day was the fruitlessness of arguing with his dark and lovely sister. Anne heard his lengthy objection to the restrictions placed on him and his cousin, then replied with irritating calm, "Jamie, in spite of your overlordship of this house, as long as you are in your minority you will abide by whatever ruling is agreed between your mother, Simon and me. I think you will find upon discussing this with your mother that she shares that opinion. Henceforth, you and Tristan will stay away from the cliff and cove after sunset. You have the freedom to come and go as you please at all other times, and indeed, your apartments have a private entrance that will allow you any company you wish at any hour without disturbing the household, but," Anne's shadowy eyes narrowed and he could sense a cold power in her, "if you are caught again near the cliff or on the sand below at any time after sunset, I will have you whipped to within an inch of your life. I have far more weighty matters to concern me than the safety and whereabouts of two canting cullies. Do I make myself clear?"

Drawn up to her full height, her fist clenched, her eyes glaring, there was no doubt in Jamie's mind that she meant her threat, every word.

"Will your mother be joining us?" Anne asked as Jamie entered the great hall where a table had been set for breakfast.

"She asked Angharad to bring a tray to her rooms," Jamie replied as he took a seat near the fire and watched Anne pour his cup of tea. "Tristan has wandered off somewhere. He was gone when I rose."

Simon strode in, stopping short at the sight of Jamie, then took a seat at the far side of the table. "Good morning," he muttered.

"I was intrigued by your professed interest in matters philosophical," Anne said, looking intently at her younger brother. "'Tis rare to find a Hawkwood with no love of business."

Jamie glanced up at her, then at the silent Simon. "Mother told me that once Father's family had no trade at all, and were deeply involved with politics and matters of faith." He cut a slice of ham and layered it on a piece of bread.

"You are referring to the past generation," Anne said, "and you are correct. Father's family was loyal to the king and fought hard to save him from the scaffold. They failed, of course, but 'twas not for lack of effort." She selected an apple from the richly embossed silver bowl in the center of the table.

"Then why have you suffered his son to be replaced by a Dutch usurper?" Jamie asked, bracing for the debate.

"Because," Simon answered as he spread butter on a slab of bread, "although we have no love for Dutchmen, Whigs and presbyters, we have even less love for papists and their Romish plots."

"King James tolerates all men's faiths," Jamie countered.

"His most recent declarations have been less than tolerant," Anne pointed out quietly, carefully slicing the apple.

"He is the king," Jamie argued.

"Was the king," Simon countered. "William of Orange is king now." He poured himself a cup of tea.

"And are we to be a people that changes sovereigns as we might a dirty shirt -- killing or disposing any who displease one small fanatical faction?"

"Why not?" Simon shrugged. "The Scots have been doing it for centuries."

Jamie's face flushed hotly and Anne held up her hands for peace. "Brothers, please."

"Have you no loyalty?" Jamie demanded, ignoring her.

Simon jerked forward, his dark eyes piercing. "Aye, little brother. The Hawkwoods have never lacked for loyalty. Our grandfather died at Naseby defending saintly Charles the First. His two elder sons fled to Holland and died in exile. Grandmother had but our father left and he was only a child. They struggled and starved to hold this house from Lord Protector Cromwell and in the end had nothing but this house left. All this because the Hawkwoods were loyal Englishmen who fought to defend their king and the English church."

"And what are you loyal to now?" Jamie asked, sitting back with a victorious smile. "Grandfather, grandmother, uncles. They are all past and dead. What of you -- and Anne? What are you loyal to?"

Simon turned away from his brother's smug smile and said, "You would like me to say that we are loyal only to money and our leisure. That after the years of struggle and hardship, we feel entitled to our reward of a rich life with no deep burning issues to cloud our bright future gambling on the markets. Then you can call us hypocrites, no better than the radicals who take the land of the bishops and papists, and while singing God's glories, keep all for themselves." Simon paused and smiled, leaning back in his chair and fondling his tea cup. "Well, you are right. We are loyal to ourselves only, to the betterment of our family. Our time of self-sacrifice ended over thirty years ago. We nearly lost everything in the civil war, and for what? A king who was badly advised and blind to the realities of the religious and political forces in this land, in Scotland and in Ireland. King James is no better, and as long as King William does not interfere with us, we will not interfere with him."

"'Tis a great pity to see such a noble minded ancestry debased by such as you, Simon Hawkwood," Jamie said hotly.

"Now, really, Jamie!" Anne protested.

"Whole families -- even little bairns -- are driven out to starve so that their land might be given to Whig favorites. What answer have you for them? And what of the clans whose only crime is loyalty to their anointed king in their own country? What of Glencoe?"

Anne spoke quickly, her words cutting off Simon's angry reply. "Jamie, we are not cruel people. I feel keenly at each reported injustice. And I am not altogether opposed to a restoration of James Stuart as king -- provided he embraces the English faith. But 'tis not in our best interest to involve ourselves with unpopular and controversial causes such as those of which you speak. There is, after all, little that we can do and we firmly believe that these unhappy matters are best left to the Crown. The King and his advisors are far better able to deal with the tide of fanaticism and to balance the several factions. Peace is a long, slow, painful process."

"And while you wait for it, how many more will die?"

"I do not know, Jamie," Anne replied with steady calm, "but as long as I am not among them, 'tis truly not my concern."

CHAPTER TWO

YE JACOBITES BY NAME

Ye Jacobites by name,
Your faults I will proclaim,
Your doctrines I maun blame,
You shall hear, you shall hear ... folksong

"Lionel," Jamie called softly, "caite a bheil thu?"

"Tha me an seo." Two cloaked and hooded figures stepped from the thicket beyond the east wing and hurried to the door that Jamie held open for them.

"Failte," Jamie greeted, then looked puzzled. "Co tha e?" he asked, indicating the burly older man who accompanied Lionel MacAlister.

"Tha Nicholas MacBride," Lionel answered.

"Dia dhuit," MacBride greeted.

"Dia's Muire dhuit," responded Jamie, shaking MacBride's hand warmly. "Indeed, sir, I have heard much of you. My apartments are on the next floor." The two visitors followed him up the narrow stone stairs to the heavily curtained chambers above. The stairs ended at a small landing. To the right a corridor led to other chambers within the house and in front of them an open door led into a warm sitting room, beyond which could be seen two small bed rooms with rumpled sheets and clothes strewn on the floor.

Inside, the visitors threw off their cloaks and stretched their chilled fingers over the coals in the small fireplace at one end of the room. MacBride was a short, heavyset Irishman with powerful arms and a weathered face. His hair and beard were thick, brown with a slight frosting of grey. His eyes, from within the lined pockets of flesh surrounding them, studied the well furnished room. His manner betrayed him as an old soldier ill-accustomed to great houses, curtained beds with silk sheets and velvet cushions.

Lionel MacAlister was many years younger, a slim handsome Scot with light brown hair and beard. His eyes were the color of steel and sparkled with some unspoken inner merriment. Far from being awed by the fine appointments, he settled himself comfortably in a chair by the fire, threw one leg over the arm and said, "Well, Jamie, you've no done badly for yourself. If the lads in Kintyre could but see you now, eh?"

"'Tis a fine house your father left you, to be sure," MacBride said, taking the chair opposite Lionel's.

"Generous, but ugly," Jamie commented with a laugh as he dragged a table from its place next to the wall and positioned it in the midst of the chairs by the fire.

"'Tis better than the huts that my people in Connemara inhabit," MacBride responded. There was a hesitant pause.

"Is Tristan here with you?" Lionel asked.

"Aye," Jamie nodded. "He'll be up here in a moment or so."

"Gle mhath," Lionel laughed, "for I have brought some brandy that will be his delight and his downfall."

"'Tis a wonder to me, MacAlister, that you do profess the stern faith of the presbyters while indulging yourself as freely as any Catholic," MacBride said with a gruff chuckle.

"'Tis because Lionel was ne'er one to let faith interfere with pleasure." They turned to see Tristan enter. "I have checked through the house, Jamie, and all are abed as they should be. We'll no be disturbed." From beneath the pile of cloaks Lionel retrieved a bundle and handed it to Tristan. "De tha seo?" Tristan asked.

"Brandy," Lionel answered proudly. "I smuggled it from France with you in my thoughts every step I carried it."

Jamie produced four glasses from a large inlaid cupboard at the far end of the sitting room and the French brandy was handed around. "And did you find aught in France -- besides brandy?" Jamie asked as he drew up a chair next to Tristan's.

Lionel shook his head and MacBride looked grim. "Dinna be looking for aid from the French anytime soon. There's no much left to them after La Hogue," Lionel said.

"Their ships were burnt," MacBride explained, "and whatever is remaining of their men haven't got the spirit to try again so soon."

"So we are to endure another winter of Dutch Billy," Tristan said bitterly.

"Perhaps," MacBride said. "Perhaps not. William is still in Holland and who knows when he will be returning." He sipped the brandy and smiled. "But when he does, would it not be to our advantage to be ready for him?"

"Then you did find the guns!" Tristan exclaimed.

"Aye, but not in France." MacBride took another slow sip. "Sure and if this isn't fine brandy."

"Sabhaile Dia sinn, MacBride, dinna be teasing us!" Jamie pleaded. "Where did you find the guns?"

"Spain, my bhuachail, Spain." The old soldier grinned.

"'Tis true, Jamie," Lionel said. "While I was running all over France trying to find such aid, and meeting only with one tale of defeat after another, this old man makes a single jaunt to Spain, has a word or two with some lads from Limerick, then fetches back to me with the news that there'll be a ship of arms ready to sail in a month."

"And so you will be needing the cove?" Jamie said.

MacBride nodded. "Aye, lad. My bargain with the Spaniards did not include navigating through the islands in bad weather. 'Tis too much risk. And a Spanish vessel in Scottish waters? Since La Hogue the seas are full of French privateers and Royal Navy patrols looking for them. We must stow the weapons here and smuggle them north as best we can."

"And when we have armed the islands and the clans inland loyal to the Stuart, who will lead us?" Jamie asked.

MacBride stared thoughtfully at his glass before answering, "I think you can safely wager that it will not be the king himself." Lionel nodded in agreement.

"Then who are we to fight for?" Jamie demanded.

"His son," Lionel answered softly, sadly. "The king is lost, Jamie. There is no Dundee to urge him on. The Boyne was an ignoble rout, La Hogue a disaster of inestimable proportion. The king, I think, fears to die as did his father, on the block at the hands of a Whiggish mob. He'll no be back again. It is for Prince James Edward that we must fight."

"But not in the field," MacBride cautioned. "There must be no pitched battles, no head to head encounters. Small bands of trained armed men could harry William's soldiers for years and never give him a moment's peace."

"We would ne'er win that way," Tristan protested.

"Aye, lad, but neither would we lose."

"But God is on our side and will protect us!" Tristan said.

MacBride sighed heavily. "When I was your age God was on my side, too." He leaned back and regarded the three young men in front of him. "I have been a soldier all my life. I was fighting Ireland's enemies afore you lads even drew breath. England is a hard foe. Her army never lacks for weapons or food or money. Her leaders are well trained, not only in the art of war, but in the butchery that breaks the spirit of the defeated. Aye, we can rout them once in awhile by surprise and ferocity, but our leaders fail to follow their advantage. They quarrel and bicker among themselves until the day of battle, then fly with the rest of us when they see the Sasanach ranks and their fine artillery. 'Tis better for small troops to harry the enemy, giving them no peace until the time comes when the French have spirit and forces to help us."

"I dinna like to rely on the French," Jamie said, pouring himself another glass. "They only help us when 'tis to their own advantage. They use us to distract William from his wars with them and will only give us as much aid as 'twill take to do that and no more."

MacBride sighed. "I know. I know. But I see no other way, for neither your country nor mine has the resources to destroy the Sasanach army as long as Dutch Billy can call the Dutchmen to his aid."

"How soon then can we expect these weapons to arrive?" Jamie asked.

"Ten days or so," MacBride answered, scratching his beard. "There is no reason to believe that they might have been delayed. Our agents are watching from Land's End and will send word as soon as they see the signal."

"And once the arms are landed," Jamie asked, "how long until they are sent north?"   Lionel bit his lip. "I have a man on Mull trying to arrange a ship. He's no yet sent word."

"You dinna fear your protestant friends will sell us?" Tristan asked.

Lionel laughed. "Dinna fear that. They are all my kin and the feeling amang them is that though James be an ass, at least he's our ass and a Scots ass is better than a Dutch usurper no matter his faith."

"Not tactful, but well said," Jamie chuckled, then his expression sobered. "There may be a serious danger here though." Lionel and MacBride looked up sharply. "The cove is just as you were told. 'Tis a fine place to land the arms, but I dinna live here alone. I am considered a child by my family -- of which I seem to have an abundance of late."

"Who besides your mother?" Lionel asked, pausing in his reach for the bottle.

"Father left me an older brother and sister," Jamie answered. "They go with property, it seems."

"But surely they will be abed when the ship comes," Lionel said.

"I dinna think so." Jamie shook his fair curls, then stood abruptly, turning toward the fire. "Tristan and I took a walk by the cliff our first evening here and would have gone down to the cove to see what manner of place it is after dark, but the servant man caught us and now we have been threatened with a whipping if we stray there again after sunset."

"And the reason?" MacBride asked, scratching his beard.

"That the footing is treacherous and they fear a fall," Tristan answered with disgust.

"Your mother's orders?" Lionel asked.

"Nay, my sister's." Jamie leaned against the mantel. "'Twas she that threatened to have us whipped if we are caught out there again."

"If you fear a beating from a sister more than the tyranny of Dutch Billy, then you'd best stay at home, buachail beag," MacBride mocked quietly.

Jamie frowned. "I dinna think you see the point, MacBride. We cannot go near the cliff or cove because my sister has ordered it so, and she has given the old servant special charge to keep an eye out to make sure we obey. Any activity in the cove is bound to attract notice."

"And would we be handed o'er to the law, do you think?" Lionel asked.

"I canna say," Jamie answered. "I have met them only this week past. My brother Simon is a silent miserable man who has a singular dislike for me. He'd no hesitate to see me taken, I think."

"And your sister?" MacBride asked, draining his glass.

"Beautiful, vain and very stubborn," Jamie answered. "She seems to like me well enough and is gracious to Mother, but I have a feeling that there is more to my sister than meets the eye."

"Her politics?"

"Williamite," Jamie said flatly. "She and Simon drank a health to the usurper the first night here, but made no comment when we didna join them."

"At the risk of a whipping, Jamie lad, I fear you must be investigating this matter further before the arms arrive." MacBride looked to Lionel who nodded his agreement. "We cannot afford discovery by them if they are not to be trusted." MacBride and MacAlister rose to go.

"Where shall we send word to you?" Jamie asked.

"We have taken lodgings in Welcombe under the names of Mr. Bell and Mr. Purke. When you have some word you may find us by those names at the home of Mistress Dunord." Lionel took a last sip of brandy, then set his glass on the table.

"Is Dunord's safe?" Tristan asked.

"Aye, safe enough," MacBride answered, donning his cloak. "Her man, Ned Dunord is my spy at Land's End. 'Twas he that smuggled us into England."

"But look you ask for us under no other names but Purke and Bell," Lionel cautioned as he pulled his cloak close around him. "The mistress is with us, but there is no need to put her to more risk than she is already."

"We'll send word to Dunord's in Welcombe as soon as there is aught to tell." Jamie followed the two men down the stone stairs to the door. "Go neirigh an t'a leibh."

"Agus libh fhein." MacBride returned. The luck wished was luck needed. MacBride and MacAlister bent low into the night and were gone.

And high in the grey stone tower, old Diggory Larsen watched them leave.

It was nearly dawn when Jamie woke. He and Tristan had dozed off after another hour of plotting over the remainder of Lionel's brandy. Tristan slept in his chair, his head cushioned on his arms folded on the table, his half empty glass spreading faint sparkles of light from the dying fire over his tousled hair. The sounds that had roused Jamie had not disturbed Tristan and he slept on.

A door had slammed and there had been the sound of cursing followed by hushed voices. Jamie shook himself awake and listened, unsure if perhaps he had been dreaming. There was silence. Jamie rose and drew on his coat, then his cloak. Leaving Tristan to sleep, Jamie ran down the narrow stairs and out into the night.

In front of the house Jamie saw several cloaked figures walking swiftly toward the cliff and he followed at a discreet distance. He had no doubt that the woman with them was Anne. She was escorted by a large man wearing a wide hat and another smaller man. The stooped figure of Diggory Larsen could be seen walking in front, carrying the lantern. The three reached a toppled stone wall engulfed in thick vines and from here one by one they vanished over the edge of the cliff, descending carefully by a steep winding path alternating with rough cut steps.

Jamie crouched behind the wall just as the big man was beginning his descent. "Damn pity about the cellar door," the man said. "This path is a hazard in broad daylight." Anne's reply was lost in a gust of wind.

Jamie waited until he could see the lantern on the sand below, and then he followed them, moving as quietly as he could over the steps and slippery gravel. Pausing to look out over the water he could make out the shape of a large frigate rolling heavily with the swell just within the cove's wide mouth. A longboat laden with casks was drawn up on the sand as grunting men unloaded the casks and rolled them down the beach. Anne and her companions stood near the end of the path, their voices just barely audible to Jamie as he huddled behind a large rock.

"I've got Devlin working on that lower door," the big man said. Jamie now recognized the voice of John Ward. "With luck 'twill be fixed by sunrise."

"Aye, well enough," Anne shouted back, her low smooth voice nearly lost in the wind, "for I dislike the path. 'Tis too visible from the house."

"What of your new kin?" Ward asked.

"My father's widow will not be a problem for us," Anne answered. "She spends all her time in her apartments. I cannot imagine what she finds to do in there, but ..." A huge wave crashed over the last of Anne's sentence. "... young ones have been dealt with. Such a pair of milksops!"

"You misjudge them, Anne," the smaller man said. His voice was familiar, but Jamie was too excited to give it more than a moment's thought. He strained to hear.

"Not in any way ..." Again Anne's voice vanished under the wind. "... no threat ..."

The longboat was empty now. Anne, Ward and the other man joined the six sailors who rowed them out over the waves toward the frigate. Diggory watched them leave, then walked quickly over the sand in the direction that the casks had been taken. Jamie followed, keeping close to the rocks at the foot of the cliff. He watched as the servant stepped inside a wide shallow cave, its entrance partially obscured by a tumble of boulders.

Jamie crouched low near the cave mouth. Just inside on the smooth stone floor were the casks and several large chests. He peered in cautiously. There was no guard, so Jamie crept in, taking refuge behind the casks. At the far end of the cave the floor sloped upward where the natural cave joined part of an old mine shaft. Two men were on their knees, working in the shadows while over them Diggory held the lantern. In front of them was a wall of stone.

"We need more light," one said crossly. "'Tis a tricky mechanism and you expect me to fix it in the dark?"

"Quit your whinin' and get on with it," Diggory growled.

Jamie noticed the markings on the side of one chest. There were similar markings on at least three of the casks. Dutch, he thought, or perhaps German. He could not be sure for the thin rays of the lantern barely reached his hiding place and illumined only that portion of each article facing the back of the cave.

"Luther and Calum'll be back soon," Diggory said. "It'd be best to 'ave this open by then. *The Cockerel* ain't goin' to stay there past dawn, y'know."

The two men grunted as they pushed a heavy bar into a vertical ridge of rock. Suddenly there was a snap and a harsh scrapping sound as the ridge separated from the wall. A rush of light filled the cave as the door opened, revealing several men with torches on the other side.

Jamie quickly slipped back among the casks toward the cave mouth and took refuge again behind the rocks. He had not moved a moment too soon. The men hurriedly hauled the chests and casks up the sloped floor and through the door.

So engrossed was Jamie in watching the work in the cave, that he did not hear the soft footfall on the sand behind him. A heavy blow struck against his skull and he fell limply onto the sand.

CHAPTER THREE

Ni Bhfuighe Mise Bas Duit

Lady with swanlike body,
I was reared by a cunning hand!
I know well how women are.
I will not die for you.

Irish poem translated
by Thomas Kinsela

His head aching, Jamie opened his eyes slowly. Above him the faint morning light rolled and swayed. Beneath him the hard damp ribs of the longboat rocked in the swell. He raised his head gingerly and looked around. The men at the oars took no notice of him. Twisting his head, he could see Diggory Larsen sitting above him.

"Morning to ye, young master," Diggory said grinning.

"What happened?" Jamie groaned.

"I warned ye to stay away from the cliff, but you're a stubborn boy," Diggory said, drawing on his pipe. "'Twas Calum there saw ye and 'it ye o'er the 'ead." Jamie gingerly touched the sore lump at the back of his head. "Don't worry, young master," Diggory laughed. "Your 'ead's like your father's. 'Ard as stone."

"Where are you takin' me?"

"To yon great ship," Diggory answered, gesturing with his pipe at the frigate. "Ye've seen a mite too much to be let go without seeing it all." Diggory fell silent and drew on his pipe.

Jamie was filled with questions that he felt strangely reluctant to ask. Instead, he watched the frigate roll closer with each stroke of the oars.

Of the eight men rowing only one seemed to take an occasional glance at the boy. He sat one bench away and studied Jamie for lingering moments between strokes. Jamie found himself staring back, fascinated in the same way that men are when they watch a cobra dance to his master's pipe.

The man was dark, not unlike Eben Carr in his looks, but there was a friendly softness in his smile, a light in his eyes as he watched the boy's reaction. The man was clean shaven, his smooth tanned cheeks unmarred except for a tiny cross shaped scar beneath his left eye. Jamie was drawn to look into the man's eyes, deep wells of rich brown surrounded by long soft lashes. Between the roll of the boat and the ache in his head, Jamie felt dizzy and weak, unable to break away from the man's increasingly steady gaze. There was a sense of sinking, of falling, then with a convulsive shiver, Jamie turned away.

Wood scraped against wood as the longboat came alongside the frigate that loomed above. The ship's bow, stern and railings were finely carved and painted gold. Her brass cannon were thrust from their many ports on the main deck and the gundeck below. The ship was alive and stirring in the rising light of dawn. Sailors clambered high into her rigging and unfurled the great canvas sails.

A rope ladder was lowered to the longboat and Jamie climbed up with Diggory following closely. The deck was cluttered with an assortment of chests and casks, not unlike those that had been in the cave the previous night. There were bundles of cloth on top of two chests and Jamie's well-trained eye recognized the silks and brocades that formed so much of his mother's wardrobe. He passed close to one chest and could smell the fragrance of coffee, while another exuded the scent of chocolate. The casks smelled mostly of smoked fish.

In contrast to the richness of the cargo, the crew were a brutish lot -- tattooed, scarred and filthy. Tarred hair bound up in bright bandannas, untrimmed beards, sunburnt faces and tattered clothing were common among them. Several bore the maimed marks of battle. One lacked an eye. Another was missing three fingers. Two men walked with pronounced limps. Every man carried some weapon, from boot daggers to cutlasses. Several carried pistols stuck in their belts.

Jamie shivered nervously as the men stared at him with open mouths. He was the oddity here, in his clean linen shirt and beribboned velvet suit, his lace frilled cravat slightly askew and his fair hair ruffled in the cold morning wind. He drew his cloak tighter around him, shrinking into it.

"I'll tell the cap'n you're 'ere," Diggory said, "then I'm off for 'ome again." Jamie felt his panic rise as the one familiar face left him. He sat stiffly on a large chest. A moment later a large calloused hand lightly gripped his shoulder and he jerked up, startled. It was the young man from the longboat.

"What's your name, lad?" His voice was soft like his features, the sort of voice that inspired trust.

"I am James Maclain Hawkwood," Jamie answered boldly as he looked into the stranger's eyes.

"Another 'Awkwood, eh?" The man gave Jamie's shoulder a friendly squeeze. "Word is that ye didn't expect to find so many kin when ye came 'ere to Devon."

"Aye, true enough," Jamie agreed. "Still, for all my effort 'twas worth the journey since my father saw fit to make me his heir and no my brother."

"Your father, rest 'is soul, was a fair man. I'm glad to see 'e did right by ye, being the fine lad ye are."

"I thank you, sir," Jamie stammered, surprised by this display of geniality in such an unlikely location. "And what is your name, sailor?"

"Luther Devlin. I be the bo'sun 'ere. Served with your father since I was but a lad and thankful I am to 'im and 'is for takin' me out of my mother's brothel when only young. 'Twas no life for a boy, eh?"

Jamie grinned and nodded, then winced. "My head hurts a bit," he explained.

"'Twas foolish to be out at the cove, ye know," Luther said, squatting down next to him. "And even more foolish should your pretty sister or any other 'ere 'ave found this on ye." Luther handed him a dainty string of beads, Jamie's rosary. "It fell out when I was bundling ye into the gig." Jamie hid the beads inside his shirt. "Above all, don't be letting Judas Jones our shipwright know. 'E's a bit fanatical about matters of faith and like most 'ere 'e don't like papes. Could cause no end of trouble if 'e'd a mind to."

"Thank you, Mister Devlin," Jamie said. "I trust my secret is safe with you."

"Off with ye, Devlin," Diggory chortled from the steps to the cabin. "That lad's not for ye." Luther's smooth cheeks flushed and he stalked away without another word.

Diggory led Jamie down the steps and through a short narrow corridor to a door. The servant knocked, then turned away, leaving Jamie alone to face whatever waited within.

"Come in," called a gruff voice. Jamie slowly opened the door and peeked into the spacious cabin, then froze with surprise. In the lantern lit room, seated around a fine oak table piled with platters of food were his sister, his lawyer and Captain John Ward. It was Stone's presence that most amazed him.

"You needn't speak if you have no words, brother," Anne said, "but pray do close your mouth. Else the crew might mistake ye for fish."

"Lawyer Stone, are you captured too?" Jamie asked in a breathless whisper, his stomach reeling giddily. There was a roar of laughter.

"Captured?" Stone gasped through his mirth. "Certainly not, boy! And neither would you have been if you heeded old Larsen's warning and steered clear of the cove after dark." Stone sorted through several papers that were stacked on the table in front of him. "Now come in and close the door."

Jamie entered cautiously, his eyes taking in every detail. The end of the cabin was dominated by the stern ports, wide windows through which could be seen the morning light on the grey water. There was little furniture, except for a half dozen fine wooden chairs around the central table and a heavy sideboard against the wall. Two doors opened on each side of the cabin, revealing smaller cabins for the ship's officers. A brazier warmed the air, the glow of the coals shining on his sister's dark hair as she regarded him with silent cunning.

"What ship is this?" Jamie asked.

"This, m'boy," Ward answered proudly, "is the Bold Cockerel, your late father's flagship and my inheritance from him. A fine vessel she is."

"And those men on deck? Those brigands?"

"My crew, of course," Ward laughed. "Surely you didn't expect uniforms like the Royal Navy?"

Hugo Stone stroked the black wool of his sleeve, then straightened his lace cuffs. "'Tis time to tell the lad all. If he saw even half of what Larsen said he might've, then he knows more than is safe. After all, this ship is his support and he is entitled to choose for himself whether he will have aught of it or no."

Anne glanced at Ward who nodded soberly, then pursing her lips sourly, shrugged. "Why not?" She gestured Jamie to a chair and handed him a tankard of rum. "John, hand here that plate of cheese and bread. This is not a tale to be told without some measure of breakfast." Ward shoved a partially picked-through platter in front of Jamie, who after a scant hesitation began to eat.

"How much has your mother told you of your late father?" Stone asked.

"A wee bit," Jamie said, between mouthfuls. "That he was a gentleman merchant, always fine dressed and well-mannered. No educated by tutors as I have been, but a great respecter of such and thus willing to send me to college. A good man, a lawful and loyal man who loved his king and country. 'Twas little else she could tell me for he was at sea so much that we rarely saw him." Their amazed looks puzzled him.

"I do not believe that your mother told you all she could have," Stone said, "although perhaps she told you all she should."

"You are speaking riddles, lawyer. Will you no come to the point?" Jamie found a slice of roast beef beneath several chunks of cheese and laid it on top of a piece of bread.

"You recall that our father's father and brothers were amongst the casualties of the civil war," Anne said, fondling her tankard and smiling. "And that our grandmother nearly lost the property because of them. During those years Father grew to an age where he could take charge to some measure and he was persuaded by some friends of the exiled prince to go to sea aboard a privateer to attack English ships."

"English ships?"

"Aye, Jamie. To worsen Cromwell's situation at home and thus aid in restoring the Stuarts to the throne. 'Twas very noble and not without great risk."

"I trust the family fortunes improved with the Stuarts?"

"They did indeed, Jamie," his sister answered. "Father was rewarded for his service with a knighthood and a fine ship -- not as fine as *The Bold Cockerel* here, but a goodly vessel nevertheless. And during those peaceful times he managed as a merchant, carrying goods back from the Indies and the Americas, sometimes India and Africa."

"And during war?" Jamie asked.

"Ah," said Ward, leaning back in his chair, "'twas then your father stopped his usual trade and took off against this country's enemies."

"With the Navy?"

"Not exactly," Ward answered, shifting a little in his seat. "With a Letter of Marque. A privateer again, this time against the Dutch. He had been robbed by that great Dutch rogue Van Wyck, and through the patronage of Lord Percival Golding he obtained the letter that would permit him to take his revenge on the Dutch pirate. Never did take Van Wyck, but many another Dutchman paid."

"Of course, Golding was entitled to a percentage of the profits," Stone said evenly. "Ten percent to be precise. When we asked him for a letter against the Spanish as well, Golding demanded a larger portion."

"Aye," Ward said grimly. "Nothing less than fifteen percent would satisfy that greedy hound. When another letter was needed four years ago, so that we might fight the French, Golding raised his fee to seventeen percent."

"And what has all this to do with those chests and casks in the cave?" Jamie demanded, his pale eyes narrowing.

"Ah, I have remembered me," Anne said smoothly as she rose to refill her tankard from a pitcher on the sideboard. "You are the Hawkwood with no love of business. But surely you can see that if Lord Golding takes an increasingly high percentage there is then that much less left to us and to our crew." She paused to drink, her hand straying over her dark red skirt. For the first time Jamie realized that she was wearing a skirt such as the country women wore, with no petticoats, and that her oversized shirt and coat were those of a man. "So it was that

Father arranged with dear Hugo here to distribute many of the goods privately -- before making division with Golding's agent in Plymouth."

"And how do you distribute these goods?" Jamie asked, one hand rubbing crumbs from his chin.

"Privately," Stone answered. "I have certain contacts in Bristol, in London and in Amsterdam. When the market is ripe for some particular commodity 'tis then we sell it and get the best rate."

"And between times you must store such goods at the Rookery?"

"Aye, Jamie, you have grasped it." Anne stood over him and patted his hand, but he flinched away.

"And the Chanticleer?" he demanded. "What part does your ship play in all this?"

"'Twouldn't do to have the Bold Cockerel seen unlading in any port but Plymouth," Ward said. "Golding has agents in most ports and we can not risk having our letter withdrawn. It would destroy that delicate balance of legality that we have managed to maintain for so many years."

"The *Chanticleer* is a Dutch prize that Father converted for the purpose," Anne continued, taking her seat again. "She has a goodly hold and, like most Dutch craft, can be crewed by a relatively small crew."

"In fine, then," Jamie replied, "an inexpensive though reliable smuggling vessel."

"Very good," Anne said. "Perhaps you will develop some sense of our trade after all."

"And the prizes are now all French and Spanish?"

Anne and Ward exchanged a quick glance before Ward answered, "Aye, lad."

"Then why were those casks in the cave last night bearing Dutch markings?"

Anne lowered her eyes, then fixed her younger brother with a sly smile. "My, but you did see a great deal."

"I'll have you all know right now that I want no truck with criminals and felons," Jamie answered her boldly, "but I do want to know if you are legitimate privateers or no."

"Those casks are --" Ward started to say, but Anne waved him to silence.

Gently she said, “Jamie dear, you must understand that Father had been all his life subject to peculiar fits and spells. ’Twas for that reason he was called ‘Mad Jack.’ He was often melancholy, despairing of life -- even as Simon is at times. This strange humor, some say ’twas a madness that afflicts all Hawkwoods -- well, in recent times it had become more apparent. As matters became more difficult with Golding, our poor father became subject to certain failings of memory and of sight.” She winked at Ward and Stone. “Poor Father lost his ability to remember precisely under which Letter of Marque he was currently operating.” Jamie looked confused. “You see, not one letter was ever withdrawn by Lord Golding. More than that, Father had ofttimes been asked to aid certain governors in the Indies in their struggles against their neighbors. So among our other papers is a French letter against the Dutch, a Dutch letter against the Spanish, and a Spanish letter against everyone. It was all very confusing and Father lost his ability to discriminate between one vessel and another. Sometimes mistakes were made.” She gave a dainty sigh.

“You mean he attacked friendly vessels?”

“Yes, dear,” Anne answered. “And as it became more profitable to do so, he did it more often.”

At first all Jamie could do was stare at her in disbelief. “You mean he was a pirate!”

“And a smuggler,” Hugo said, “but mostly he was successful. Very successful. The notorious Mad Jack Hawkwood.”

“Father always said that if a man takes up a trade he should strive to be successful in that trade and to hold fast to his principles,” Anne added grandly.

“How can you speak of piracy and principles in one breath?” Jamie demanded.

Ward leaned forward. “Piracy is but a scant step from privateering. Privateering is legal. Piracy is not. All that divides them is a piece of paper -- and we have that piece of paper.”

“Indeed,” Jamie replied sarcastically, “you have several.”

“We are operating within the law,” Ward maintained stoutly, then added, “well, mostly.”

Jamie sat back and took a long drink from his tankard, then paused reflectively. Finally he said, "And you want me to turn a blind eye to your felonies while you use my home for your stock house and leave me and my kin to face the law should you be caught at your criminal trade?"

"That would be advisable," Hugo cautioned. "You would find it hard to claim total innocence of these dealings since you have been their beneficiary all your life. Still, there is no reason for any of us to face the law if you are sensible and do nothing to endanger our operations here. We, in turn, will see that you, your mother and cousin are amply provided for and protected."

"And if I refuse to cooperate?" Jamie challenged.

"Then there is the legal recourse to your father's will," the lawyer continued, tapping the papers in front of him. "You will recall that there is specific mention that you will in no way interfere with the family trade."

"I didna ken what that trade was," Jamie protested, "but now that I do you wouldna dare enforce that clause for I would take you to court to contest it."

Hugo smiled. "'Twould avail you nothing, boy. Long before any inspection could be made all the evidence would be gone. As for a legal contest of the will, I think I should warn you that there is, in fact, a second and later will." Anne and Ward exchanged only a surprised look, but Jamie started sharply. "Your late father began to doubt the wisdom of leaving the Rookery to you instead of to Simon. The original document was drawn up at a time when your brother was distinctly out of favor with your father. Then some two years ago the late captain asked me to draw up a second will that would protect Anne's right to inherit while reversing the portions left to you and your brother."

"It has not been necessary to bring this second will into play, but let me assure you, young man," the lawyer peered closely at the boy, "rather than lose what has become a very profitable livelihood, I will see both you and your lovely mother put out on the road without a copper."

"So you see, brother," Anne said, "the consequences are grave if you interfere. If you attempt to stop us or go to the law, you and your kin will lose not only the Rookery, but also very possibly your lives."

"You wouldna murder us?" he asked aghast.

"I wouldn't," Anne answered, "and neither would John here. But we can not speak for the others. Simon or some member of the crew might well be persuaded to be rid of you, and there'd be little to stop them."

"I know Simon doesna like me,_ Jamie protested, "but surely he'd no commit murder!"

Anne laughed derisively and again Jamie sensed the chilling power in her. "He could. Oh, trust me, little brother, your death would weigh nothing on his conscience if it meant he might have the Rookery and know that our trade was safe. Simon is a very greedy man with expensive tastes and extravagant habits."

Jamie lowered his eyes, his usual disdain replaced by cold fear. "Then I have no choice but to cooperate." Slowly he raised his eyes again as his own bold plans reminded him that he had more at stake than they could know. "I trust that from now on you will see fit to include me in your plans and to tell me when your ships will be using the cove." Anne's suspicious gaze prompted him to add, "So that I might be sure my kin dinna learn of all this. For their safety and ours."

"Agreed," Anne said. "Welcome then to our company. In time you will be treated as a full partner." Ward and Stone nodded. "But for now you may be witness to the remainder of our meeting that was interrupted by your arrival."

"There is little else to discuss," Stone said. "I have told you that grain prices are so high in France that there is little profit to be made on other commodities for the nonce." He turned to Jamie, who stared uncomprehendingly. "When bread is scarce, there is no market for luxuries." Turning again to Ward and Anne, "We should sell this cargo here in England. Otherwise, it will have to wait until the famine is over."

Anne nodded. "Make the arrangements, Hugo," she said. "I have no wish to risk a trip to Amsterdam now."

"Besides that," Ward added, "as though the infestation of French privateers was not bad enough, there has been added to their numbers here yet another."

"Who?" Anne's low voice was little more than a whisper.

"Who else? LeBoutellier, of course." Ward's tone betrayed his exasperation and Anne's disgusted expression confirmed hers.

"Damn that fop!" she said crossly.

"Aye, mistress," Ward continued. "We spotted him just off Land's End. I am not sure whether or not he saw us. I think not."

"Who?" Jamie asked.

"Captain Pierre Henri LeBoutellier," Anne answered with a flourish of her dainty hand. "A notorious French pirate who dresses like any coxcomb of the Court and sails a gaudy painted frigate called *La Panache.* He is an errant fop who preys on English vessels with the blessings of the French crown."

"He and your father were great rivals," Ward added. "Many's the duel we fought with that peacock, but none could be called decisive. I suppose it will fall to me to take up where Mad Jack left off and finish LeBoutellier."

"'Tis to you or to me," Anne said thoughtfully. "Aye, we will have our duel, but in our own time and a place of our choosing."

"Damned difficult with LeBoutellier's uncanny sense of timing," Ward replied, with a deep chuckle. "I have never known that Frenchman to make an appearance at any time but the worst possible."

"Then his arrival in these waters should be no surprise," Anne said. "He is, without doubt, the last person on God's green earth we have any wish to see."

The meeting ended soon after. Anne accepted Ward's offer of his cabin and withdrew to take a nap. Ward went to the quarter deck, while Hugo Stone commandeered the mate's cabin to read and rest. Left to himself, Jamie soon dozed off in his chair, exhausted by excitement, rum, long hours and his still aching head.

When he awoke it was many hours later, and stepping onto the deck he was shocked to find that the familiar and reassuring sight of land was nowhere to be seen.

"Never fear, boy," Anne said, coming up behind him as he stood at the railing, "we shall return you to land at nightfall. For safety's sake we put out to sea to keep the Royal Navy's eyes away from the Rookery." Jamie nodded and said nothing. Anne smiled and walked away.

For a time he watched the grey water and the white chop slap against the hull, but the crack of gunfire drew his attention to the stern. Luther Devlin and several others were tossing bottles into the sea and attempting to shatter them with shots from their wheellocks before the targets bobbed away. Only Luther and the man they called Calum were having any success in the exercise.

"Luther has a fine aim," Jamie commented to the man nearest him. The man turned and gave him a slow appraising look.

"Aye, 'e 'as that. Perhaps the best shot on the ship. Our gunner there finds 'im to be worthy competition. You're young 'Awkwood, eh?"

"I am, sir. And you?"

The man stroked his grizzled chin. "Judas Jones, ship's carpenter and sometimes preacher." Even though his lined face creased into a smile, Jamie noted the steady gleam in the old man's eyes.

"'Tis a strange craft to have a preacher," Jamie commented as he surveyed the ragtag crewmen around them.

"All the more reason to tell 'em of the power of Jesus Christ," Jones said. "For all their weapons and dominion on the seas, they will be as dust before the throne of the most 'igh God. A wheellock will avail 'em nothing in the fiery pits of 'ell, nor will their stolen wealth buy 'em into 'eaven. They will all stink of abomination before the face of God and 'is angels will cast 'em down, yea into the depths of the pit!" Judas Jones' thrust his finger into the air as his voice rose. Suddenly he seemed to come to himself again as he saw Jamie's amazed expression.

"If these pirates are doomed to eternal damnation as you say," the boy asked, choosing his words carefully, "then why do you remain with them?"

"I mean to save 'em," Jones explained. "Save 'em from the fiery pit 'cause they're me mates. I take no part in their crimes and keep me eye on the carpentry and the Scriptures. When there's time to spare I tell 'em of Christ's salvation and of 'ell's torment for those who will not 'ear 'is call."

"Still, it must be difficult for you," Jamie said, "if you must see some ship plundered and know that 'tis against holy writ."

Jones grinned. "Mostly we strikes against French and Spanish and there's no sin in takin' from papist dogs what was not theirs by right to begin with. Thems that follow Rome are doomed to damnation and the quicker we send 'em there, the better."

"Aye, of course," Jamie agreed nervously, turning back to watch the man with the pistol pick off his target in the waning afternoon sun.

Evening was drawing into night when Jamie again entered the Rookery's foyer. Simon was waiting for him at the foot of the stairs. "I took the liberty of concocting some tale to appease your mother and cousin," Simon said. "Remember it. That you saw the Chanticleer -- not the Cockerel -- in the cove at dawn and asked Anne if you might go aboard. Anne invited you for a day's sail and you are only just returned." Jamie nodded. "Diggory will tell Anne," Simon added, then led Jamie into the main hall. "He reported your entire escapade to me shortly after you sailed this morning. You are a very lucky young man." There was as usual no trace of humor in Simon's tone.

"Anne says I am now to become a partner in the enterprise," Jamie said, stopping to look Simon in the eyes.

The eyes, hard and black as onyx, appraised him, then Simon answered, "I see no reason not to abide by Anne's decision." There was a pause. "See that I am never given one."

There were other private entrances to the house that allowed the passage of guests at late hours. At least so it seemed when on the following morning Jamie entered the great hall to find that the Rookery had acquired a visitor during the night.

Simon introduced his guest as Doctor Patrick Hartley, a physician of Exeter. Jamie had but a moment to consider the tall, bony, red haired man who rose to greet him when Anne burst into the room and flung herself into the doctor's arms.

"Patrick!" she exclaimed. "How glorious to see you! Have you come to stay?"

"For a time, for a time," he answered, kissing her on the cheek and releasing her. "I heard of Simon's fortune --"

"And raced to congratulate me out of it," Simon laughed. The sound caused Jamie's blonde brows to rise in silent amazement

"Nay, good Simon," Hartley replied, slapping him on the back. "I mean my greetings sincerely. And my condolences on the loss of your father, who for all else was a fine man." He smiled broadly, his blue eyes sparkling. "And I came to see Anne who is so often to Amsterdam that I fear she will forget her native tongue and speak naught but Dutch."

"'Tis a great lie you tell," Anne said. "I speak not a word of Dutch and well you know it."

Turning to Jamie, Hartley regarded him for a moment, then said, "Simon has told me of you and your pretty mother. Quite a surprise, I dare say." His voice was friendly.

"'Twas a surprise for us as well." Jamie liked this freckled, smiling doctor and was intrigued that such an ebullient spirit could have so immediate an effect on Simon's sour disposition. The four took seats at the table, helping themselves to the bread, cheese, fresh butter and slabs of ham. Angharad appeared, bearing a pot of thick fragrant coffee.

"Not chocolate?" Hartley asked plaintively.

"Your fondness for drinking chocolate will be your undoing," Anne cautioned laughingly. "This coffee is newly fetched from across the Channel."

"At the Dutch Company's expense," Hartley added with a knowing smile. Jamie looked startled. "Oh, you needn't look so surprised, Master James," the doctor said. "I am well acquainted with your family's exploits -- as they are with mine."

"The doctor and Simon are old friends," Anne said. "They met through their mutual fondness of dice and young ladies -- and their lack of scruples."

"I find it hard to believe that a physician as yourself, Dr. Hartley, would be so involved with gambling and women that you'd let your scruples suffer for it." Jamie sipped the bitter coffee, grimacing at the unfamiliar taste.

"I did not lack for scruples, Jamie," Hartley said, his manner radiant. "I lacked for money, and then your brother led me astray."

"I did nothing of the sort," Simon protested. "I was in some sorry straits and you were kind enough to oblige."

"As though I had some choice," Hartley countered.

"Well, Jamie," Simon continued, "here it is the way of it. I was then only some few years older than yourself and working for my keep in Bideford as Hugo Stone's clerk. Father was having financial difficulties with Lord Golding. Our patron's share kept increasing while ours was decreasing, and as yet no steps had been taken to redress the balance. 'Twas at this time I learned of Mister Stone's total lack of ethics. I took care not to trust him more than necessary, which policy I maintain to this very day."

"Very wise, Simon, very wise," Hartley said, nodding his red curls.

"To continue," Simon smiled, "I had but little money -- Father being the most ethical of privateers and having for counsel one of the most unethical of solicitors --"

"And for patron one of the greediest of noblemen," Anne threw in.

"Aye, so that for a time there was little money for me to pursue my twin interests in dicing and doxies. I was forced by these circumstances to collect donations from passing travelers."

"Which is to say, he became a common bandit," Hartley said with genteel nonchalance. If this admission caused Jamie any surprise he did not show it.

"I had seen this doctor," Simon continued, "win well at cards in a particular salon that night, so I lay in wait for him on the road beyond. I relieved him of a burdensome amount of coin and went straightway to a dalliance with a young lady I fancied."

"Lady my arse," Anne laughed. "Some tavern whore belike."

"Well, I fancied her," Simon said without remorse. "'Twas nigh to daylight when I rose out again and who should I meet but the same good and noble young physician armed with sword and pistol, and he, bold rascal, bids me to stand and deliver."

"Which I noted you did with all speed and respect." Hartley added as he selected another slice of ham. "You see, Jamie, I had taken a fancy to the same young lady as had he and was seeking her tender company for solace when I recognized his horse behind her house. So there I waited and was well rewarded for my patience. 'Twas later I found that a goodly portion of the money had been spent in those few hours."

"So he tracks me down," Simon said. "Follows me even to Hugo Stone's doorstep and there demands the remainder of the money. Father overheard the accusation and went into a towering rage that I his son had become a felon."

"So embarrassed was I by the breach of domestic harmony I had caused, that I found myself apologizing to the Captain and fabricating some great fantasy that I was his son's good friend and comrade, and that I had used the term 'rob' only in a figurative sense -- as one might over a loss at the gaming table."

"Then so embarrassed was Father," Simon laughed, "that he invited my recent victim to visit us here at the Rookery."

"And I, though skilled in medicine, being impoverished, accepted," Hartley concluded. "And that is how I came to stay here."

"And stay and stay and stay," Anne added with a giggle. Never had Jamie met a woman so changeable. "Ah, such girlish love I had for you then, Patrick. I was quite infatuated."

"I know," Patrick replied teasingly, "but what was I to do with a lover scarce twelve years old and having the manners of a Barbary pirate and a dangerous father watching over her."

In the midst of their laughter Tristan walked in. He paused for a moment when he saw the doctor.

"My cousin, Tristan MacDonald," Jamie said as the doctor rose to shake Tristan's hand. "Tristan, this is Doctor Patrick Hartley, a friend of Simon's who has come to visit for a time."

Tristan absently accepted the doctor's warm handclasp, then motioned Jamie from the room. In the corridor beyond, he whispered, "There's been word from Welcombe. The Spanish ship is sighted and only wants word from us to land. Shall we send it?"

Jamie thought for a moment. "We must bide awhile longer, cousin. There are family matters to consider."

"We canna bide forever, Jamie," Tristan pleaded. "That Spanish ship will no be safe in our waters long, and if she is seized by a Navy patrol we will lose all."

"I know that," Jamie argued, "but we must be sure of the cove before we can land aught here. As I said, there are certain family matters to consider."

"I thought you said we have nothing to fear from your kin."

"Aye, and that is the truth," Jamie answered, "but there is more at stake here than I can tell you. You must trust me, Tristan. 'Twill no be long."

Tristan looked far from satisfied. "You are acting most strange, Jamie Hawkwood, ever since you disappeared yester morning."

"I didna disappear. I was with Anne on her ship."

"Aye, so we were told. And you come home with some new affection for your kin. 'Tis strange."

"'Tis no affection," Jamie said with a sly grin. "'Tis understanding only. As I told you, cousin, I understand them now. And they are no danger to us. No danger at all."

CHAPTER FOUR

JOHN BARLEYCORN

There were three men come from the west
their fortunes for to try;
And these three men made a solemn vow
John Barleycorn should die. folksong

"Commander Hargrove sends his greetings, Colonel. He trusts his absence will not prove an inconvenience."

Colonel Andrew Campbell slowly raised his eyes and stared at the fresh faced young officer who handed him a sealed document, then stood at attention in front of the table. "And who might you be, Lieutenant?" he asked, just a trace of Scots in his voice.

"Lieutenant Philip Gilchrist of His Majesty's ship *Rainbow*, sir."

"Are you Hargrove's aide?"

"I am, sir."

Campbell motioned to a chair across from him. "You may sit, Lieutenant." Gilchrist accepted the offer, his gaze never leaving the colonel's humorless face for a moment. "There's ale in the pitcher there if you wish it." With a nod of thanks Gilchrist took an empty tankard and filled it. There was a pause as Campbell continued to study the papers in front of him.

Downstairs could be heard the rowdy sound of the Red Cock's common room, its dockside patrons crowding the benches for their midday meal. The general roar was occasionally topped by a woman's high-pitched squealing laughter, then the clatter of a falling plate.

In the upper chamber, the noise was muffled and far away. The only distinct sound was the rustle of paper as Colonel Campbell read again the letter Gilchrist had presented to him.

"Your commander speaks very highly of you, Lieutenant," the colonel said, his eyes still on the letter. "A commissioned officer of good family. Ah, I see 'twas you that captured the smugglers in Prussia Cove last June."

"Aye, sir," Gilchrist nodded proudly, his fair hair catching the few dimmed rays of light that shone through the oil paper on the windows. "I had a good crew, some good information and some very good luck."

"Let us hope that your luck hasna diminished," Campbell said, laying the letter down and looking earnestly into the young lieutenant's face. "Hargrove has told me that you are a man of the law, a scrupulous officer loyal to king and country. Is that the truth?"

"Every word of it, upon my honor," Gilchrist answered, his eyes shining as he looked into the colonel's hard creased face.

"Good enough then," Campbell said, leaning back with satisfaction. "If you have Desmond Hargrove's approval, you shall no lack for mine. Have you been told aught of this matter?"

"Very little," Gilchrist answered. "Commander Hargrove thought it best to let you give me the particulars."

"Did he mention the Spanish ship?"

"He didn't have to, sir, for I saw it with my own eyes."

"I have a man in Cornwall -- lad by the name of Varick – who has been following a man named Ned Dunord. Dunord it seems was making inquiries of certain Irish fisherman and the like as to whether or no they had seen a Spanish warship in the nearby waters. When one said that he had seen such a vessel, Dunord took horse and rode for his home in the village of Welcombe. My man Varick followed him there and during his vigil saw two men he knew to be Jacobite agents."

"And you believe there is a connection between the ship and these two men?" Gilchrist asked, seriousness clouding his youthful face.

"I do indeed, Lieutenant," Campbell answered, rising and pacing across the room. Gilchrist noted the shortness of the man, the stockiness that tended toward fat in the belly, the reddish tinge to his face and eyes that bespoke of middle-aged indulgences. "I know my fellow Scots and they'll no let a French defeat such as La Hogue interfere with their treasonous designs. With our good king now in Holland and perhaps no to return soon, 'tis likely the more misguided clans in the islands will attempt to rise up in support of the papist James."

"And for that they need weapons," Gilchrist observed.

"Aye, lad, weapons they canna get from France for the French need all that they have now. But Spain!" Campbell turned back to the lieutenant. "Aye, Spain might spare such a cargo for the cause of a papist king."

"Then the question remains of where they might land their cargo and who would receive it." Gilchrist's eyes followed the pacing Colonel.

"Indeed, Lieutenant, and that is why I need you. You know the ways of smugglers in these waters and along these southern coasts."

"But why, Colonel, do you think they will attempt to land here?" Gilchrist asked perplexed. "Surely it would make more sense to sail directly to the islands or to Ireland?"

"I agree," Campbell said, returning to his seat, "but I think 'tis safe to say that because this ship remains in these waters that she intends to land her cargo here. Perhaps that is the best deal that could be made or possibly that 'tis here she must make some contact to learn where she is to go next."

"Well, you can be right sure there will be no landing without great care." Gilchrist spoke with authority. "'Tis all rocks and cliffs. There are a few quiet coves here in the Bideford area and some fine spots to the north, but most of them are in places of population. Such a ship and a landing would be seen by the locals. South toward Hartland Point and 'tis all wild water and rocks. Perhaps they mean to land in Cornwall."

"Varick says that Ned Dunord sent out two men. One went south toward Tintagel Head. The other came here to the Red Cock."

"Some manner of relay?"

"Could be. 'Tis our work to find out."

"I see." Gilchrist took a thoughtful sip of ale. "And how do you propose we go about it?"

Campbell smiled and patted the breast of his uniform coat. "I have the necessities here. If Dunord's man met with someone in this tavern, then perhaps some other saw or heard them. Lord Golding has entrusted to me a sum of gold to pay for any such information as might be available. Other than that, we are to make formal inquiries of the coastal estates, to learn if such a ship has been seen or if preparations have been made for a landing."

"'Tis a good course," Gilchrist said, nodding agreeably. "When shall we start?"

"Why, immediately, lad," the colonel answered in surprise. "In this tavern. 'Tis run by an old scoundrel named Blackistone and has among its locals such as had dealing with all manner of seafaring men."

"Blackistone," Gilchrist said thoughtfully. "I seem to recall that he sailed with the privateer Hawkwood. Was his mate once, I believe."

"Aye, lad, the very same." Campbell rose. "Shall we go?"

"Aye, sir." Towering over his superior, Gilchrist followed him down into the common room.

It had quieted down deal in the room below. There were a few sailors and tradesmen lingering over their tankards. Two men were rolling dice on a table improvised from a barrel and a wide board. A small black haired beggar boy stood near the door, hand outstretched as a brawny blonde blacksmith huffed past him on his way back to the forge. "Out of my way, scum," the smith laughed. The boy dodged the massive boot just in time, then retreated to the corner by the fire.

The auburn haired serving girl was attempting to gather up the empty tankards and platters while ignoring the brash youth who had thrust his hand inside her bodice to massage her breast.

"Here now, lad," a big Irish sailor reproved. "This is a wench for a grown man. A slip of a lad like yourself should be rogering the dairymaids afore takin' on the likes of the Red Cock's Jenny."

Jenny shook her bright curls and laughingly removed the boy's hand. "Young, but learning he is. Darcy, m'lover, you've been long from me. And Simon comes so rarely at times."

Darcy pulled her down into his lap and kissed her warmly, then tickled her. It was in the midst of her laughter that she noticed the two officers standing at the foot of the stairs. Blushing, she leapt from the Irishman's lap. There was a sudden hush in the common room. Campbell and Gilchrist traded an uneasy glance, then took a table in the corner.

The two men at the neighboring table watched them suspiciously, then returned to their conversation in quiet tones.

"I get the unmistakable feeling that our company is not much desired," Gilchrist said. The two men at the next table abruptly rose and joined the Irishman.

"Aye, Lieutenant," Campbell agreed. "'Tis the authority of the uniform." He signaled Jenny for ale.

"Is the proprietor here?" Campbell asked her as she approached the table with the pitcher.

"Mister Blackistone is having his meal with his wife and children today," Jenny answered warily. "Some complaint you have?"

"Oh, nay, lass," the colonel answered giving her a friendly appraising smile. "'Tis an official matter."

"Aye," the lieutenant said. "We're looking for a bit of information."

"What sort of information?" she asked bouncing nervously on her heels.

"About a man from Welcombe who met with someone two days ago in this tavern." Campbell watched her reaction, but was disappointed.

"I recall no such man," Jenny answered easily. "No strangers at all, save for you gentlemen." She returned the colonel's steady gaze. "If that will be all, sir?"

Campbell nodded and for a moment watched the sway of her rounded backside as she moved off. He started to turn back to Gilchrist when the young lieutenant's changed expression prompted him to look again at the departing barmaid. She had paused to whisper to the three men at the other table. The big Irishman's ruddy face darkened, then looked relieved. He and his two companions laughed loudly. The Irishman slapped Jenny on the bottom as she returned to work.

"Know them?" Campbell asked.

Lieutenant Gilchrist studied the men for a moment. "Not the old man or the dark one. The big Irishman I have seen before on the docks here in Bideford." He stroked his smooth chin. "Think they know of our Welcombe man?"

"'Twouldna harm us to ask." Campbell rose, tankard in hand and, followed by the lieutenant, boldly joined the three sailors. The handful of other patrons watched with guarded curiosity. "Good day to you, gentlemen."

"And to you, sir." The Irishman's broad, red bearded face broke into an open friendly smile.

"May we sit?" Gilchrist asked politely.

"Aye, sirs," Darcy answered, "we'd be hard pressed to stop you." On this uncertain invitation, Campbell and Gilchrist took their seats on the long bench.

"I am Colonel Andrew Campbell of Argyll's Regiment."

"Ah, the treachery at Glencoe," the Irishman said with quiet mockery.

"I was no in Glencoe," Campbell answered curtly.

"And your mate?" asked the young man with the cross-scarred cheek.

"I am Lieutenant Philip Gilchrist of His Majesty's ship *Rainbow*," Gilchrist replied, regarding the man carefully.

"O'Flynn. Darcy O'Flynn," the Irishman said. "These lads be Judas Jones and Luther Devlin." The older man and then the younger nodded in turn. "Now what may we be doing for you, gentlemen?"

"'Tis information we want," Campbell answered. "Down in Welcombe we know that two agents of James Stuart have been seen. And now off Land's End a Spanish ship has been sighted."

"And what is that to us?" Darcy asked bluntly.

"A man came here from Welcombe two days ago and met with someone in this tavern. Would you know aught of that?"

Darcy shook his leonine head of russet hair. "We were not on land that day." There was an increasing density to the unseen wall between the two officers and the sailors.

Luther Devlin gave them a beguiling smile. "Perhaps if you told us more about these men you're seeking, we, in our loyalty to our good King William, could watch for 'em in future." Darcy shot Luther a warning look that went unheeded.

"We know nothing of the man who came here to the Red Cock," Campbell said, "but we do know something of two Jacobites in Welcombe. One is Nicholas MacBride, a man of some forty years, brown haired, an Irishman like yourself." Darcy gave a wry smile and turned his attention to his tankard. "MacBride is with a man some many years younger, named Lionel MacAlister. He is perhaps twenty five years old, tall, thin, light haired, a Scot --"

"Like yourself," Darcy chuckled.

"Aye," Campbell said impatiently.

"And the ship you spoke of?" Judas asked, running a hand through his thin hair. "Spanish, you say."

"Aye," Gilchrist answered. "A fifth rater at best. We spotted her from the Rainbow near the Scillies. We have reason to believe they mean to land arms for the papist rebels in the north."

Ignoring Judas' muttering about papists, Campbell said, "There is a reward for the man who gives us the information we need. We have taken lodgings with Mistress Pease not far from here should you have need to find us."

"As I said, we'll bear it in mind." Darcy rose, standing a full head higher than the colonel. "If that be all, sir?"

Colonel Campbell said a stiff, "Good day," and then retired with the lieutenant to the corner table. There was a long pause as the two enclaves settled into their conversations again, each table casting wary glances at the other.

The tavern door opened, admitting a chill October gust and Blind Kate. On her back was strapped a harp and in her right hand was a cane. She may have once been an attractive woman, but a hard life had left its marks. Her face was strong and lined, smudged with greasy dirt. She was dressed in an odd mixture of clean but shabby gifts from various patrons. Her green skirt had once been the height of fashion, but was now thin and patched. A tattered shawl was draped over her long tangled brown hair, her threadbare black bodice and her wrinkled linen shift. Her sightless eyes stared squarely at the ale cask, though her sense was more directed by a keen nose.

"Jenny!" she called. "Jenny m'girl, where are ye? Kate's come and she's thirsty, by all the saints." Jenny ran out from the pantry, still wiping her hands on her apron, and led the blind woman to a chair by the fire, then helped her unstrap the harp. Moments later, several men pushed through the door, clamoring for drinks and music.

"Ah, you do bring the custom with you, eh, Kate?" Jenny laughed.

"Well, lads," Kate said, making some adjustment to her harp's tuning, "what would ye hear?"

"Give us a jig," Darcy called, "and I'll give you a step or two."

With skilled sure fingers Kate began to play a merry tune and there was raucous laughter from the men at the sight of the big ruddy faced Irishman skipping and capering to the rollicking dance. "'Tis a great pity I cannot see ye," Kate called. The tune ended, and puffing and panting Darcy dropped a coin into Kate's hand. "A few more such as you, Darcy O'Flynn, and I shall drink all this day and into the morrow."

"I can afford but one jig from you, Kate," Darcy said breathlessly. "I am not so nimble these days."

"Ah, and what a liar ye are," she laughed. The room became quiet as she picked out a sad aire.

Darcy returned to his table long enough to drain his tankard. "Are you lads coming?" he asked his companions. "Luther?" Luther nodded and finished his ale. "Judas?"

The old man shook his head, running a gnarled hand over his balding scalp again. "I will sit 'ere a time longer, I think."

"But you said we --" Luther broke off his protest.

"I say I wish to stay 'ere," Judas answered firmly. "I want to 'ear the 'arp playing."

Darcy took Luther by the arm and pulled him from the table. "Let the old man be, Devlin." The two sailors had a brief word with Jenny about their tally of chalk marks on the wall near the tap. They paid and left, Luther pausing briefly in the door for one last appraising look at his friend Judas and then at the two officers at the corner table.

Judas listened enraptured to Kate's music for a time, then drew out a small book of scriptures and began to read slowly. He looked up once as Kate sang a Gaelic love song composed a century ago. He looked up again when a shadow fell across his page and he found that the two officers had joined him once more.

"God's truth, gentlemen, I ain't got any information," Judas said, with an uneasy glance around the room.

"No, man, we came no for that," Campbell said. "'Twas to be nearer the music."

"If we may?" Gilchrist asked, indicating the empty bench. Judas nodded resignedly.

"I heard the Irishman call you Judas," Campbell remarked. "'Tis a strange name for a Christian, surely."

"My gran give me that name in the 'ope that I would rise above its shadow."

"And had your parents no say?" Gilchrist asked.

Judas shook his head. "My mother was a young woman of good family who died abearing me. My father was some roving sinner who seduced 'er and was ne'er seen again. 'Twas 'e that was the shadow o'er my conception and my gran, thinking that weren't shadow enough, named me Judas and schooled me in the way of salvation through the scriptures. Better to be a good man with an evil name, than an evil man with a good name, as she would say."

"And you are a good Christian and a devout Protestant, are you not?" Campbell leaned forward.

"Aye, Colonel, and loyal to me king," Judas responded with satisfaction.

"I take that to mean King William and not the papist James Stuart," Campbell said.

"Aye," Judas replied, "but I still know nothing about your man from Welcombe and the Spanish ship." He looked at them craftily, grinning through several missing and broken teeth. "Those papists, they'll all burn in the fires of eternal damnation for their abuses and corruptions that are abominations in the eyes of God."

"Then," Campbell said, "we could trust you to be telling us if you were to hear aught of these spies of whom we have spoken. There would be gold in it for you."

Judas grinned again. "But since I know nothing of 'em, 'tis no matter. Nor am I likely to know of 'em, gentlemen, since I am soon to sail and 'ave me work to keep me from the affairs of this sinful world."

"And your friends?" Campbell asked. "What of them? I suspect the Irishman to be in faith with the papists."

"I wouldn't know, Colonel," Judas replied. "I meet 'im but rarely. We are of different vessels."

"And young Devlin? What of him?"

Judas beamed warmly. "An 'andsome lad, isn't 'e? Although somewhat given to the sin of pride, which, as ye know, goeth before a fall, but, aye, 'e could be trusted I think." Seeing the light in the colonel's eyes, Judas hastened to add, "But there ain't nothing to tell. We 'ave only just made port and are off again soon enough." He leaned closer to the officers. "Still, I do 'ave one bit of advice from an old man who 'as seen much of the world, both the righteous and the evil." The officers listened expectantly. "Offering bribes in a tavern amongst local sailors and tradesmen will only net ye an empty pocket and a fine cargo of useless lies. This lot 'ere will tell ye anything ye want to 'ear, even to bear false witness against one another, in order to take your money and then they will leave ye looking the fool. 'Tisn't that they are disloyal, just merely out for coin at some other's expense." Judas opened his book of scriptures, thus shutting out the two officers and ending the conversation.

Resignedly, Campbell and Gilchrist returned to their own table. Kate played on, now singing a lively drinking song and the men around her joined in heartily.

"I dinna agree with that old man," Campbell said. "Any fisherman knows if you throw out a large enough net, something is bound to be caught. Offer gold to these lads and one of them will take the bait."

"So far it doesn't look very promising," Gilchrist sighed.

"Oh, I dinna think you see, lad," Campbell said with a cunning smile. "I have already found our man."

CHAPTER FIVE

RIDDLES WISELY EXPOUNDED

> Oh, envy's greener than the grass,
> lay the ben tae the bonny broom;
> and the Devil's more wicked than
> any woman there was. folksong

Margaret laughed prettily and flashed a beautiful smile as she revealed the strength of her hand and so won another round. Simon grumbled as he watched her sweep up the coins and stack them neatly beside her other winnings. "I shall be a poor man again before the clock strikes nine," he said ruefully.

"If your father never told you aught of me, he did you and your purse a great disservice," Margaret said lightly. "I was always clever with cards."

"Clever or lucky?" Anne asked, taking a sip of wine and glumly surveying the newly dealt hand in front of her.

"Aye," Margaret said with a delighted giggle. She, the two elder Hawkwoods and Dr. Hartley sat at the table near the fire in the great hall. In the far corner by the brazier, Jamie and Tristan drank manful amounts of brandy and conversed in low voices. The evening at cards had been most profitable for Margaret who, despite her sweet features and helpless manner, was an absolutely ruthless card player.

Simon again threw down his cards in disgust and rose from the table. "Well, I can ill afford to have my stepmother hold my inheritance in its entirety. I shall therefore withdraw." He refilled his glass, lit his pipe and leaned against the carved stone mantel, watching as Jamie took the empty chair at the table and Patrick dealt a fresh hand.

Tristan left his place by the brazier and sat on the bench inside the wide fireplace, warming his hands over the coals, and twisting awkwardly as he attempted to be comfortable in his tight velvet knee breeches. "I shall ne'er understand why such garments are in genteel company considered superior to the breacan feile," he said, loosening some of the ribbons at his knee. "Nor how it was that I was convinced to wear them."

"I think you will adjust in time," Margaret said. "Would you care to play a hand, Tristan?"

"Nay, Aunt Margaret," he answered. "I have no skill with the cards." He added with a slight blush, "'Tis pretty women that are my vice."

"Both can lead a man to his downfall," Simon said with mock seriousness.

"You are talking like a Calvinist, brother," Anne replied, not looking up from her cards, "and for a man of your reputation 'tis a sorry thing to hear."

"I doubt if Simon's reputation would be harmed by such statements," Patrick said as he laid his cards down in front of him and started collecting the coins. Margaret frowned.

"I didna see where you came by that king," Jamie remarked.

"'Tis the hand of a skilled surgeon -- very deft, it is," Simon laughed.

"'Twas the luck of the draw and nothing more," Patrick answered as he started to deal a new hand.

The door opened and Diggory entered, concern ill-hidden on his antique face. "There be two officers wanting to speak with ye," he said quietly as he reached the table. Behind him could be seen two uniformed men waiting by the door. An uncomfortable look passed between Anne and Simon, then between Jamie and Tristan.

"Show them in, Diggory," Margaret said, unaware of the anxious glances around her. Colonel Campbell entered first, looking short and thick in contrast to the tall slender form of Lieutenant Gilchrist who followed him at a respectful distance.

"And to what may we ascribe this honor?" Margaret asked.

"We are here to make formal inquiries," the colonel answered, smiling stiffly. "I am Colonel Andrew Campbell of Argyll's Regiment, and this is --" He got no further. Margaret was on her feet, her small white fists clenched and shaking. Behind her both Jamie and Tristan had risen. Jamie was forcibly restraining his cousin.

Anne rose and put a light hand on Margaret's arm. "Perhaps it would be better, madam, if you retired with your kinsmen and left this matter to us." Without a word Margaret strode from the room, Jamie pulling Tristan along after her.

"What on earth was that about?" the lieutenant asked.

"Glencoe," Anne answered with a sharp nod at the colonel.

"I was no in Glencoe," Campbell answered defensively, "but 'twas a legal action for the peace and security of the nation."

"Of course," Anne said.

"I see," the lieutenant said, smiling at the elegant young woman in front of him. "Well, 'twas not our intention to cause dispute, only to make inquiries."

"Please be seated, gentlemen," Anne said, gesturing graciously to the empty chairs at the table. "Simon, be so kind as to fetch some more wine." Grateful for the escape, Simon quickly left. "You must forgive the bad manners of my family. I believe the interruption prevented proper introductions." The gaze of her shadowy jet eyes lighted on the lieutenant. "Your comrade, Colonel?"

"Lieutenant Philip Gilchrist of His Majesty's ship *Rainbow*." Gilchrist snapped a fine bow. Neither officer noticed the slight shiver the Navy vessel's name produced in Anne.

"I am Anne Hawkwood, and this is our good friend, Doctor Patrick Hartley." Patrick bowed. Simon returned with a decanter of wine, which he set on the table in front of Anne. "My older brother, Simon Hawkwood." Simon also bowed, then withdrew to sit with Patrick, each of them eyeing the distance to the door. Anne poured wine for the two officers as they took the offered seats across from her. "You had some questions for us?"

"Aye," the colonel replied. "We came to ask if you had noticed any activity in the cove below this house." Anne felt her body stiffen, and sensed the same current pass through her brother and Patrick.

"There is a Spanish warship further down the coast." Gilchrist explained, "and we suspect that she may be trying to make some contact in this vicinity."

"This is a hard stretch of rock," Anne commented coolly, sipping her wine.

"Precisely why we are making inquiry of those with quiet water near their homes," Campbell replied.

"I would hardly call the Rookery's cove quiet," Anne said. "'Tis high waves and white chop most of the time."

"But a ship could put down a boat there," Gilchrist persisted.

"Aye," Anne nodded, "but surely we would see it if it did. Is that what you wish to hear?"

Campbell's flesh-pocketed eyes narrowed as he studied her. "Aye," he answered slowly. "There is also the matter of two enemy agents."

"Colonel," Anne said, leaning forward, "let me assure you that the Hawkwoods have long had a reputation for loyalty to their king, who is at present the Prince of Orange. My late father, Sir John Hawkwood, of whom you may have heard, built our family's fortune on his loyalty after the restoration of the crown. I think you needn't fear treason in this house."

"And your kin who left upon our arrival?"

"They are newly arrived here, Colonel," Anne replied. "I hardly know them, but I can assure you that all three have refrained from any social contact, being in mourning for our late father." She lowered her eyes coyly, avoiding the colonel's unrelenting perusal. She sensed that his interest in her was steadily passing that which was required for formal inquiry. Such interest could be used to advantage.

"Who are these men you are seeking?" Patrick asked.

"An Irishman named MacBride and a young Scot named MacAlister. Both have been seen in the village of Welcombe."

"Then why do you not seek them in Welcombe?" Simon asked.

"Because I had report from one of my men that they had come to the Bideford area." Campbell turned his attention from Anne to her brother.

"And could you not arrest them?" Patrick asked.

"We could," Gilchrist answered, his smooth cheeks glowing in the firelight, "but that would give away the game and we would not be able to take their other contacts here."

"Ah, these matters are far too complex for the likes of me," Anne said with a demure flutter of her long soft lashes. "I am sorry, gentlemen, that we cannot be of more assistance. It is always our intention to aid the forces of the king whenever we are called upon to do so. Feel free to inquire of us further if you think such will help you capture these rebels."

"Thank you, mistress," Gilchrist said, rising. "You are most kind."

"Aye, indeed," Campbell said, also rising. "We will bid you then goodnight."

Gilchrist cast one last look on Anne as he followed the colonel out. "A comely young woman," Gilchrist said as he untethered his horse from the hitching post by the front door.

"Aye, but with too much command," Campbell replied as he led his horse across the cobblestones. "She wants taming. 'Tis no good for a woman to be so much in charge."

Gilchrist mounted his horse. "I think it shows a fine spirit."

"Aye, but a woman is like a horse," Campbell said, mounting and riding close to Gilchrist. "A fine spirited horse may be a beauty, but 'tis of no value if you canna ride it." Campbell looked sternly at the lieutenant. "God gave man dominion o'er all the earth, to humble and to tame all within it."

Setting spurs to the horse the colonel trotted away down the dark drive. Gilchrist followed, offering no further argument, but in his heart those dark eyes were still shining.

"I do not like having royal officers as guests," Anne said crossly, settling herself in her chair by the fire. "Most disturbing."

"Well, thank God that their business has naught to do with us," Patrick said, filling his pipe by the mantel. "I could hear Simon's heart pounding the entire time."

"Simon, for a man who was born to hang," Anne said with a wily smile, "I do not understand why you worry over it so much."

"'Tis not the gallows I fear, sister. 'Tis my manner of reaching it." He drained his glass and refilled it.

The door was flung open as Margaret entered, followed by Jamie and Tristan. "What did they want?" Margaret asked sharply.

"You should have stayed to find out," Anne said. "Quite a spectacle you made of yourselves and for no reason at all."

"No reason!" Tristan fumed. "That man was a Campbell!"

"Aye," said Jamie, "and every jackass in Scotland knows the high feeling that runs between the MacDonalds and the Campbells."

"Well, this is not Scotland," Simon replied coldly. "Your clan disputes have no place here. 'Tis no matter to us that the colonel is named Campbell."

"Perhaps it would if you knew more of them," Jamie said, anger heating his white cheeks. "It was his sort who sold your beloved Charles the First to the rabble. It was the Campbell who let seven hundred and sixty men of Clan MacLean die at Inverkeithing for want of reinforcements that he withheld. It was the Campbell who dangled young Charles betwixt the throne and Cromwell. It was the Campbell who arranged the barbarous execution of the great Montrose, and it was the Campbell with a Dalrymple who planned the slaughter in Glencoe."

"Are you finished?" Anne demanded impatiently.

"No, and neither am I," Tristan said, pushing forward. "I know that man who was here tonight. He is a near cousin to that dog Robert Campbell of Glenlyon whose orders it was to cut off the clan of MacIain 'root and branch'." Tristan's eyes blazed, his fist shook. "You have no doubt heard the tale told by the Crown -- how 'twas for the good of the country that this nest of highland thieves be exterminated. 'Twas no Glencoe alone they would kill. They would have killed all the MacDonalds, but they dinna dare. So they decided to attack the smallest clan, the MacIains in Glencoe."

"If your chief had taken the oath of allegiance to King William as had been required by law, nothing would have happened," Patrick said steadily.

"He did take the oath," Jamie said, "but 'twas no reported to the Master of Stair, or if 'twas the fact of it was suppressed from the Council."

"Aye," Tristan agreed, "for the Master of Stair was eager for our blood." He looked straight at Anne and Simon. "I will admit that our chief took his time o'er the oath and was a day or two late in the taking of it, but 'twas deep winter and who could expect an old man to walk with speed o'er the glens."

"Obviously, someone did," Anne commented, accepting a glass from Simon and sipping delicately.

"Aye, but that someone didna wish to see MacIain take the oath and suppressed the fact that he did," Tristan said. He sat next to the fire, and gazed on the flames as though he were seeing another fire. "A month after our chief's return with assurances of our safety because he took the oath, the Campbells came. 'Twas Argyll's Regiment, under Glenlyon. He was kin by marriage to the chief's son and as such was welcomed. He asked for quarters and we took all his men in, billeted them in our homes. We fed them and kept the fires warm for them. They diced with us and drank with us. No kindness was spared nor was any refused.

"Then in the wee hours of the thirteenth day of February last they rose from their beds under orders from Glenlyon and slaughtered all within reach. Some two score died at the hands of the soldiers. Many more died running through the glen to escape, caught as they were in a snow storm and ill dressed for the weather."

"Your presence here shows that the soldiers did a less than thorough job," Anne observed.

Tristan smiled bitterly. "Well, no MacDonald would e'er give a Campbell credit for competence. They might have killed us all but for the conscience of some and the stupidity of others." He turned from the fire. "There were among the soldiers a few who gave signs of warning to our people, though no soldier spoke outright of his orders. Two soldiers were heard to say that they wouldna mind fighting the men of Glencoe in the field, but that they didna think much of murdering them in their beds. So on that night there had been some little warning from men of conscience."

"And the stupidity of others?" Patrick asked, smoke from the pipe curling around his red hair.

"The soldiers used their guns to kill the first of us. With those shots the glen awoke and those who could fled into the snow." Tristan looked back into the flames. "MacIain was shot through the back of the head as he was ordering drink for Lieutenant Lindsay who had come to call. MacIain's lady was stripped naked of her clothes and jewels, treated shamefully, and eventually escaped into the night. We found her dead of cold the next day.

"The man who had let Glenlyon's into his home and eight men with him were bound hand and foot, then shot one at a time. Wee children and helpless women were butchered." The horrible memory seemed alive before his eyes in the dancing of the fire. His voice barely rose above a whisper. "I saw my sister -- a child of not four years with her head smashed against a rock, my parents dead in the snow beside her."

Tristan paused and smiled softly to himself. Behind him Margaret stood, Jamie's hand clasped in hers, their faces betraying the deep emotions the tragedy invoked. Anne, Simon and Patrick remained in respectful silence.

"'Twas the Campbell gunfire and poor timing that allowed most of the clan to escape. Another four hundred men had been sent to block all the passes so that none of the clan might leave, but a fierce snow delayed them so that the passes were open to us when we reached them. And in the snow the soldiers that followed couldna see us. Those who survived ran to the Stewarts of Appin and were given sanctuary with them. From there the story was carried through the highlands, and so the attempts to bury the truth with the dead were to no avail."

"And how is it that you escaped being murdered in your bed?" Simon asked, refilling his glass.

Tristan smiled and a blush of color flooded his drawn face. "I wasna in my bed that night," he admitted. "As I told ye earlier I have a fondness for the lassies. On that night I was lying snug in the shieling with my sweet Meggie, all covered with straw and my plaid we were and warm enough. Then we heard the shots and the screams and there was the smell of fire in the air. We dressed and ran down to our homes. There was naught left for me to fight for, so I gathered up my lass and we ran to Larig Eilde. 'Twas unguarded and we escaped in the snow." He rose and poured himself a glass of wine.

"I am glad that you and the girl were saved," Anne said kindly, sensing a new compassion for her Scots kin.

Tristan shook his head. "My Meg died two days after. The cold killed her -- the cold and the grief."

"I am sorry," Anne said gently.

Tristan drained his glass. "Dinna be sorry, Anne. Be angry." He looked expectantly into her face. She smiled gently.

Patrick refilled the youth's glass. "Of course, we had heard of the killing there, but always couched in some semblance of official necessity, that 'twas for the peace of the nation."

Tristan laughed sourly. "My wee sister's death was for the peace of the nation?"

The silence was finally broken by Margaret. "You can well see why I canna allow any Campbell nor his minions into my home. I canna change what is past nor can I raise up the dead again to life." She tossed her blonde curls defiantly. "But I can forbid my hospitality to those who are no to be trusted with the privilege. Where we come from the obligations of host and guest are held as a sacred trust. Glencoe proved that the Campbells have no respect for that trust and therefore should be turned away no matter their need or desire."

"There is no one here who desires the presence of men such as the colonel on this property," Anne replied reassuringly, "though perhaps not for such noble reasons." Her baleful gaze rested first on Margaret, then on Jamie and Tristan. "However, the Hawkwoods have long had a reputation of dealing fairly with all inquiries and inquests from the authorities. In future, should Colonel Campbell and his lieutenant come here again there is to be no mention of Glencoe nor any matter of clan politics. Keep your peace and leave me to send the officers on their way as soon as may be. I believe that is a fair compromise." It was only when both Jamie and Tristan had given a nod of agreement that Margaret nodded as well.

It was sometime later, after they had returned to the cards and the visitation seemed almost forgotten, that Jamie asked, "Anne, what did they want? The officers, I mean."

"'Twas naught to do with us, Jamie," Anne answered unconcernedly.

Hours later, a man who had been hiding in the woods just beyond the house saw the flash of a lantern in an upper window of the east wing. Silently he slipped forward to the side entrance where Jamie was waiting for him.

And of the three men keeping watch in the tower, only one noticed.

CHAPTER SIX

SUCH A PARCEL OF ROGUES

But pith and power, till my last hour,
I'll mak' this declaration,
We're bought and sold for English gold;
Such a parcel of rogues in a nation. Robert Burns

In the cold night air that smelled faintly of dawn Gilchrist ran along a narrow alley in Bideford after a man, grabbing him by the arm. "A word with you," the lieutenant said in a rushed whisper, his breath turning to smoke.

"I promised ye the information," the man protested. "Ye must be patient, Lieutenant."

Gilchrist took a breath and shook his head. "'Tisn't that, man. I just wanted to be certain. 'Tis only Jamie Hawkwood and his cousin that are involved, is it not?" he asked the sailor anxiously.

The man thought for a moment. "Aye," he said, "those two along with MacBride and MacAlister."

"And none else at the Rookery has aught to do with these crimes you have reported?"

The man patted the rattling pouch beneath his coat. "There be no others than those I 'ave named." He started off again, then turned back to the lieutenant. "And ye swear to keep your word and ne'er tell 'twas me that told."

"I will keep my word," Gilchrist answered. "I have neither the wish nor the means to identify you."

"Ye'll 'ave your information then," the man said as he melted into the shadows of the alley.

In the morning Jamie escorted his cousin to the stable. "Tristan, I canna go with you to Welcombe," he said. In answer to Tristan's surprised look he added, "Anne has some business to discuss with me."

"I thought you didna like talk of business," Tristan said as he led a sleek mare out into the early morning sun.

"Aye," Jamie answered hesitantly, "but Father left all the money to Simon and none to me for the keeping of the house, so I had better get canny as to the trade if I am to keep this property and us in it, eh?"

"Indeed," Tristan agreed. He looked around, then said in a low voice, "Are you aware that your mother has found an old chapel in the tower here and is making shift to put it into use?"

"Jesu!" Jamie hissed.

"Aye, she'll have us all caught with such indiscretion," Tristan added.

Jamie then laughed softly. "But I dinna think that any here will hand us o'er to the law. My brother and sister, believe it or no, have a lot to lose if they lose me." His cousin looked at him quizzically, but mounted the mare without comment. "And, Tristan, you are no one to talk of indiscretion. How many days did it take me to convince you to leave off your plaid and dress in clothes of English cut?"

Tristan grinned. "And naked I feel without my plaid about me," he replied, studying his suit of brown velvet trimmed with gold braid and silk ribbons. "But if 'twill help our designs for me to go in disguise, well enough then." He wrapped his cloak tightly about him and settled his plumed hat on his head. "I feel like some court fop."

"'Tis the fashion here," Jamie replied as he handed him a gold headed riding whip. "Here. 'Twas one of my father's and now 'tis a fine whip for the lord of the manor's kinsman."

Tristan laughed as he accepted the gift, admiring the elaborate 'H' engraved on the head. "Now all will know me for a gentleman and no a highland savage." He gathered the reins and turned the mare. "Well, 'tis off to Mistress Dunord's." He trotted across the stable yard. "Slan," he called.

"Slan," Jamie answered as he watched him ride into the chill shadows of the tree shaded drive.

Hugo Stone arrived at midday and was shown into the great hall where Anne, her two brothers and Doctor Hartley were seated around the table by the fire. Taking a chair at the head of the table, the lawyer spread several papers before him while Diggory poured him a glass of wine.

"Thank you, Diggory," Anne said. "You may leave the decanter on the sideboard. We can fend for ourselves."

"Aye, mistress." The old servant gave an awkward little bow and left.

"I suppose if we are all here, we may get on with our business," Hugo said. "I trust that we will not be disturbed."

"My mother is occupied elsewhere in the house," Jamie replied, "and my cousin Tristan has found reason to ride abroad for the day."

"Some wench, I'll wager," Simon grinned.

"Aye, I fear so," Jamie nodded with shy smile.

"Very well then," Stone continued, "I think we need not spend over much time on formalities." He handed each of them a paper. "I have reports on both the London and the Amsterdam markets. The price of wheat has doubled."

"Has it indeed?" Simon asked with a suspicious glance at the paper in his hand.

Stone's piercing eyes glared at Simon, then his beaky face worked itself into a smile. "Really, Simon, you must not distrust everything I say. I am perfectly capable of the truth."

"Whenever 'tis to your advantage," Simon retorted dropping the paper on the table and draining his wine glass.

"And in this case, it is," Stone replied, then returned to his papers, lifting one. "As of the wet summer and the French defeat, there is nigh to famine in that country."

Patrick rose. "There is word from Bristol that silver has lost value," he said as he filled his pipe from the tobacco box on the mantel.

"I have the same report from Amsterdam," Stone replied.

"Pity," Anne said, "for I have two chests of Spanish coin in the cellar."

Stone patted her hand. "'Twill regain its worth in time, my dear. Simply keep hold of it until the bulls push the price up again."

"I fear my younger brother comprehends little of this," Anne said with a compassionate glance at Jamie who sat quietly with his hands folded on the table.

"Let me listen and I will understand it all soon enough," he answered with a secretive smile. "Go on, Lawyer Stone. You were discussing the famine in France and the price of wheat."

"I do believe this boy is a Hawkwood after all," Patrick chuckled. "He sounds as much like the old captain as any I have heard."

Once the laughter abated, Stone started the matter of markets again. "My recommendation is to hold back the silver, coffee, tea, chocolate and miscellaneous fineries. With the famine the best item of trade will be edible and cheap."

"We have ample cod, herring, sugar and some grain," Anne said.

"Excellent!" Stone rubbed his hands together, the greedy gleam in his eye apparent to all. "When can the Chanticleer sail?"

"I can send word to Eben tonight," Anne answered. "He can sail from Bideford tomorrow night to pick up the stores, and we can be on our way to Amsterdam or to Dunkirk by dawn following."

Jamie paled. "Surely, sister," he stammered, "surely 'twould be wiser to wait another few days." They all stared at him. "I mean, with those officers searching for a ship and all."

"What officers?" Stone asked sharply.

"A Scots colonel and a Navy lieutenant were here two nights ago," Anne answered. "Nothing to do with us, but ..." She thought for a moment. "Jamie may have a valid point here. If there is no hurry, perhaps we should wait."

"But not too long," Stone cautioned. "With winter moving in and the market good, we should take advantage of this famine while we can."

"Hugo, I have never heard of a famine that lasted not long enough," Simon said dryly.

"Aye, Simon is right," Anne agreed. "This famine will not lessen with the coming of winter. Indeed, the price of food may rise beyond all expectations."

"But the sailing weather will be bad," Stone argued.

"The *Chanticleer* can manage," Anne answered confidently. "We will wait. If there is word of the market failing, we will sail at once."

"Has the Bold Cockerel sailed?" Stone asked.

Anne shook her head. "Tomorrow morning with the first tide."

"Ward has stayed over long as it is," Stone complained. "We don't want Golding's spies reporting the Cockerel in Bideford even if it is to report the death of the late captain. Did you leave some token in her hold for Golding's share?"

Anne laughed. "Aye, little enough for that simpering old thief. There is a small chest of silver, some silk and brocade, pepper, sugar and tobacco. It will fetch him a good profit, but not near compared to what we removed."

"Ward did remember to repack the Dutch goods this time, I hope," Simon asked Anne.

"Aye, Simon," she replied. "The scare on the last cargo when that barrel of cheese was found has certainly schooled his crew. There are a few such containers in the cellar that must be repacked before the Chanticleer sails again, so 'tis well to take an extra few days to see to it."

Throughout the remaining conversation of markets won and lost, no one noticed that Jamie had abandoned them for the realm of his own thoughts, smiling shrewdly all the while.

Half asleep, Tristan let the horse pick its own way along the rocky path on Hartland Point. Far below at the foot of the magnificent cliffs the crash of wild waves sang a violent lullaby to the drowsy youth. It had been a hard ride down to Welcombe, tiring both horse and rider. Twilight settled over them, the horse ambling along while Tristan's dozing dreams were filled with glorious plans and noble endeavors. He would arm his kinsmen and they would drive King William from the highlands. Then would MacIain and his murdered kin rest easy in the Pass of Glencoe.

The powerful grip pulling him from the saddle and the taste of the road against his mouth jerked Tristan to consciousness. He lay face down in the dust while strong hands roughly pinned his arms behind him and bound his wrists with coarse cord. He struggled and might have cried out had not the cold point of a knife touched his throat. "Quiet, brat," the man hissed. "Ye'll 'ave plenty of time for talk."

Bound and frightened, Tristan let the cry die in his throat, offering no resistance as he was hauled to his feet. Dragging him by the arm and leading the horse, his captor led him into the woods. To the left he could see the little roadside chapel. "A favorite meeting spot for the 'Awkwoods, this little chapel," the man commented. "A good spot to wait for them what's on the road from Welcombe." He laughed and slung Tristan to the ground.

"What do you want from me?" Tristan asked.

"Information, lad."

"Of what sort?"

"What are ye and Master James planning that involves the cove?"

Tristan's heart thudded to a stop, but he forced a laugh and said, "Why, 'tis no more than stealing a lass away from under her father's watchful eye."

The man laughed with him. "Is that all then?" Tristan nodded with relief and began to breathe with ease. Suddenly the man seized him by the hair and brutally jerked his head back. "Ye lie, boy! Two nights ago your friend from the Red Cock came by for a visit. I know 'cause I saw 'im. That and them officers put me on to ye."

"You know all you will," Tristan declared boldly. "I willna tell you more."

"Oh, ye'll talk, ye little pape." The voice softened to a cruel whisper. "Ye'll tell me all I want to know afore the night's 'alf done. I 'ave a ship to catch and 'ave no time to be delicate about this business." A pale streak of moonlight slipped between the clouds and trees, and in it Tristan saw the greedy glint in the man's eyes. "Ye'll beg to talk when I'm done with ye. Aye, lad, ye'll beg."

In the moonlight there was a flash of the gold handle as the riding whip came down.

It was late the following afternoon when Tristan's mare finally walked wearily into the Rookery's stable. She was exhausted, streaked, scored and lathered.

"Like someone rode her hard all night," Simon remarked when Diggory showed him the animal. "And Tristan?"

"No sign of 'im, Master Simon," Diggory said as he carefully washed the mare's flanks.

"He never struck me as the sort to abuse his mount," Simon said reflectively stroking his black moustache. "Could the horse have been stolen?"

"Aye, perhaps," Diggory replied plunging his sponge into the washbucket again.

Anne strode into the dim stable. "What is this I hear about Tristan's horse coming home without him?" Her brisk manner was an odd contrast to her fashionable gown and piled curls.

"Aye, Cap'n," Diggory said, "'E may 'ave met with ill fortune."

"Take care of the horse," Anne said flatly. "We will search if he does not appear by tomorrow morning." She took Simon's arm and turned to go. "Oh, Diggory?" He looked up. "Never call me Captain here."

Diggory lowered his eyes. "Aye, Mistress Anne."

Inside the great hall, Anne warmed her hands over the fire. "Dear God, but this house is cold," she said. "I'm all ashiver. 'Tis the same feeling I get when there is a storm brewing at sea."

"I hope young Tristan's disappearance proves to be no more than a folly of youth," Simon remarked. "I cannot abide the thought of dealing with Margaret and Jamie under any circumstance more emotionally fraught than a game of whist. Where are they, by the way?"

"In the tower, cleaning out the old chapel up there," Anne answered with disgust. "You realize that they're papists, the three of them, don't you, Simon?"

He looked shocked. "I had no idea!"

"Neither had I until I found Margaret's rosary in her room this morning. I had wondered what she did in there all the time. What was Father about when he married her!?" Anne pressed her lips together in a firm line. "We must tread very carefully, brother. If Jamie has talked, then they all know enough to hang the lot of us."

"Aye," he said. "Well, to me 'tis a better death than to die sick as did Father, or to vanish without trace as did my mother."

"Well," Anne declared, "I have no intention of hanging. 'Tis a damn good thing *The Bold Cockerel* sailed this morning. Until I better know Jamie's mind Ward is safer in Plymouth."

"And the Chanticleer?"

"She is still docked in Bideford," Anne said. "It may be best to send her elsewhere, too."

"I cannot think that Margaret is so much a threat, even if she is a Catholic," Simon commented, half to himself. Anne nodded. "And I doubt me if Jamie has the wit for it."

"All the same, dear brother," Anne replied, "I think we must be wary of them all for the nonce." She rose and stood in front of him. "And I am concerned about Tristan," she admitted. "Of the three I like him best and I dearly hope that no harm has come to him."

"And what shall we say of his horse?" Simon asked.

"Best to say nothing at all for the present," Anne said thoughtfully. "No need to upset Margaret and have Jamie riding all over the countryside calling attention to himself. Indeed, Tristan may have found a willing wench and in youthful exuberance forgot to tether the mare properly." This idea seemed to please her. "Aye, no doubt he will be home tomorrow."

"And if not?" Simon looked intently into his sister's sly dark eyes.

"Well, at least it is one less person who can hang us."

CHAPTER SEVEN

THE CRAFTY MAID'S POLICY

You knew not my meaning,
You wrong understood me,
and away she went galloping
down the long lane. folksong

It was deep night when the first shots awakened Anne. She leapt from bed and ran to the small window overlooking the cove, but could see nothing. Below her she could hear the sharp crack of muskets and from over the water the roar of cannon.

She hastily pulled on her dark red skirt and a shirt that had once been her father's. She had just donned one of his full skirted coats and was shoving a brace of pistols into her sash when Margaret rushed through the door between their rooms.

"What is happening out there, Anne?" Margaret cried breathlessly, then stopped short at the sight of the young woman's attire, "And why are you dressed ... like a ..."

"There is no time to explain, Margaret," Anne answered brusquely, throwing a cloak over her shoulders, "and no time for corsets and petticoats." She shoved a dagger into her boot. "Now stay here and do not come down until I send word." Anne strode from the room, leaving a distraught Margaret watching anxiously by the window. At the foot of the stairs Simon and Patrick waited, also fully dressed and armed.

"I thought you said Ward had sailed this morning," Simon said tersely as he followed Anne to the front door.

"He did," Anne answered. Patrick started toward the fireplace in the great hall. "Not that way, Patrick. We go by the path."

"And get shot?" the doctor asked incredulously.

"I see no reason to risk the cellars to these interlopers until I know who and what they are," Anne said as she pulled open the front door and stepped into the cool night air.

There were more shots as the three made their way to the path. Crouching in the thicket above they could just make out the figures on the sand below. Several men on horses were chasing a handful of men along the water's edge. "How in God's name did the get horses down there?" Patrick whispered.

"There's a place of easier descent about three quarters of a mile to the north," Anne whispered back. "See? They ride for it now." The mounted men galloped up the sand, one turning to fire at a short thickset man who fell near the foot of the path.

Again there was the sound of cannon, and in the flash of fire could be seen a Navy man-of-war in close pursuit of another warship. "Not the Bold Cockerel surely," Patrick said, as they started their cautious climb down the cliff.

Anne shook her head. "She's Spanish from the shape of her. I fear we shall soon be seeing Colonel Campbell on this matter."

They reached the bottom of the path. The shore was empty except for the body of the fallen man. Patrick stepped out carefully. On his signal Anne and Simon joined him at the man's side. Gently Patrick turned him over. His eyes opened and he stared into Patrick's face.

"I am a doctor," Patrick said reassuringly as he examined the bloody hole in the man's chest.

"Will he live?" Simon asked kneeling beside him.

Patrick shook his head. "The wound is mortal."

"Naimhaid faoi cheilt," the man whispered.

"'Tis Irish," Anne said. "This must be the rebel MacBride that Campbell is seeking."

MacBride suddenly tensed at the sound of his name. His breathing was weak, his eyes unfocused. "Naimhaid faoi cheilt," he said again. His eyes fixed, his breathing stopped. Patrick laid him back on the sand.

"What do you suppose he meant?" Simon asked.

"'A hidden enemy'," Anne answered. "I have not sailed all these years with Darcy O'Flynn without learning something of the Gaelic gibberish."

"Well," said Simon rising, "I have no wish for his enemies, hidden or otherwise, to find me here."

"Aye," Anne agreed. "Those soldiers will be all through the Rookery within half an hour. We must get back and fend them off." They left the corpse on the sand and ran toward the shallow cave. "Now we shall go by the cellars, Patrick," Anne said as she led the way through the damp stone passage up to the door hidden in the rock, past a small chamber neatly stacked with casks and chests. When they emerged through a small door at the back of the huge fireplace in the great hall they found Diggory waiting for them.

"Ye 'ave seen the soldiers?" he asked hurriedly.

"Aye," Simon answered, "all over the cove."

"'Tis Master James they want," Diggory said.

"Are you certain?" Anne asked, turning in surprise.

"What has he done?" Simon demanded.

"I don't know, sir," Diggory answered, "'but 'tis something powerful criminal by the looks of things. 'E's in the wine cellar with Eben looking after 'im."

"Eben's here?" Anne asked.

"Aye, Mistress. Come up from Bideford to ask for orders. Arrived just afore the soldiers and come to warn ye," Diggory said, as he turned the dying coals in the fireplace and added kindling to build up a blaze. "Ended up rescuing Master James and pulling 'im into the cellar."

Anne threw off her cloak. "Here then, gentlemen, are my orders. Simon and Patrick, saddle horses and ride for Plymouth. Get there as quickly as you can and find John Ward. Tell him what has happened here and that I will sail to Mousehole if I can, but he is not to wait for more than a week. If I do not come and send no word, then assume the worst and put to sea. Diggory, stow Jamie in the lower cellar, then return to your room. When the soldiers come, act as though you have slept all night."

"What are you going to do, Anne?" Simon asked anxiously.

"I? Why, dear brother, I am going back to bed, of course," she announced airily. "'Twouldn't do for the soldiers to find me up and about at this hour." She raced up the stairs.

Colonel Campbell pounded long and hard on the door before a disgruntled looking Diggory opened it. "A bit late for calling, ain't it?" he grumbled as Campbell pushed past him, followed by Lieutenant Gilchrist and a dozen soldiers, filling the foyer.

"We have a warrant for the arrest of James Hawkwood, Tristan MacDonald and Lionel MacAlister," Campbell announced. "I have reason to believe that they are hiding on these premises and demand to search for them."

"Well," Diggory replied slowly, scratching his grizzled chin, "I 'ad best be asking the lady of the 'ouse."

"Ask me what?" It was Margaret. She stood on the landing above, her golden hair loose and tousled, her face unpainted, her nightdress and robe flowing behind her.

"We must search this house," Campbell repeated, brandishing his pistol. Already his men had pushed into the great hall and down the corridor into the pantries and the kitchen.

"For what?" There was no sweetness in her voice.

"Your son and your nephew."

"They are no here and you are no searching this house," Margaret said coldly. She glared witheringly at Campbell. "Diggory, show them out."

"Madam," Campbell said with full authority, "you dinna have that privilege."

"I will no allow --" Margaret began, fury breaking her words.

"Margaret," Anne said firmly, coming down the stairs behind her, "we cannot prevent this search and when it is done, the colonel will be satisfied and will leave. We are innocent and therefore have nothing to hide." Anne smiled hospitably at the officers. She was in her robe, her thick hair in a tangled ebony mass about her shoulders, her thin face sweet and sleepy.

"No Campbell is allowed here," Margaret snapped. "That is the policy of my house."

"Was the policy, Margaret," Anne whispered sharply as she took her by the arm and turned her upstairs. "Now go to your room and stay there." Though the order had a good deal of threat behind it, Margaret still resisted. "Diggory," Anne called, "please escort this good lady to her chambers and ensure that she remains there." The old man climbed the stairs with an unusually spry step, took Margaret by the arm and led her upstairs.

"Search wherever you wish," Anne invited as she stepped down the stairs, "but, if you plan to look in Dame Margaret's apartments, you do so at your own risk," she added with a chuckle. The soldiers swarmed up the stairs and down the corridors while Anne led the two officers into the great hall where they found warmth beside the fire.

"'Tis a fine blaze for this hour of night," Gilchrist observed.

"You would like me to say that we were expecting you," Anne replied, a seductive slyness in her eyes. "In fact, I retired early this evening. Perhaps my brother Simon and his friend built it up." She poured brandy for the two men. "Exactly what has my dear younger brother done to command so much attention?"

"Treason, mistress," Campbell replied with relish, pacing in front of her. "We have certain information that he, his cousin, and the two rebel agents were meaning to receive a shipment of Spanish weapons for their rebel friends in Scotland and Ireland."

Anne froze for a moment, and it was all she could do to speak calmly. "I find that hard to believe."

"Nevertheless, 'tis true," Gilchrist said as he accepted a glass from her. "It is as we suspected when we came here before. Your cove is perfect for such a venture and we caught them at it tonight -- landing weapons, including small cannon, and hiding them in some caves above the beach. Those arms can now be sent to our own troops in Flanders."

"You saw my brother and Tristan?" Anne asked, gracefully taking a chair while modestly arranging her robe.

Campbell hesitated. "We no saw young MacDonald," he admitted, "but we did see your brother scramble up the path, and MacAlister take to his heels up the strand."

"And MacBride?" Anne lowered her eyes.

"Is dead," Campbell answered. "Never has it been such a pleasure to shoot a man. There were some few others, lads from Stoke and Welcombe."

A soldier entered the room. "Your pardon, Colonel," he said, "but we have searched and found nothing."

"You have inspected every room on every floor?" Campbell asked.

"Except the lady's bedchamber," the soldier replied. "The old man would not let us in, so we set a guard and thought it best for you to intervene."

"Idiot!" Campbell groaned. "This is no a social visit with niceties. 'Tis a search for traitors against our lawful king. I will come at once." Campbell rose.

"Nay, Colonel," Anne said sweetly, "let the lieutenant go. I think my stepmother will accept a perusal of her apartments better from him." To Gilchrist she said, "Tell Diggory that I ask you to be admitted to the lady's room and that he should restrain her from opposition." Gilchrist snapped a quick bow and left with the soldier.

"You aid is much appreciated," Campbell said.

"My stepmother is a gentle creature most of the time."

"Save when it comes to Campbells, it seems."

"No doubt this late night visit of yours only reminds her of what may seem to be a Campbell trait," Anne said with a slight smile. "Attacks on the sleeping innocent?"

Campbell frowned. "I had naught to do with Glencoe," he replied testily.

"It makes no difference to her and she will neither forget nor forgive that your cause and kin murdered her brother's family."

"I trust her cause is none of yours," Campbell said, his eyes tightening as he studied Anne.

"Not at all," Anne answered. "I am a loyal English woman and a faithful member of the English Church. I want no more of James Stuart than you do."

"And you had naught to do with your brother's crimes this night?"

"None at all," Anne said with perfect calm. "I was in my bed asleep until you awakened me."

"And I can trust that you will in no way aid your brother?" Campbell leaned closer.

"He is my brother, Colonel," Anne answered. "He is also a traitor. I will not assist in his capture, but neither will I hinder your efforts."

Campbell sat back and smiled. "I suppose I canna ask for more."

Gilchrist returned. "Search the grounds and the stables," he ordered, dismissing the soldier at his heels. "Your stepmother is in a fine temper, but suffered me to look about her apartments without bludgeoning me overmuch," he chuckled. He sat down again, giving Anne a long searching look.

"And you found nothing of the boy?" Campbell asked.

"Nothing," Gilchrist answered absently, his eyes still on Anne. "And there would be no means to smuggle him in or out of that room without going through Mistress Anne's chamber, which, I understand, she was in until our arrival."

"That is correct, Lieutenant," Anne answered, lowering her eyes to avoid his. "I was sound asleep the entire time."

"Yes, of course," he replied, his eyes never leaving her.

Suddenly a soldier burst into the room. "There are two horses missing from the stable and fresh tracks in the road!" he shouted.

Campbell was on his feet and almost to the door before he turned to Anne. "So your brother and MacAlister were hiding in the stable, eh?" Anne numbly shook her head, chilled by the lieutenant's steady gaze. Campbell strode forward and seized her by the shoulders. "I have no proof against you, mistress, but when I have got it, you will wish you had no made a fool of Andrew Campbell."

"'Tisn't they that --" she started to say.

Campbell shook her roughly. "You want taming, mistress!"

He might have gone on shaking her, but Lieutenant Gilchrist pulled him away. "She is not our quarry, Colonel. Let her be." Campbell released Anne and strode angrily from the room. "My apologies, Mistress Hawkwood," Gilchrist said, gallantly kissing her hand. "I hope we will have no need to trouble you again this night." He started to leave, but turned back at the door. "And may I suggest that you have your boots cleaned of sand and salt water before we come here again."

Anne watched him go, her heart pounding, until all that remained was the echo of hooves clattering away.

In the chill of the cellar Jamie poked curiously into a chest of coffee, then plunged his hands into a box of pearls. "Got those off a big galleon," Eben explained. "A fine Portuguese she was. One of our better prizes."

"I have heard those big ships are hard to take," Jamie said.

"Aye, that they are," Eben replied, tapping his pipe and dumping the ash on the floor. "We usually stay clear of the big money ships -- unless we have an advantage, which in the case of the Portuguese we did. She was leaking and like to sink, so your father and Captain Ward offered their aid."

"Aid?"

"Aye, we lightened their hold for them and thus we saw the crew safe to shore. They were in no position to argue."

"Have you always been a pirate?" Jamie asked, sitting on a pile of perfumed silks and brocades.

"Not always," Eben replied, stuffing his pipe from the tobacco atop a barrel. "Your father took me off a Bristol dock when I was just a lad, maybe eight year old or so. He sent me to school, which I did not much like, but in gratitude I did well to please him. I was his cabin boy on *The Black Swallow*, later served on the Bold Cockerel, and then three years ago Captain -- uh, Mistress Anne your sister asked me to join the Chanticleer's crew to work the smuggling trade here in England. I have been her quartermaster for six months now."

"And you dinna find her difficult to serve?"

Eben grinned. "I take it you mean her vagaries of mood, eh?" Jamie nodded. "She's like your father. 'Twas not for nothing he was called Mad Jack. Like two persons he was. A fine dandy now, a vicious cutthroat a moment later -- especially if he was crossed. Didn't happen often, I can tell you that." Eben drew hard on his pipe, its coal lighting his face. In that moment Jamie noticed how much the quartermaster looked like Anne, like Simon, like his childhood memories of his father. "Why do you look at me like that?" Eben asked.

"I was just thinking that you looked a wee bit like my brother Simon," Jamie answered, idly fingering the cloth beneath him.

"'Tis no accident, most say," Eben replied airily. "The late captain laid his seed in many a furrow. I could well be your brother, but there's no proof other than my mother's word. Anyhow, my looks have done well by me."

"You didna press your claim?" Jamie asked. "Even a bastard is entitled to some share and there's so much here." His hand swept in front of him, indicating the cellar of illicit goods.

"The Hawkwoods have done fine by me and the late captain was hard on those who got above themselves. I remember once when Mistress Anne was just beginning to fill out and look a woman. There was a lad in the crew -- a mate of Luther Devlin's, I recall -- who took a fancy to your sister. Quite a change for him, since he was known to be a capon, if you get my meaning. Anyway, he had some mad scheme to woo Anne and to marry into the Hawkwood family, to better himself. Luther -- and others, mind you -- tried to talk him out of it, but he would hear none of it." He paused to draw on his pipe. "Well, he made no progress in courting your sister, as you can well imagine. She's far too grand for the common sea rat and let him know it. He got angry -- went raging mad -- and tried to rape her in the cabin. Mad Jack heard her scream and broke down the door."

"What happened to him?" Jamie's voice was little more than an awed whisper.

Eben shivered slightly. "He came to a horrible end, worst I've ever seen. That was a lesson for all the crew, one that did not need repeating." He drew on his pipe. "Mad Jack wasn't one to let his daughter consort with the crew. They were fine for friends or for work, but not meant for courting."

"I wish I knew what was happening out there," Jamie said as he jumped up and glanced anxiously at the stone door.

"You'll be finding out soon enough," Eben replied. "If you're lucky your sister might have pity and not hand your over, although I'll wager she has thought on it."

"She wouldna hand me over," Jamie said, suppressing his panic at the thought as the stone door scraped open. "Aye, she knows I have too much to tell."

"There is a remedy for that," Anne said as she pushed the stone door closed behind her.

"Morning, Captain," Eben greeted. Anne made no reply. She walked straight over to Jamie and looked him hard in the face.

"I knew you would no turn me in!" Jamie reached out to embrace her. Without a word she struck him a stinging slap across the mouth with the back of her hand, her eyes flashing with anger.

"You impudent little fool!" she said hotly. "Have you any idea of the trouble you have caused? Have you the least perception of the danger you put us in?"

Jamie pressed his hand over his lip and found a small trickle of blood. "'Tis my house."

Anne laughed coldly. "Well, young lord of the manor, you are free to roam your estate, and the soldiers you find there are your guests." She turned to go.

"Wait!" Jamie ran to her, catching her robe. "Please. I am sorry. Dinna go." He swallowed hard. "Help me."

She paused. "Very well, because it is the only way to protect our assets and for no other reason. I despise your politics. You are a traitor and deserve to hang."

Jamie straightened up and looked her in the eye. "And are you no equally deserving of the gallows, Mistress Smuggler!" He ducked as she swung to strike him again. "You darena wax righteous with me, Anne. Mine is a noble cause, to restore our anointed king, as did our father's father. Let that be my crime, but never have I broken the law for personal gain."

Anne frowned, her eyes little more than slits. "I do not have to offer you my aid and no one will force you to accept it." She drew a pistol from beneath her robe. "And as I said, there is a remedy for any threat that you will betray me or any member of my company." Jamie looked doubtful.

"If you are thinking that your own sister will not kill you in cold blood," Eben remarked through the haze of smoke that wreathed his lank hair and swarthy features, "let me assure you, Jamie lad, that I have seen her do far worse."

Jamie stared at the stone floor. "Forgive me, Anne."

"'Tis much better," she said, shoving the pistol into her sash.

"Have I alone escaped?" Jamie asked.

"MacBride lies dead on the sand," Anne replied. "There were some men captured."

"MacAlister?"

"Seems to have escaped. The soldiers are still looking for the two of you and have taken to the road in pursuit of Simon and Patrick, thinking they are you and MacAlister." She sat on a tea chest. "If aught ill befalls Simon or Patrick you may find yourself begging me to hand you over to the law," she threatened. "Mister Carr can tell you the fate of those who anger me." Eben grinned and nodded.

"Has there been word of Tristan?"

Anne looked at her brother perplexedly. "The soldiers are looking for him as well. Campbell seems to think he is somewhere hereabouts although he did not see him tonight."

Jamie shook his head, returning to his seat on the piled brocade. "I have no seen my cousin since he rode to Welcombe yester morning. I know he reached Welcombe and set off again in good time to arrive here last night, but he didna come. I am nigh sick with worry for what might have befallen him."

"First we must get you out of here," Anne said. "Then we will search for Tristan." She turned to Eben. "Mister Carr?" Eben looked up from his pipe. "Fetch the Chanticleer. Bring her here tomorrow at dawn."

"This cove?" he asked in surprise.

She thought for a moment. "Nothing is safe here now. There's another inlet about two miles down. Do you know it?"

"Aye," Eben answered, nodding.

"It's rougher water and more rocks than our cove, but 'twill do for this. One longboat -- no more," Anne cautioned. "And keep an eye on the shore. If you see any trouble keep the Chanticleer well out of it."

Eben rose. "Will that be all, Captain?"

"Aye, Mister Carr. Now off with ye." Eben pulled his hat low over his face and wrapped his cloak about him. He gave a mocking salute and left by the passage that led into the house. "I pray God to keep him safe," Anne whispered as she watched him go. "No thanks to you," she said, turning on Jamie. "You have jeopardized our entire livelihood, do you realize?"

Jamie raised his eyes boldly and said, "For something I truly believe in."

Anne gave him a grim nod. "I hope your belief is worth hanging for because, if the venture fails and you are taken, there is very little I can or will do to save you."

Jamie watched her walk from the chamber, her shadow swaying in the lantern light. There was again the scraping sound, then silence.

Halfway across the open desolation of the moor, the small band of soldiers were still riding hard after the two men they believed to be Jamie Hawkwood and Lionel MacAlister. Simon and Patrick had a good headstart and had changed to fresh mounts at a posting house before entering the moor. The soldiers had found a shortage of horses at the posting house and now dropped further behind to rest their tired mounts.

Campbell reined in and Gilchrist pulled close beside him. "I have a strange feeling about this, Lieutenant," the colonel said.

"You think we are being led away?"

"Precisely. Corporal Fielding?" he called. One man rode closer.

"Yes, Colonel?"

"Take twenty men and continue pursuit," Campbell ordered. "Lieutenant Gilchrist and I will take the remaining three men and return to the Bideford area."

"Yes, sir." Fielding saluted and rode off.

"What do you expect to find in Bideford?" Gilchrist asked. "And who have we been chasing if not Hawkwood and MacAlister?"

"I dinna ken," Campbell said, "but I suspect that Mistress Anne Hawkwood could tell us."

It was still dark when Anne and Jamie made their way out of the cave. The small lantern she carried illumined little more than the rocks and sand beneath their feet. They said nothing as they climbed the steep path to the top of the cliff. There was no sound but the water below, no light but the lantern, no living creature but themselves. They walked along a narrow path on the cliff's edge, the sea on their right, dense woods on their left. They walked on toward the inlet, the dawn and escape.

They had reached the boundary of the Hawkwood property when a man stood up from behind a thicket. "A Sheasmuishin," he called softly. "Tha Lionel anseo."

"Lionel!" Jamie called. To Anne he said, "Wait here." Before she could protest he was off to bring his companion from his hiding place. They returned deep in conversation.

Lionel stopped when he saw Anne clearly in the lantern light. "Co tha i?"

"My sister Anne," Jamie explained. "She is taking me to a ship and to safety."

"And if we don't get on with it, 'twill be of no avail," she said crossly.

"Forgive me, lady," Lionel said with a respectful bow. "In that coat in the dark I took you for some gentleman." Anne nodded curtly, then took her brother by the arm and started to pull him after her. "These cliffs are full of caves," Lionel observed. "Some are deeper than others. I found refuge there." His voice turned sly. "I found other things as well."

Anne stopped and stared at him. "So?" she said stiffly.

"You had best take me with you," Lionel continued. "If I am left to capture I may under duress tell what I found hidden in the caves."

"Your threats are meaningless to me," Anne answered. "Your venture here has already ended the safety of our operations." She paused, Jamie whispering in her ear. "Yet, you may have a point. And no Christian would leave even a dog to the mercies of that man Campbell. Come then." She started off again, Lionel falling in beside Jamie.

They had just left the cover of the wood when a voice from behind them yelled, "There, Colonel, there they are!" A glance back at the road revealed five mounted men.

"Down!" Lionel cried as he ran for a rough path down the cliff and began the climb he knew no horse could make. Anne and Jamie scrambled after him, madly clutching the scrubby growth for support. A shot whistled past them. The tide was out and a wide swath of sand broken by rocks stretched out from the cliff's foot. Lionel leapt the last twenty feet and tumbled onto the sand. A moment later Anne joined him and both looked up at Jamie who had lost his footing and dangled from the cliff's edge high above them. Gilchrist aimed his pistol at the boy.

"Surrender, lad," Gilchrist ordered. Jamie hesitated.

"If he doesna surrender now," Campbell shouted, "shoot him."

Jamie looked back at Anne and then resignedly reached up to Gilchrist who seized his wrists and pulled him up.

"Come on!" Lionel ordered Anne who watched numbly as her brother was shoved to his knees and roughly manacled. "We must go," Lionel pleaded, pulling on her arm. She shook her head. Never one to waste time on dangerous chivalry, Lionel dashed across the sand and was soon out of sight amongst the rocks.

Anne crouched down among the rocks, hidden from the view of the soldiers who peered over the cliff edge. "They're gone," one called back.

"Damn!" the colonel swore. "You two, take the prisoner into Bideford and hold him there until I come to collect him." Turning to the remaining soldier, he ordered, "You are to ride for reinforcements. The lieutenant and I will remain here and do what we can to apprehend MacAlister and the woman."

Anne heard the clatter of hooves as the men obeyed. She peeked out and could just see the outline of two mounted men at the edge of the cliff. A glance out to sea confirmed her other fear. Already the sky was lightening and the point of rendezvous was still over a mile away. She crept quietly among the rocks at the cliff's foot, but realized that she would not be able to reach the inlet from the shore. A ridge of rock divided the sand and beyond the ridge the sand vanished into a long stretch of rocks and deep crashing water. Anne made it to the ridge, and climbed along its spine to another rocky path up the cliff face. At the top she looked about for Gilchrist and Campbell. Seeing no one she started off again along the cliff path.

"There she is!"

Anne spun around to see the two officers riding toward her through the thicket. They slowed their pace when she made no move to run.

"'Tis early for walking, Mistress Hawkwood," Campbell said, his lips curling into a bare hint of a smile.

"But not too early for a ride, eh, Colonel?" she replied, boldly.

"'Tis no time to be saucy, girl," Campbell retorted. "We have your brother in irons and you are soon to follow."

"On what charges?"

"The harboring of traitors is a felony," Gilchrist explained soberly. "If you are found guilty of harboring your brother and MacAlister you could well hang for it or face transportation to the Indies."

"And that would please your sense of justice?" she asked nimbly.

Gilchrist looked away. "No, not mine."

"Well, 'twould please mine," Campbell said. "You tried to make a fool of me, mistress, and 'twill be the greatest pleasure to teach you a woman's proper place in life."

Anne eyed him cunningly. "And what if I were a good pupil and allowed you to tutor me here and now, would you let me go?"

"So that you could leave on the ship that's coming? Oh, yes, we made a guess about the ship and our inquiries in Bideford turned up one that was victualed yesterday all in a hurry. And she'll come for you here, won't she?"

Anne looked away. "About my offer? You have my brother and 'twas he you wanted. You'll probably have no trouble taking MacAlister, since he cannot have gotten far. You do not need me. We could say, my freedom to leave here as I wish and in return I shall take betwixt my legs what does at this moment lie betwixt thine."

"'Tis a tawdry way to put it, mistress," Campbell said, his eye lighting with a lecherous gleam, "but if you will hold to it."

"Every word as I spoke it," Anne promised.

Colonel Campbell turned to Gilchrist, noting the lieutenant's disgusted expression. "You have witnessed our agreement. Now stand off and give us a bit of privacy."

"Yes, sir," Gilchrist said sourly, avoiding Anne's gaze. He pulled his horse away and rode close to the ridge, his eyes on the sea. Campbell removed his pistols and his sword and hung them on his saddle. He dismounted and strode to a patch of grass a few yards off. "This will do," he said. "I'm going to enjoy this, mistress." He started to unfasten his breeches. "Now come here, woman."

Anne smiled and started toward him, then with the speed of a striking hawk she leapt astride the colonel's horse and seized the reins.

"Every word as I spoke it!" she yelled and galloped through the trees for the road.

"After her, Gilchrist, damn you!" the red faced Colonel screamed. "Dinna let her get away!"

Stifling a laugh, Gilchrist spurred his horse and chased the fleeing woman. She leaned over her horse's neck and lashed it again and again with the long reins. Gilchrist followed, goading his horse, slowly gaining on Anne. He glanced to the sea to see a ship in the lifting morning fog, and from the ship a gig was already making for the rocky shore.

Suddenly she stopped and turned, a pistol in her hand. Gilchrist slowed to a trot. "Surely, mistress, you have no intention of ..."

"Killing you?" She laughed, then the mirth faded. "'Tisn't a matter I'd wager on, if I were you, Lieutenant." He raised his reins to move closer, but the pistol jerked up. "Any closer and you are a dead man." He stopped. "Much better," she said. "Now dismount, Lieutenant." He hesitated. "I said, dismount!" She spanned the wheellock. He swung down from the saddle.

"Remove your weapons," Anne said, "slowly, mind you -- and toss them over the cliff." There was a clatter of metal on stone as he complied. "Now start walking away from the cliff. I shall tell you when to stop." As he walked from her he heard a slap and saw his horse race away through the woods.

"That's far enough," she called. He turned and saw that the boat was nearly to shore.

"Now turn around," she called. "Turn your back to the sea and drop to your knees."

He obeyed stiffly, turning his face toward the trees, then dropped slowly to his knees, feeling the crack of twigs beneath them. "Are you going to kill me?" he asked simply, without fear.

"Not if there is no need," she replied as she dismounted and sent the colonel's horse cantering away. "If you stay put and make no move to hinder my departure, you need not die." She was impressed by his courage.

"Mistress Hawkwood, before you go, may I ask why?"

"Why?"

"Why a fine lady like yourself has taken such risk for a brother whose crimes have naught to do with you?" He heard a stick crack as she stepped closer to him.

"Your question answers itself," she said.

"But the risk," he protested.

"Is not unknown to me," she answered. He started to turn his head toward her. "No, do not turn around. I do not wish your death -- although killing you would lessen the risk to me."

"That thought, I admit, has occurred to me," he said, "not that I am in any way displeased by having my life."

"I will not kill you, Lieutenant, because you have been gallant and honest. And there is the kindness you did me by not informing Campbell that I had been on the beach the night you searched the Rookery."

"'Twas my pleasure," Gilchrist said. "Had I not paused to savor the sweet scent of your chamber I surely would not have noticed the rumpled clothes and wet boots."

"Your life then is your reward," Anne cried as the gig slid onto the sand behind her. "Gallant gentleman, I bid you adieu."

He remained on his knees, facing the woods as Anne climbed down the steep slope to the sandy inlet. He heard the sounds of greeting and the splash of the oars taking lovely Anne Hawkwood to what, in his heart of hearts he felt, was a well earned escape.

CHAPTER EIGHT

The Newry Highwayman

> I never robbed any poor man yet,
> nor honest tradesman did I beset;
> But I robbed lords and ladies bright
> and stole their jewels to my heart's delight. folksong

Ward refilled his glass, then leaned back in his chair. For a moment he stared through the wide stern ports of the Bold Cockerel's main cabin at the sunlight on Plymouth harbor. "And you have no idea if Anne and young Jamie escaped?" he asked.

Patrick shook his head. "We rode out immediately after the ambush."

"With all the soldiers on our heels, I might add." Simon reached for the decanter. "I have wondered if my sister meant for us to lead them off."

Ward grinned. "It would in no way surprise me. She is a most cunning woman."

"Well, 'tis no matter," Patrick said, "for here we are, alive and at liberty."

"Aye," Simon agreed, "and if drawing the soldiers here has spared my stupid little brother the gallows, however well deserved, then I suppose it was worth the risk."

Ward studied his wine thoughtfully. "You say that it was left to Diggory to keep an eye on the boys."

"Aye," Simon nodded, pausing to drink. "Anne gave him charge over them, to keep an eye on their comings and goings and to keep them from the cove after dark."

"Keeping up with two lads like that is a heavy task for an old man," Ward commented.

"Oh, he was not above enlisting aid," Simon replied. "On one or two nights he invited men from your crew to drink with him in the tower while he kept watch." Ward was amused.

"'Twas nigh a fortnight ago when two men paid a visit to the east wing." Simon rose and paced the cabin like a barrister making a summation. "We now believe that when Jamie was aboard this ship young Tristan went to Bideford to meet someone at the Red Cock. There may have been another visitor the night before Tristan went to Welcombe, but Diggory could not be certain. Seems that he didn't see this fellow for himself."

"And you did not find all this coming and going strange?" Ward asked.

Simon paused and shook his head. "We thought nothing of it. Diggory made but scant reference to it, thinking it was naught but some of the lads' drinking acquaintances." He turned to face Ward. "John, I tell you 'twas a great shock to realize that my pristine young brother with all his fine graces is a more wanted man than I."

"And Tristan?"

"Missing," Patrick answered bluntly.

"Could he have been the hidden enemy the dying Irishman meant?" Ward mused.

Simon shook his head, resuming his seat and lifting his glass. "I think not. Not willingly, anyway. He has no one but Margaret and Jamie and was an ardent Jacobite from all appearances."

"And his horse returned alone," Patrick added. "If he had betrayed Jamie, then fled, surely he would have taken the horse."

"Well, considering all you have told me," Ward said slowly, as he packed a pipe with tobacco, "'Twould seem that young Master James and his friends are traitors of the first order, bound to hang."

"And it may be well to assume," Simon added, "that young Tristan is either a prisoner or dead."

"Is anyone making a search to determine which?" Ward asked.

Simon shrugged. "If Anne is free, I think she will send Diggory out to find news of the boy. Perhaps there will be some word when we reach Mousehole."

"How could we have been so blind?" Patrick said suddenly, leaping to his feet. "Damnation! We should have seen all this but for our over-confidence."

Simon nodded. "I don't understand it either. Once Tristan had vanished and we learned that all three were papists there was still a day when we might have prevented this. We should have seen the connection between three Scots and that official inquiry into rebel agents, but we didn't. Anne didn't seem worried. And I," he paused and sighed, "I did not give Jamie credit for wit enough to create such trouble."

"It seems he is a Hawkwood after all," Patrick commented, "much as you are loathe to admit it."

"No son of my father would betray his country," Simon snapped indignantly. "For whatever else we are, we have always been loyal to our king."

"And willing to risk all for him," Patrick added. "Can you not see, Simon, that Jamie is as loyal to his king as you are to yours?"

"Sounds like a Hawkwood to me," Ward said with a wry smile. He sighed. "'Tis no matter now," he said gravely, "for our future operations are hampered at best, and most probably destroyed. We must seek a new base for surely the Rookery will be well watched for a time."

"Aye," Simon replied, "and until we get some word from Anne or from Hugo there is no way to find out how much damage has been done to our business and our name."

Ward drew on his pipe, his features momentarily obscured by the smoke. "If the lower cellar went undetected in the search, then all may be well in time. 'Tis possible to disavow any knowledge of the remaining caves and their contents. If, however, that lower cellar was found, or *The Chanticleer* implicated, then the problem is much more extensive."

"In which case, John," Simon said, "you should put to sea at once."

"There's the reckoning with Golding first," Ward answered. "He'll be here later this afternoon and most likely wondering what kept us up in Bideford."

"No respect for my dead father, eh?" Simon laughed.

"We'll sail for Mousehole in the morning. No doubt you two wish passage."

"Nay, John," Simon replied with a wave of his hand. "You know how I hate the sea. Patrick and I will bide the night here, then take horse to Mousehole in time to rendezvous with Anne."

"Deo volente," Patrick muttered.

On the Bold Cockerel's deck, the crew sat idle in the midday sun. It was a warm day with only a hint of the chill autumn. Judas Jones quietly read his scriptures while listening appreciatively to the lively tunes played by Morgan and Estey in the fo'c'sle. Next to Judas sat Luther Devlin, mending sail and talking about guns with Calum who was carving a bone button. Jonathan stitched a leather buff coat and occasionally threw a comment into the conversation.

"A good day to you, gentlemen," Patrick said as he politely tipped his hat to the crewman.

"The doctor 'as 'ad a dram too many if 'e sees gentlemen 'ere," Luther laughed.

"And where are ye gents off to tonight?" Jonathan asked, running his hand through his trim beard. "To Jane Trower's brothel, I'll wager."

"Nay, man," Simon replied. "Why, the good doctor and I will spend our evening in the theatre and then resort to one of the finer salons for a turn or two at the dice."

"Aye," Calum laughed, as Simon and Patrick started their climb into the longboat, "and wind up at Mistress Trower's without a shilling to pay her custom."

"'Tis a sinful waste of coin," Judas muttered. No one paid him any attention.

The voices faded as the longboat slid over the short distance to Plymouth dock. On the Bold Cockerel's deck, Calum and Jonathan continued their work while the two musicians played another dance. Luther's soft eyes closed in sleep, while Judas smiled over his scriptures.

The theatre was crowded when Simon and Patrick arrived. The building itself had served some other purpose during the years of

Cromwell and the ensuing ban on the activities of all players. Now, regilded and draped, filled with the gentry of Plymouth and the estates surrounding, the building hosted a traveling troop's performance of Wycherly's comedy The Country Wife.

Simon and Patrick settled into their box and watched with amusement as two brashly enterprising prostitutes hawked their wares in the pit below. They were followed by a flower seller and then a girl with a basket of oranges. The play itself was a pale performance compared to the exuberance of the audience who frequently bandied words with the actresses and hooted encouragement to the hero.

"That girl playing Mrs. Pinchwife has a lovely face," Simon remarked, "but, dear God, so stiff with her play."

"She is no Mrs. Bracegirdle," Patrick agreed. He caught the eye of the infamous Jane Trower in a neighboring box. "Jane's here. Over there," he said, pointing discreetly to the pretty young madam. "Shall we pay a visit to her most noted and respected establishment after the play?"

Jane flashed them a seductive smile, waving delicately with her handkerchief. Simon took a moment to regard the young henna haired beauties with her, then said, "Perhaps." His attention was drawn again to the stage, and so engrossed did he and Patrick become in the laughter of the 'China scene' that neither noticed the flashes of red appearing in the pit below.

"Corporal!" called saucy Jane. "Corporal Fielding! Hallo, lover!" She waved at the distracted officer. Simon and Patrick immediately started. There were now more than a dozen soldiers scattered throughout the crowd below.

"Surely they are not looking for us," Patrick said.

"I don't like it," Simon answered and started to rise.

"There they are!" Corporal Fielding bellowed, pointing to the box. The actors bravely continued despite the sudden burst of chaos in the pit as the soldiers pushed through the crowd and made their way to the stairs that led to the boxes.

Certain now that they were the quarry, Simon and Patrick ran to the stairs. There they were confronted by two soldiers. They dashed back to the boxes, diving into the one that held Jane Trower and the sampling of her merchandise. "There!" shouted a soldier from below. Patrick quickly unhooked the heavy drape from the front of the box and dropped it down to the stage where the actors now stood watching the audience. He climbed down, was across the sloped stage and out of the door when there was a shot. He turned to see Simon stagger out, blood pouring from his left shoulder.

"This way," Patrick said as he seized his wounded friend.

"They're getting away," shouted a voice.

"To the stage," shouted another.

Behind the theatre Simon and Patrick found horses, and mounting quickly, rode away through the winding streets. Simon leaned weakly over the neck of his mount, his left arm useless. Behind them clattered the soldiers in disarray. Soon hunter and hunted were parted in the night streets of Plymouth.

The alley was cold and dark, lit only by the blaze of light from the front windows of Jane Trower's lavish brothel. The man who stood in the shadows squared his shoulders and pressed his demand again. "The colonel promised me that money and 'e said ye 'ad some papers I'm wanting." The man's eyes were cold, their glint only slightly hazed by his chilled breath in the night air.

Lord Golding stood passively, one pallid hand toying with a curl from his powdered wig. "Indeed, sir, I have no idea what you are talking about," he said with exaggerated boredom.

"Mad Jack's papers," the man said. "I was to 'ave 'em and gold for telling ye 'ow to take young Jamie and 'is papist friends."

"At the last word to reach me," Golding said. "James Hawkwood had been captured, but not MacAlister. MacBride is dead, and young MacDonald is missing."

"'E'll be no trouble to ye, I promise," the man laughed.

"But still with MacAlister free," Golding shrugged. "Well, you have been paid by the colonel. Do not think to ask me for more coin."

But the man seized Golding's brocade covered elbow. "I give ye good information on Simon 'Awkwood and 'is friend."

"And both of them escaped," Golding countered, pulling his arm away.

"Ain't my fault if your lads don't take the prize, is it?"

"There is a saying in your trade, is there not? No prey, no pay. 'Tis the same here." Again Golding turned away from the man, looking into the brightly lit windows of Jane Trower's establishment. "If you will excuse me, I have a comely young whore who awaits my bidding within."

"All I want is them papers," the man pleaded. "The Cap'n's diary and all."

"What good are they to you, man? You can't read," Golding sniffed. "Any papers I have are from Lawyer Stone and you can be certain that he gave me nothing of importance to anyone. There is no diary, no journal, no log. There were a few letters and a ledger."

"I want them," the man persisted. Golding turned away. "I know things about you, m'lord. Things that could do ye some 'urt if I was to tell."

"You could not do half the harm that I could do to you with a word to your captain. Bear that in mind." Golding was gratified to see the man's face pale at the thought. "This interview is at an end." Golding abruptly turned away and reentered the brothel. The light and sounds of rowdy laughter drifted into the background as the sailor stalked down the street.

Simon and Patrick found refuge in a small house of pleasure near the docks. The gaudily painted tart who showed them to an empty room required no explanations, only a sum of silver. Then she left, happy to have made her wages without having so much as to loosen her drawers.

Patrick helped Simon to the room's only furnishing, a ragged narrow bed, and proceeded to strip back the bloody cloth over the wounded shoulder. "Not too bad from the looks of it," Patrick said cheerfully.

"'Tis easy for you to say," Simon replied through gritted teeth as the doctor's skilled fingers probed the wound. "You should experience it from my vantage point."

"Indeed," Patrick chuckled. "Why, Simon, with a tight bandage and some hot rum in you, you'll be riding the roads again in two day's time, I'll wager."

"Aye," Simon muttered, "to Mousehole -- to see if my kin still live."

"The ball passed through. Looks as though it missed the bone entirely. Lucky thing that." Patrick began to tear strips from Simon's shirt to bind the wound. "I'll fetch you another shirt in the morning," he said apologetically.

"Do you realize," Simon said philosophically, "that in all these years of banditry upon the highways, though I have ofttimes been shot at, I have never been shot?"

"Damn lucky, I'd say," Patrick said, continuing his work. "But why, pray tell, did your luck choose this particular evening to run out?"

"Perhaps because I stopped to kiss Jane Trower."

"Idiot," Patrick groaned. "You might have been killed."

"Ah, but what a grand exit," Simon laughed. "And she did save our lives by calling to that corporal."

Patrick paused in his bandaging. "I have been wondering how the soldiers knew where to find us." He tied off the last strip. "Or that they should even look for us at all. We are not exactly notorious, are we?"

"I should hope not," Simon answered. "I never work without a mask and I sincerely doubt that any of my former acquaintances on the roads could identify me."

"But who else might?"

"You think we were betrayed?" Simon asked in surprise. "By whom? John Ward? I think not."

"Not Ward," Patrick said. "He wouldn't, and besides, I don't recall telling him where we would spend the evening." Patrick opened a flask and handed it to Simon who took a long drink. "But it must have been someone aboard the Cockerel because we have spoken to no others that I can recall."

Simon handed the flask back to Patrick who also took a long drink. "It could have been nothing more than someone who saw us ride in last night with those red monkeys on our arses and assumed that we must be desperate felons. Perhaps that same person then saw us enter the theatre and sought to earn a coin or two by telling the soldiers."

"But who was there to see us?" Patrick argued. "It was nigh dawn when we arrived. Even the ugliest whore in town had quit the streets." He rose suddenly. "I do not understand you, Simon. You spend half your life glaring at the world in suspicion of the hangman, and when he is breathing down your neck you seek excuses and assumptions."

Simon smiled. "I simply want to be very sure of your argument. If there is such a traitor on *The Cockerel*, we must tell Ward without delay for such a one must be found and silenced."

"Well, we daren't attempt to reach the ship tonight, and by morning she will sail for Mousehole. Our suspicions will have to wait until we can reach the rendezvous." Patrick took another drink and then gave the flask to Simon. "Is it possible that the trap set for us and MacBride's 'hidden enemy' are the work of the same hand?"

Simon bit his lower lip as the idea sank in. "Aye," he said slowly as he took the flask, "but if 'tis so, then the danger is so much the greater. Think on it. Considering what the crew is capable of, not to mention Anne when the rage is on her, is there such a one who so hates my brother and me as to risk his life just to see us hanged?"

"I do not know," Patrick said, "but I can think of one who might." He smiled and drank.

"If you think that I will go anywhere near that rascal Campbell --"

"Not Campbell, Simon. Golding." The wisdom of it was plain enough. "He will ride for his estate in Salcombe tomorrow, having collected his fee from Ward."

Simon beamed. "This could be a very profitable little venture." Patrick nodded.

In the chill of morning the following day Simon and Patrick rode out of Plymouth in the direction of Salcombe. Simon, still pale and weary despite the night's sleep, rode gently, his wounded arm bound in a sling beneath a clean shirt stolen from an unwary laundress. They slipped unnoticed through the half lit streets, then turned onto the track toward Salcombe. About a mile further on they found a copse of trees and there waited for their prey.

After two carts, a plowhorse ridden by a farmboy and a carriage they nearly robbed out of boredom, they spied Lord Golding riding toward them, alone.

"Shall we take him now?" Patrick whispered. "He rides straight for us."

"Not yet," Simon answered. "We do not know if he has aught to give us and I am in no condition to force him if he should prove difficult."

"Then leave this ruse to me," Patrick advised. "You ride ahead and wait in ambush up the road." With that they separated, Simon galloping ahead while Patrick waited at the crossroads.

Lord Golding rode closer and drew to a halt when he saw the waiting stranger. "Hallo, sir," Golding said cautiously.

"And a good morning to you, m'lord," Patrick replied, taking in at a moment's glance the much beribboned, laced and plumed gentleman whose patched face and powdered curls marked him for a dandy. And a very wealthy dandy, thought Patrick as he admired the blue brocade suit beneath's Golding's heavy cloak. "Indeed, we are well met."

"Are we so?" Golding smiled wanly and sniffed.

"Indeed," Patrick said, drawing his horse alongside Golding's. "I am traveling to Salcombe, and as it seems that we travel the same road, I thought we might do well to do so together."

"I do travel to Salcombe," Golding responded in his gratingly nasal voice. "My winter estate is there. But why, pray, should you have need to join me?"

"Oh, have you not heard?" Patrick looked around uneasily, then said in a low confidential tone, "There was a shooting last night in the Plymouth theatre. Soldiers chasing some notorious felons or so I heard. The blackguards escaped and are loose in these parts. Hence my desire to travel in company."

"I know something of the men that were sought," Golding said as he nudged his horse forward and gestured for Patrick to follow. "I sent the soldiers for them."

"Indeed!" Patrick raised his reddish brows.

"A brother of a well known traitor and thus wanted for questioning," Golding said, pleased to find a listening ear for his gossip. "I have had some acquaintance with that family in the past and can fully believe their complicity in numerous other crimes. But treason! What am I to think of that? 'Tis a dangerous world we live in, young man. A dangerous world."

"Aye, I can well believe that," Patrick agreed. "And carrying as I am a sum of money that I would not care to lose, you can understand my desire for companionship, even on such a short excursion as this." He patted his boot. "A tidy sum, indeed, and hidden here. There is only a bit of coin in my purse to satisfy any robber I may meet."

"How clever!" Golding remarked, impressed. "For myself, I carry a goodly sum as well as papers of no little worth."

"Not in your purse I hope?" Patrick asked, concerned. "Why, 'tis the first thing a thief will take!"

"Oh, to be sure," Golding said. "But you are not the only clever one. You see, I have hidden all that I value in the lining of my cloak. I think 'twill be safe enough there."

Patrick nodded. "Certainly, m'lord. Tell me, how came you to know about the traitor's brother in the theatre last night? Surely a gentleman like yourself would not consort with such men."

Golding smiled proudly. "I consort with all manner of people, friend. As it happens, I have a spy in near contact with the traitor's family. 'Twas from him that Colonel Campbell and his men arranged an ambush on the landing of some contraband arms up near Bideford, and then he, this common sailor, comes to demand more pay from me in Plymouth, even though the traitor slipped the net, and nearly escaped. This informant -- I do not know his name -- told me where the brother might be found and that he was in some way implicated, then returns still later to make further demands, even while this second man escapes." Golding sniffed petulantly, then added with a lecherous smile, "And I was trying to have my pleasure at Trower's with this impudent spy on my heels, I say." He paused. "You are familiar with Trower's?"

"I am indeed." Patrick grinned broadly as they rounded the bend where the trees ran down close to the road. From the shadows leapt a dark horse, its rider masked, a pistol in his left hand held close to his body, a sword in his right.

"Stand as you are, gentlemen," Simon yelled as the sun fell full upon him. "Your purses, if you please."

"'Tis not his purse you want," Patrick laughed. "'Tis his fine cloak." Patrick's own sword was out and pointed at Golding's back.

Sputtering with rage, Golding dropped both his cloak and his purse over the extended point of Simon's sword. "I'll see you both hang for this, I swear," he cursed as he watched Simon skillfully slip the cloak down his bending sword and lay it neatly across his horse's neck. "How dare you!"

"I can well understand your feelings," Patrick said in mocking sympathy, "but times being what they are -- please, m'lord, do not turn around to look at me again," he warned, poking his sword against Golding's brocade coat. "You have seen too much of me already, do you not think?"

"Off your horse, m'lord," Simon ordered. Golding dismounted, glaring wrathfully at the masked man. Simon slapped the horse's rump and sent it galloping down the road to Salcombe. "Now your mount can herald your arrival home. I suggest you walk briskly, m'lord. 'Tis a long way to Salcombe."

Golding turned away, then stopped. "Your voice is known to me."

"We have never met," Simon answered flatly.

"And yet I know your voice." Golding walked a few feet, then stopped again. "I will remember this."

"Good day to you, m'lord," Patrick called. With that he and Simon galloped back toward Plymouth, leaving the hapless lord stranded in the dusty road.

The two thieves had ridden for no more than a mile when Simon began to show signs of fatigue and they took cover away from the road in a small grove. While sampling Patrick's flask, Simon drew a knife and ripped open the stolen cloak. Out tumbled a quantity of gold coins and several papers.

"'Twould seem that m'lord chose to convert his share of cargo into a more immediately useable form," Simon mused.

"He said he had been the night at Trower's," Patrick remarked.

"And what else did he say?"

"That he has a paid informant with connections to the Hawkwoods. If he means a sailor who was last night in Plymouth, then he must have been on the Cockerel."

"'Tis true then. We were betrayed," Simon said gravely.

"Golding admitted sending the soldiers on this spy's information. He also made mention that your brother 'nearly escaped' Campbell's net."

"Then Jamie is taken." There was no pity in Simon's voice.

"Aye, I fear so." Patrick began perusing the papers. "Ah, what have we here? A warrant for the arrest of your lovely sister."

Simon looked up sharply. "On what charge?"

"According to this," Patrick glanced over the paper again, "the 'harboring of traitors in that she did conceal one James Hawkwood and one Lionel MacAlister, both wanted for crimes against His Majesty King William', and for horse stealing."

"Horse stealing!"

"'In that she did by trickery steal the horse of one Colonel Andrew Campbell, thereby making good her escape in resistance of rightful arrest by that same officer'."

"Ah, she is free," Simon sighed.

"But Jamie is not," Patrick said. "And according to this other document he is to be transferred to the Citadel in Plymouth to be tried under Golding's jurisdiction."

"Well, if the lad is guilty of treason," Simon said crossly, "I can scarce feel any sympathy for him."

"Ah, but, Simon, if he is convicted -- no matter how deservedly -- his worldly property is forfeited to the Crown." Patrick watched the effect of his words on Simon. "And we cannot have that, now, can we?"

CHAPTER NINE

HANGMAN, HANGMAN, SLACK THY ROPE

Hangman, hangman, slack thy rope,
Oh, slack it for awhile;
For I think I see my mother coming,
coming many a long mile. folksong

As evening fell over the tidy granite cottages that lined the narrow streets of Mousehole, the Bold Cockerel rocked in the swell just beyond the little harbor's mouth. Inside the cabin Ward, Simon and Patrick had been joined by Anne and Eben. Not far away, the Chanticleer was moored inconspicuously among the local fishing vessels.

"Jim lad, more rum, then off with you," Ward ordered. The cabin boy pushed back a loose lock of honey colored hair and poured rum into five tankards, then ran off to the galley. "Fine boy," Ward commented, watching the sturdy legs climb the steps. "I have trouble keeping the crew's hands off him."

"'Tis no wonder," Patrick said. "Pretty lad like that and a crew half full of sodomites."

"If they but do their work, I care not how they get their pleasure," Ward replied, "but not with my cabin boy. Enough of that. Again to serious matters."

"Aye," Anne said, looking first at Eben and then at Simon, "as I was saying afore the boy came with dinner, if there was ever doubt that Hugo Stone is an errant knave and as crooked as a thorn bush, 'tis now dispelled -- but since 'tis all in our favor, well enough." She took a hearty bite of chicken. "Word has come from the Rookery. Jamie is disinherited."

"In whose favor?" Simon asked.

"Yours, dear brother." Anne smiled over the chicken.

"Your father made another will," Ward explained to the surprised Simon, "and entrusted it to Hugo. If Jamie or his mother proved to be trouble the later will could be brought into play, giving you the Rookery and Jamie the money."

"You knew of this other will, Anne?" Simon asked.

"Aye, Simon, but I did not know what it contained until recently and was sworn to say nothing of it, to let Jamie have his chance to prove himself a Hawkwood." She smiled ruefully. "Greatest mistake I ever made."

"Well, I think I preferred having the money," Simon responded glumly.

"Indeed, brother, but we must now use that money do to what we can to extricate ourselves from this situation, and that will be better accomplished with Hugo holding the fortune in trust."

"And no doubt Hugo will ensure that not one copper remains on the day Jamie hangs," Simon retorted.

Anne nodded sadly. "He may hang alone. 'Twould seem that MacAlister is escaped entirely and that the other men taken were but hirelings who are worthy of no more than transportation."

"How in God's name did Jamie become involved in such treason?" Patrick asked.

"'Twas that fellow MacAlister," Anne answered. "He was tutor to both Jamie and Tristan, and though a Protestant, is an ardent Jacobite. He ran off to the Boyne and from there to France where he met MacBride. MacAlister has been slipping in and out of Scotland for months now, and always with a letter for Jamie." She took another bite. "I met this MacAlister just before Jamie was taken. He is a sly cunning fox of a man, and still I helped him to escape, though God knows why."

"True hearted Anne," Simon teased. "Always ready to aid the unfortunate."

"Well," Anne growled, "when I find the unfortunate who sold us to Campbell, I will aid the bastard straight to hell."

Eben, who had been mostly silent the entire evening, now emptied his tankard and refilled it. "I think that is a matter bearing some discussion." His voice was low and soft, full of tension. "'Tis, I think, safe to say that it could not be one of us. Nor could it be O'Flynn."

"I should certainly hope not," Ward laughed. "Good God, boy, we have the most to lose."

"He must be on your ship, Captain," Eben said, leaning forward and jabbing a finger for emphasis, "and I for one want him found and soon."

"As do we all," Anne said, gently patting Eben's large rough hand. She turned to the other three. "We have some word of Tristan."

"He is found?" Simon asked.

Anne shook her head. "That, I fear, is the word we have of him. Diggory made a search of the road as far as Welcombe."

"And?" Simon leaned forward.

"Show them, Eben." The young quartermaster pushed his hair out of his eyes as he picked up a bundle from the floor and unrolled it onto the table amid the platters of roast chicken, yams and bowls of barley soup. On the ragged canvas lay a gold headed riding whip engraved with an 'H' and a torn piece of shirt covered in brownish stains. "Diggory found these near the old chapel on Hartland."

"The whip was one of Father's," Anne said. Simon nodded.

Patrick picked up the whip and flexed it. A shower of red brown dust drifted down. "'Tis blood, I'd say."

"Aye, but horse or human?" Anne raised her tankard to her lips.

"There is no way to tell, of course," Patrick answered, "but 'tis safe to assume that it need not be horse's. After all, if this was dropped on Hartland Point, then it couldn't have been used by a rider to whip the mare back to the Rookery."

"Then you are saying that young MacDonald was met on the road, taken into the woods and beaten severely enough to loosen his tongue," Ward concluded.

"And is now very likely dead," Anne added with a sad sigh. "The body was probably pitched over the cliff to be lost in the waves and rocks below."

"But did Campbell and his lackey lieutenant murder the boy?" Simon asked, "or did our spy?"

"There is no way to answer that until we lay hands on one or the other," Eben answered.

Patrick gazed thoughtfully at the darkening ports where the last of the sunlight glowed. "Could this spy be a forced man?"

Ward shook his head. "I cannot think it. Mad Jack was never one to force a man. All here have signed articles -- well, except my shipwright Jones. His religion, you know, prevents him from joining in the more distasteful aspects of our trade, except against the shipping of papist countries. I pay his skill in wages rather than a percentage of the prize."

"He could well be the one to set a trap for a papist conspiracy then," Anne remarked.

"And he was late in returning to the ship when we sailed from Bideford," Ward added, scratching his beard. "But then so was Luther Devlin. And Morgan and Estey were slow, too."

"Well, I would certainly discount Devlin," Anne said. "He liked Jamie well and was kind to him."

They paused to think and the silence was broken by Eben. "It might have been Diggory, you know. That old scoundrel would sell his own mother. And he did have extraordinary luck in finding where the deed was done, eh?"

"So why bring us the whip and Tristan's shirt?" Simon asked.

"To throw us off, perhaps," Anne mused, then shook her head. "He has been with us too long for me to think aught against him. And he wasn't in Plymouth to betray you two."

"Anne, Anne, no matter how much we are distressed by the possibility, we must face the truth that someone known and trusted by us has betrayed us and that someone could well see us all on the gallows." Patrick gripped her hand, then released it with a sigh.

"It simply doesn't seem possible," Ward said. "There isn't a man on either ship who would take royal gold, save by force from a prize."

"And yet we know that one of them did." Anne leaned back, tapping her fingers together thoughtfully. "May I suggest that we say nothing of this rat in our hold for the nonce. Let him think he is safe, but let us be watchful and when next he betrays us we shall find him out."

"In the meantime," Ward scowled, "I can hardly trust my ship to any profitable action, knowing that one of my own crew might bring the Navy down upon me."

"You may have less to fear on that than you imagine," Eben said. "After all, when the Navy cannon pounds this vessel, your traitor must run the same risk as the men he has betrayed. If he wants to live to spend his blood money, he'll commit his treason from the land, but never from the sea."

"And that is why, John, you must put to sea as soon as possible," Anne said. "This spy has betrayed both my brothers and I am a hunted woman. I cannot afford to have him on land."

"'Tis poor season for sailing," Ward grumbled. "Nigh to November and the cold storms of winter."

"I did not say you must sail far," Anne corrected, "but as long as this rat is in your hold you must isolate him, confine him so that he does no more harm. Take a prize or two from the French or the Spanish. Much warmer 'twill be in Spain's waters."

"Aye," Ward agreed. "And what will the Chanticleer do?"

Anne paused and drank, glancing speculatively at Eben. "What say you, Mister Carr? Shall we stay a time in Mousehole? Among these fishing smacks and flytes we shall not look amiss."

"Aye," he said. "I think O'Flynn will agree. Are you certain Lieutenant Gilchrist cannot identify us?"

"I doubt that he can or will," Anne replied. "I kept his back to the sea. He caught no more than a glimpse of the Chanticleer and that at dawn."

"Very well then," Eben nodded, "we stay in Mousehole. Once 'tis quiet again at the Rookery we can return for that last cargo and trade it in Amsterdam." This brought general nods of agreement.

Anne rose, staring out at the darkening water and the twinkling lights of the town. "And what of Jamie?"

Simon looked at her in surprise. "What of him? He is a traitor and will hang."

"He was captured because of a spy amongst our ranks," Anne reminded him.

"Will you plead for his life, dear Anne?" Patrick asked teasingly.

"And get myself arrested!" Anne threw back her head with laughter. "Not even for my brother," adding, "if indeed he is my brother." Her mirth calmed. "No, that must be Margaret's duty. I shall remain in seclusion aboard my ship. If Margaret can win her son's life, I will win his freedom. I will do no more -- even if he is my father's son."

"Surely no more could be expected," Patrick said quietly.

In the small bare chapel at the top of the Rookery's tower, Margaret knelt silently, her fingers clicking bead against bead as she said her rosary. In front of her stood a priest, a young man with kind eyes.

"And I always thought him to be a shoemaker," Anne whispered to Simon as they stood at the back of the chapel with Patrick.

"Resourceful, these papists," Simon whispered back.

Patrick nudged them to respectful attention as Margaret stood and the priest solemnly pronounced the final words of the funeral service for Tristan MacDonald.

"May God grant rest to his soul," Anne muttered. She glanced around nervously. Down in the cellars, Eben and the crew were hauling out the chests and loading them aboard the Chanticleer. Every moment in her childhood home was a danger now, and Anne would not have returned but for Margaret's pleading and a certain inborn greed.

There was a long silence after the benediction while the priest prayed with Margaret. Finally they stood and Margaret turned to Anne. "My deepest thanks to you for coming here. It didna seem right that his body be lost and none to mourn him but myself."

Anne drew her cloak closer, covering her less than ladylike attire from the priest's curious gaze. "Aye, madam, I understand." For a moment her eyes rested on the priest. "'Tis a marvel that you so quickly found a minister of your faith."

"Though we must practice mostly in secret," the priest answered, "yet amongst our own we are known to one another."

"Well, if you want to keep it that way," Simon said tensely, "you had best get out of those robes and return to your shoes. There is danger enough, what with Anne here and the ship in the cove -- and to be caught with a papist priest in the house . . ." His fears needed no further statement.

"Good night to you, Father Robert," Margaret said as she pressed a few coins into the priest's hand. "And my many thanks for your comfort."

"Bless you, daughter."

"Pray for him, Father," she said, her voice tremulous. "Tristan and my son. Pray for them both."

"I will. God keep you." The priest left through a side door under Diggory's watchful eye.

In the heavily curtained great hall the family sat while Diggory poured out fine Melaga wine into goblets of Venetian glass. Anne threw back her hood and looked around anxiously. Simon and Patrick, both soberly dressed in black, seemed equally ill at ease, moving restlessly in the shadows near the fireplace.

Anne shivered in the chill musty air. She was again wearing her old red skirt with Mad Jack's coat and shirt, both awkwardly large on her narrow shoulders.

"If you wore more petticoats, it wouldna seem so cold," Margaret said.

Anne took a dainty sip of wine. "Aye, but there is no place for petticoats upon a ship. So Father always said."

Margaret looked from one to another, then suddenly burst into tears. "They mean to hang my Jamie," she wailed, sinking down onto a bench before the fire. Anne sat beside her, putting an arm around Margaret's shaking shoulders. Over Margaret's black-veiled blonde curls Anne shot her brother a desperate look. He sat stiffly on Margaret's other side. Patrick smiled at this odd display of family familiarity.

"Now, now, Margaret," Anne said gently, although it was clearly difficult for her, "he is not hanged yet, and as long as he is alive there is always a chance."

Margaret continued to weep uncontrollably. Patrick opened his pouch and removed a phial, adding its contents to Margaret's wine and offering it to her drink. "This will calm her," he said as she took the goblet from his hand.

Margaret drained the wine, took a deep breath and said, "I have racked my brains to find some answer, but I canna think of any way to save my son."

"We know of one," Anne said, "but it depends greatly on you." Margaret looked up expectantly, tears streaking her painted cheeks. "Jamie is held now in Plymouth and our old friend Lord Percival Golding could do much to sway the verdict. You could, of course, do much to sway Lord Golding."

Margaret blushed hotly. "Are you suggesting that I go to Golding and . . ."

Anne shook her head. "You must do as you see fit. I merely offer this as a possibility if you wish to save your son. Golding is fond of gaming and has never enough money. Hence the association with the Hawkwoods. And if I recall correctly, you were once his paramour with an eye on a mesalliance."

"I was little more than a child then," Margaret protested. "And Golding is a repugnant little man. He was ever interested in more -- unnatural practices."

"Still such things have been survived," Simon replied, "and by women with far less to lose."

"I will need money," Margaret said, a calculating gleam replacing the sorrow in her blue eyes. "A great deal of money. Enough to make my way into his company."

"Hugo has that arranged, as well as lodgings for you and a servant in Salcombe. The lady of that house has a husband, a barrister named Ned Bear. 'Twill be he that will plead Jamie's case in court. But he is also a great one for gaming and will see to it that you meet with Lord Golding."

"And if I do," Margaret said, "if I go to Golding and submit to him -- and if this lawyer pleads well for Jamie's life, then what?" she demanded. "Will my son no be transported or left to rot in some prison?"

"Aye," Anne said, "but he will be alive. Alive, Margaret, and if he is transported he must go by sea. 'Tis a great and wild ocean betwixt sweet England and Jamaica. A great ocean and some two months a'sailing."

"And you would take this risk for me?"

Anne rose, her face drawn and pale against her stream of ebony hair. "I would do this for you, but mostly I do it for Father. 'Of my blood, For my blood' -- remember?"

Eben poked his head through the door behind the fire and beckoned. "Ship is ready," Patrick noted as he began to pull the burning logs away from the little door, making a narrow path along one stone wall.

"Aye," Anne replied. She rose and again pulled her cloak about her, lifting the hood to cover her head. Her face vanished in shadow as she turned to follow Simon and Patrick into the passage. "I will await word in Mousehole. You may promise Golding anything you wish. In the end it will not matter, except perhaps to him."

A week later Margaret with her serving girl Angharad in attendance took up residence in the vicinity of Salcombe. Her host saw to her introduction and within a fortnight Margaret MacDonald Hawkwood had made a name for herself in several noble houses for her large wins at whist and lanterloo. Amongst those most heavily in her debt was Lord Percival Golding.

"He will not be acquitted," said Mr. Bear as he entered Margaret's sitting room. She bit her lip and said nothing. "There will be little I can do if he is removed to London and my informants say that he will be after tomorrow's hearing. 'Twould seem, madam, that your son's best hope lies with you and your visit with Golding."

Margaret nodded slowly and sipped her wine, her eyes intent on the note in front of her. Finally she said, "I will go tonight, if he will receive me." She looked up at the lawyer who filled the doorway to her right. "And will you, Lawyer Bear, strengthen my hand by giving me the note of payment owed to you from Golding."

"Will Hugo see it paid? I dislike losing a thousand crowns if it can be otherwise avoided."

"You will be paid. Rest assured," Margaret answered as she took the paper handed to her and added it to the one she had already, "And with these I must gamble for my son's life."

"Dame Margaret Hawkwood, m'lord," the servant announced formally as he showed the lady into Golding's much gilded private apartments. Golding received her warmly, the delight of his greeting but poorly hidden by his embroidered silk robe.

"My dear Margaret," he cooed as he kissed her cheek.

"Yes, Percival," she answered coyly. "I am come again. A widow's life is a lonely one."

"Black does not become you, my dear." He crossed to a small table and poured her a glass of wine. "Some refreshment, my dear?"

Margaret nodded her thanks as she took the glass. "It has been such a long time since I was in these rooms," she said, her eyes falling first on the bed, its curtains drawn back invitingly.

"'Tis no fault of mine," Golding said, his tone not quite a whine. "No one was more grieved than I to find that you had absconded with that scoundrel Hawkwood."

She laughed lightly. "He abducted me, you know. Stole me away on his ship."

"You did not resist overmuch," he chided.

"Aye, I suppose not," she admitted. "After all, I was only young and had ne'er been abducted before."

"And now, nigh a score years later and you come back to me."

"After winning all your purse and holding a note for some five hundred crowns more," she added.

"And your son to be tried tomorrow for treason," Golding replied bluntly, the humor gone from his voice. "He will hang."

"Not if you determine otherwise."

"He is a traitor Jacobite and deserves to hang," Golding retorted. "Indeed, there are far worse torments for such as he, and, but for his youth, he should suffer them."

"Could you not, also for his youth, spare his life?" She gave Golding a sideways calculating glance, then quickly lowered her eyes.

"I could," Golding said, now enjoying the game, "but why should I?" He sniffed petulantly. "He is nothing to me."

"And I?"

"After seventeen years, you think you should still matter?"

Margaret blinked back tears that had not formed and flung herself against Golding, her breasts firm and round over his beating heart. "Oh, Percival, dinna say that. After all, I am a widow -- a very rich widow. We could begin anew."

He stroked her golden curls, his hand stealing down over her back. "But you would only wish to if I spare your son, eh?"

"Is it so much to ask?" She looked imploringly into his eyes, still pressing her ample bosom against his chest and sensing the gratifying change in his heart rate.

"It is when it does nothing to offset my debts." His heart rate might be increasing, but his generosity was not.

"I had thought that my late husband's associate was still paying you quite handsomely for your patronage," she said, nuzzling closer.

"For all that my patronage is the only thing that stands between Captain Ward and plain piracy, he seems to make little profit for me," Golding replied. "I have long suspected that he lands his cargo elsewhere and leaves me the dregs."

"If your share of Ward's profits were increased," she again raised her eyes to his, "then could you make shift to spare my son?"

Golding's fingers carefully unlaced her bodice and strayed inside. "I want coin, a set sum."

"But name it."

He led her to the bed, sitting down beside her while drawing open her bodice and exposing her full white breasts. She made no effort to resist. "Two thousand crowns," he whispered, his painted lips moving down from her ear to her shoulder. "Half to be delivered by tomorrow morning. For that I will ensure that your son is not removed to London."

"A thousand crowns by morning," she said silkily. "'Tis much to ask on such short notice."

"Nevertheless," he said as he stroked her breasts, "'tis the fee I require to postpone the trial and hold him in Devonshire."

"You are in debt to me for such a sum," Margaret said, feeling her blood rising under his attentions.

"Indeed?" Golding asked, looking up at her as he unfastened her over skirt. "I recall being in debt to you for half that sum."

Margaret smiled as she pulled the two notes from a stay casing in her open bodice. "And here is your note to me for that debt," she said, handing him one of the papers.

"I expect one thousand crowns besides being released of this debt to you," he answered, crumpling the paper. He noted with cruel satisfaction her dismayed look, then was puzzled by her sudden indifference. "It is nothing to me if your boy dies, but I should think that an old whore like yourself could find such a sum, even with the little time at your disposal."

Margaret smiled and handed him the other note. "And here is a note for another thousand crowns, owed by you to Lawyer Edward Bear. This debt has been duly recorded and witnessed so destroying this note will not make it go away unless I so choose. Your fee is paid."

If Golding was disappointed by her success, the greed over his pallid features masked it. "Well done, Margaret," he said as he tucked the note away in his robe. "So your boy will sit in the Citadel some little time longer. Tell Edward Bear that the trial is postponed." His hands crept beneath her voluminous skirts and into the smooth wet crevices hidden beneath. "I will arrange for the boy's trial when I receive another thousand crowns. Until then he rots in prison."

"And once we pay that fee, you will let him go?" The words caught in her throat.

"I will spare his life. I can promise no more than that." Golding smiled to himself as he pulled away that last of her bulky undergarments and opened his robe. "Your son will be transported," he whispered as he stretched himself out over her and pushed between her legs. "There must be some justice done."

Margaret was no longer listening. Despite her revulsion of Golding, her widow's life had indeed been a lonely one.

"How could you let that boy go!?" Campbell demanded.

Golding carefully knocked a croquet ball through the wicket and slowly turned his attention to the fuming officer as they stood on the grass in the warm May sun. "I did not let him go. I merely spared his life. By God, Campbell, that boy is but sixteen years old and bound for the living hell of a Jamaica plantation. I do not see my action as particularly merciful." Golding strutted to the next wicket.

"Unless, of course, his clever sister finds some means of rescue at sea," Campbell said angrily.

"I have thought of that already," Golding said proudly. "Commander Hargrove was here yesterday with that lieutenant of his -- what is his name? The fine looking lad you worked with to capture young Hawkwood."

"Gilchrist," Campbell answered, his tone betraying some uncomfortable memory. "The damned fool let Anne Hawkwood escape."

"Well, nevertheless," Golding said, brushing past him, "Hargrove has permission from the Admiralty to escort the transport vessel. They can keep an eye out for the Bold Cockerel, as well as watch for that other ship Gilchrist saw, and rest assured that no Hawkwood ship would go against a fifth rater like the Rainbow. Captain Ward is far too cautious for that." Golding took a delicate pinch of snuff, then offered the pearl inlaid box to the colonel. "I should like to end all ties with the Hawkwood enterprise. I never did trust Mad Jack when he was alive and I certainly do not trust him more now that he is dead. Your spy, Colonel, is a threat to me. He seems to know much about the personal workings of my patronage. There are some details I would have kept from Court."

"I would give him his money and have done with him then," Campbell suggested.

"I would prefer to give that money to you, Colonel," Golding said, "and you may do with the spy as you think best." Golding paused and smiled. "After all, he has served his use."

CHAPTER TEN

WHO'S THE FOOL NOW?

I saw a mouse chase a cat,
Saw a cheese eat a rat;
Thou hast well drunken, man,
Who's the fool now? folksong

On the bright spring morning of departure, the transport vessel *Swiftestake* loaded the chained and stumbling prisoners bound for sale in Jamaica, set her sails and pulled away from Plymouth. At the side of the *Swiftestake* rolled the mighty *Rainbow* under Commander Desmond Hargrove's stern and able command.

"'Tis rare that a fifth rater is sent to escort a simple transport vessel," one of the *Swiftestake's* crew commented to the ship's surgeon as they watched the big thirty-two gun *Rainbow* take a parallel course about half a mile away. "We've no cargo but criminals and any pirate is welcomed to 'em."

"Aye," the doctor nodded absently, his eyes intent on the Navy vessel, his red hair glowing like fire in the sun.

Rounding the rocky Cornish coast at evening the lookout high in the *Rainbow's* mainmast sang out, "Sail to starboard! Ship hoy!" Hargrove lifted the glass to his weathered face and scanned the dimming horizon. Just barely visible in the setting sun were the sails of a frigate. Chuckling deeply, Hargrove handed the glass to Gilchrist who raised it to look at the point indicated.

"What think you, Mister Gilchrist? 'Tis the vessel you saw the morning that Mistress Hawkwood escaped you, eh?"

Gilchrist shook his head. "Nay, Commander," he said, handing back the glass. "That was a small vessel. From this distance such a ship would not be seen by us at all. Yon frigate looks to be nigh as big as we."

"Then perhaps 'tis the *Bold Cockerel*," Hargrove said as he snapped the telescope closed and pocketed it. "We will know by morning."

In the clear light of the following day Hargrove came on deck and found Lieutenant Gilchrist studying their lately acquired companion vessel. "She keeps pace with us, sir," Gilchrist reported.

"And her distance," Hargrove commented, squinting at the ship which now lay abreast and far to starboard of the *Swiftestake*. He drew out the telescope and studied the frigate. "Ah," he said grinning broadly, "'tis the *Bold Cockerel* without doubt." He handed the glass to Gilchrist. "See for yourself -- the flag with the black kestrel on it. Aye, 'tis the Hawkwood ship. Tell the helm to stay with her."

"But should we not stick fast to the *Swiftestake*?"

"Aye, Mister Gilchrist," Hargrove answered, "but trust Captain Ward to go where the *Swiftestake* goes, and after all, 'tis not the *Swiftestake* we want."

"Aye, sir." Gilchrist marched off to give orders to the helmsman and soon the *Rainbow* maneuvered between the transport ship and the frigate.

On the deck of the *Bold Cockerel* John Ward watched the *Rainbow* drifting closer. "Keep your distance," he ordered his helmsman. Again the frigate pulled further off.

Aboard the *Swiftestake* the prisoners, Jamie amongst them, coped as best they could with the crowding, the chains, the stench and the waves of nausea brought on by the conditions, augmented as they were by seasickness. It promised to be a wretched voyage followed by the miseries of enslavement should any survive to reach the auction block in Jamaica.

On that first day and late into the night, his belly rolling with every shudder of the ship, Jamie wondered if it might not have been better to hang with dignity and make a noble end. There had been those long anxious days of waiting as he grew thinner and weaker from worry and mistreatment. Hugo had gone to some lengths to secure for Jamie a cell worthy of a young gentleman, but this had the disadvantage of leaving him prey to the baser instincts of his guards while depriving him of the protection of his fellow prisoners.

And now in this hold full of companions, Jamie felt more alone than ever before. Most of all he missed Tristan. He knew that his mother had held a funeral service for his missing cousin, but something inside him would not accept the disappearance as death.

The next morning a guard entered the hold and announced, "Ship's surgeon to inspect the prisoners." The guard stepped back and a tall thin figure ducked past him. In the glow of light from the hatch all Jamie saw clearly was sunlight on red gold hair, then another bout of nausea seized him and he bent his head over a nearby bucket, already brimming, to deposit the vile meal he had consumed earlier. Jamie lay back on his filthy pallet, too weak to sit when the doctor approached.

"You must find more buckets and empty them more often." The doctor's voice was startlingly familiar. Jamie opened his eyes and would have cried out had not a warning hand come down over his mouth. "There now, easy with you," Patrick said. "Do not speak. 'Twill only tire you, boy." Jamie looked into Patrick's smiling face. The guard, he noted, had moved off to shift a bucket. "You do not know me," Patrick instructed in a whisper. Jamie nodded. A quick glance around confirmed that the exchange had gone unnoticed.

"I have seen all that I need," Patrick said to the guard. "I can now make my report to the captain."

Whatever Jamie hoped might happen did not that second day nor the third. Conditions improved only slightly. More buckets were found for the prisoners' use and the hardier of the prisoners were assigned to empty the buckets more frequently. Other than that, there seemed no hope for the weeks of crossing.

Late in the afternoon of the third day, Jamie was brought to the main deck with several others and allowed some exercise. Doctor Hartley stood at the railing, thin wisps of smoke trailing from his pipe. Very casually he turned as Jamie approached.

"And how are you, Master Hawkwood?" Patrick asked quietly.

"Well enough for one so nearly dead."

"Fit for travel?"

"Aye."

"The captain has been persuaded that some better care of the prisoners will improve their sale value once we reach Jamaica," Patrick said, watching as a sailor passed. "One can always count on human greed, it seems." His voice dropped to a low whisper. "Come dawn tomorrow I will fetch thee out of yon hell hole, but tell no one, not even your dearest comrade below. I am sent to save you alone and no other. Is that clear?"

Jamie nodded. "But how? How came you here? And how are we to escape?"

"In good time, m'boy, all your questions will be answered." Patrick warily scanned the deck. "Suffice it to say that I came here through Mister Carr's ministrations to the ship's regular doctor, rendering him unfit to serve. Thus, I took his place. As to our leaving, your lovely sister is contriving that at this very moment, I'll wager."

"Against a Navy warship?" Jamie asked aghast.

Patrick eyed the great vessel, now grown small with distance. "Aye, Jamie, even against the *Rainbow*."

What Commander Hargrove and his lookout failed to see of the *Bold Cockerel* was the small merchantman keeping pace on the far side. And in the blackness of night following the third day no one noticed the watch aboard the *Swiftestake* fall into a drowsy lull after accepting a kindly dram from the ship's doctor.

Patrick turned the *Swiftestake*, slowing her as the *Rainbow* sailed by in the dark, then veering her off to starboard. The watch on the warship, intent upon the well-lit *Bold Cockerel*, never noticed the *Swiftestake* slip away nor the appearance of the small merchantman as she left her shelter behind the frigate and sailed to intercept the wandering transport vessel.

There was the faintest hint of dawn when Patrick stole the keys from the sleeping gaoler, and unshackled Jamie from the chains that bound him to a poacher. None of the prisoners took notice as Patrick led Jamie through the sleeping bodies and up to the clean free air. Jamie, still weak, leaned on Patrick and very nearly stumbled over a fallen guard.

"Don't worry about the guards," Patrick whispered. "I gave them and all the officers enough laudanum to keep them sleeping for hours. We will be far and away before their heads clear."

"And when they do, will they no give chase?"

"I think not," Patrick said with a sly smile. "At least not until they straighten out their rigging and splice the lines I cut."

There was a splash of oars, then the grinding of wood as a small gig touched the transport's side. "Hallo, Patrick," called a low voice, "have you got the boy?"

"Aye, Anne," Patrick replied. "Safe and well." He followed Jamie down the ladder into the waiting gig. There Jamie found his sister, Eben Carr and a huge African at the oars.

"Where's Simon?" Jamie asked.

"In Plymouth, I believe," Anne answered. "He wishes you well, but says he has no desire to go to sea for you. He will mind the Rookery while we are away."

"'Tis his now," Jamie said, settling himself in the boat beside Anne. "Perhaps he will give up the roads and find a place in life."

"Well, if LeBoutellier has a place in life," Eben said suddenly, "I wish to God he'd find it. Look!"

There in the faint light, wildly gilded and festooned, *La Panache* was bearing down on the *Chanticleer*, the sleeping *Swiftestake* and the little gig that rowed hard between them. The soft haze of dawn glinted on the carved gold cupids and nymphs that adorned *La Panache's* bow and high stern, and the dark, much plumed figure of her captain on the quarter deck.

"Damn that Frenchman!" Anne hissed. To the African she said, "Row, Jubilee my man, row!" The thick black shoulders strained at the oars and brought the gig scraping against the *Chanticleer* where the passengers scrambled up the ladders. As the gig was rapidly hauled up, *La Panache* sailed closer until she lay between the silent *Swiftestake* and the *Chanticleer*.

"'Tis LeBoutellier with his usual impeccable timing," Anne said stormily as Darcy helped her onto the deck.

He nodded. "We had no way to warn ye, not without risk of waking the transport's crew."

"We have got to get away -- now," Anne said. "Are we --"

"Bon jour, mes amies," LeBoutellier shouted, cutting her off. "And have I the honor of addressing the most beauteous Anne Hawkwood?"

"You have, LeBoutellier," Anne shouted back, her voice harsh. Behind her the crew continued their frantic preparations for departure. "What do you want, you pox infested fop?"

"Ah, but where is your comrade John Ward? Shall I be forced to fight this great sea duel with a mere girl in a tiny Dutch shoe with no cannon?" Anne did not answer, signaling Patrick to take Jamie below to her cabin. "Perhaps you and I shall have our little duel, no?"

"No," Anne answered, her eyes nervously scanning the *Swiftestake* for signs of life. "No duel today, Frenchman."

"But your dear late father promised, eh?" The accent did not hide the laughing sarcasm and the distance did not diminish the gleaming greedy looks of his crew as they lined *La Panache's* railing. "Here I find you preying upon a filthy prison ship. Hah! Cher Anne, this is not worthy of you. Indeed, I shall believe I am the greatest of flibustiers unless the English Hawkwoods prove me wrong."

"We must not tarry here longer," Eben whispered hoarsely to Anne. "Patrick says he only had enough laudanum to reduce the watch and the officers. The crew and cargo will be up and moving any time now."

"But name me the greatest of flibustiers and we will put an end to our silly contest," LeBoutellier called wooingly. "Let us be lovers then instead of rivals, eh, ma petite?"

"In a pig's arse!" she yelled. Already the *Chanticleer* was moving away from both the *Swiftestake*, which now showed disturbing signs of life, and *La Panache*, which gamely tried to block the merchantman's path.

Aboard the transport ship the tangled rigging and severed lines were quickly discovered by the awakening sailors, and with cries of dismay they fired their two small cannon upon the supposed perpetrator, which they assumed to be *La Panache*. LeBoutellier, now distracted from his ship to ship wooing of Anne Hawkwood, fired on the transport vessel, bringing down her mizzenmast and more rigging.

The *Chanticleer's* larboard gunports opened as she passed *La Panache* and sent a withering barrage of chainshot high into the French ship's sails, ripping her topgallants and staysails. The *Chanticleer* sailed on while *La Panache* limped behind, like a wounded lover after his faithless sweetheart.

When the sun was fully above the horizon, Hargrove raised his telescope and saw to his satisfaction that the *Bold Cockerel* was holding her course. He smiled to himself and started to lower the glass when a slight swing to larboard caused him to notice that while the frigate had held her course, the *Swiftestake* had not. She was nowhere to be seen.

"Gilchrist!" Hargrove bellowed. "Gilchrist, by damn! She's slipped us."

The lieutenant rushed to his side, then stopped. "Indeed not, sir. There they are, as before," he said, pointing to the *Bold Cockerel.*

"Not the frigate, you fool," Hargrove said impatiently. "The transport ship." Gilchrist took the glass from him and searched the ocean, then nodded glumly in agreement. The watch was summoned from bed. Only one man had noticed the *Swiftestake* fall behind in the night.

"But I didn't think to rouse you, sir," the man said, "since your orders was for us to keep an eye to yon frigate."

Hargrove bit his lip. He might have ordered the man flogged for negligence, but deep in his heart he knew that the fault was his own. "Turn about then and find the *Swiftestake*," he ordered. "She is our convoy and no other."

Most of the morning was spent locating the transport ship, who now with her rigging mended made all speed to find her erring protector and to report the unexplained removal of one prisoner and the ship's surgeon.

"This doctor," Gilchrist asked the *Swiftestake's* captain, "what sort of fellow was he?"

"Tall, thin with red hair," the captain answered. "Not our regular surgeon. That fellow took sick just before we sailed. Then this fellow Hartley turned up and --"

"Hartley!" Gilchrist said. "I might have known."

"Why? Do you know the man?" Hargrove asked.

"Aye," Gilchrist replied. "Doctor Patrick Hartley. I met him at the Rookery when I went there with Colonel Campbell."

Hargrove sighed. "Thank you, Mister Gilchrist. Captain, please return to your ship and keep your course. We will rejoin you as soon as we have made a thorough search of these waters for the two vessels you sighted."

The *Rainbow* deserted the *Swiftestake* once more, and the sun was already on the downward path when the lookout spotted two ships far to starboard.

All day the *Chanticleer* had run before the wind and the pursuit of the amorous Frenchman. When her lookout announced the approach of a large frigate, Anne sighed with relief. "'Tis the *Bold Cockerel*," she cried happily. "Mayhap John Ward can convince this Gallic goose to go to the Indies or to hell, but without us."

Minutes later the lookout reported that *La Panache* had turned and was no longer following them. Anne laughed heartily. "No doubt they have seen our good brethren and fear a more equal contest." She drew out her spyglass and watched the French ship's gilded stern grow smaller in the afternoon sun. "Farewell, LeBoutellier, and to the devil with all Frenchmen." She turned the glass to the approaching vessel, still too far off for any detail of her deck or crew to be seen, but clear enough to be recognized for what she was.

"Sweet Jesus!" Anne swore. Clearly dismayed, she handed the glass to Darcy who reacted similarly, then passed it to Eben.

"What is it?" Patrick asked, climbing up to the quarterdeck with Jamie behind him.

"'Tis Hargrove, worse the luck," Anne replied grimly. "And no sign of Ward to rescue us from their big guns."

"We have cannon." Jamie said.

"Aye," Eben replied. "Ten small guns below, two swivel guns in the bow and some forty men. The *Rainbow* is a ship of the line with three times our cannon and a crew of nigh two hundred." Eben started to turn away. "If you have some popish prayers you'd like to say, this is an excellent time to be about it."

Suddenly Darcy spoke. "Leave the Pope out of it, Eben mo bhuachaill. Besides, I have given the matter some thought and there is a way out of it, I'm thinking."

"Well?" Anne demanded.

Darcy scratched his beard. "Do you remember when your father had that other little sloop and was nearly taken by that big Spaniard?"

"Aye," she said, then exclaimed, "Mad Jack's fever!"

"The very same," Darcy continued. "It may keep them from wanting to board us, and buy us the time we need for the *Cockerel* to reach us."

"Very well, gentlemen, get to work," Anne said.

Darcy and Eben shouted orders and the deck came alive with men. Yards of spare sail were unfolded on the deck while bundles of rope and gear were arranged to look like the forms of prone men. The white canvas was then draped over the bundles and the deck took on the appearance of a floating morgue. A dozen men, pistols and swords at the ready, lay down amongst the bundles and pulled the cloth over them. The cannon and swivel guns were loaded and primed and the remaining crew hidden on the gun deck below.

"I want you to go below with the cannon crew," Anne said. Jamie looked startled.

"I dinna ken cannon," he stammered.

"Best learn then," Anne said. "With any luck there will be no fight. The men on deck are merely a precaution. Get below, Jamie. I have not risked so much to have you killed within hours of your rescue." Grudgingly, he obeyed.

As the *Rainbow* drew nearer, the few men who remained visible on deck took on a seeming lassitude while those under the canvas pulled it over their faces and lay still. Anne and Patrick retired to her cabin. "Are you sure 'tis wise to leave Jamie with the cannon?" Patrick asked. "He is still weak from prison."

"I know," she nodded as she took one final look at the *Rainbow*, her deck and men now distinct, "but if the lad is indeed Mad Jack's son, then there will be no keeping him from the fight, so we might as well put him where he will be in least danger and of most use."

A single shot was fired from the *Rainbow* across the *Chanticleer's* bow. Eben answered the warning by dutifully turning the ship into the wind, letting the sails luff loudly overhead. The warship sailed closer and was not far from grappling distance when a voice called, "This is Commander Desmond Hargrove of His Majesty's ship *Rainbow*. We are searching for pirates in these waters."

"We have seen none," Darcy called back, staggering against the rail. "And none would come nigh us even if we begged. There is plague here."

There was a pause as Hargrove conferred with his aide, then over the sound of luffing canvas, he called, "My lieutenant feels that there is some cause to search your ship. Prepare to be boarded."

"At your own risk, Hargrove," Darcy answered. "Nigh half my crew lie dead from this fever. Come closer and you'll infect your own men with this contagion."

After a long pause, Hargrove called, "We have noted the corpses on your deck. Are there those alive who have this fever?"

"Aye," Darcy answered, coughing and swaying. "'Tis I myself have it. And my helmsman," he waved at Eben who clutched at the wheel like a demented child. The two men huddled by the swivel guns slumped lower, hiding their slow match. "There be a few more below -- all sick. You'd be a damned fool to board."

There was another pause. "My lieutenant still feels that a search is in order. If you are not the vessel we are seeking, we will do what we can to help you."

The *Rainbow* veered off, widening the gap between the two ships. Darcy watched as the longboat was lowered and noted that only a dozen men had joined the lieutenant. The warship drifted ever further from the suspect merchantman, the Navy crew revealing their revulsion of the shrouded deck.

"My apologies," Gilchrist said as he stepped onto the deck, his men lined up behind him and shuddering as they viewed the still white forms hidden under the canvas. "This ship is very like another I have seen and --" Gilchrist stopped and stared at the big Irishman. "I do remember you."

"Then you remember too much," O'Flynn growled.

There was a hot spark of realization, then Gilchrist yelled, "Search this ship -- every inch!" One of the boarders jerked back the canvas and dropped with an axe in his chest.

"Fire!" Eben bellowed, leaping up. There was a blaze of pistol fire and several uniformed men fell. The two men in the bow touched the match to the swivel guns and a hail of grapeshot raked the *Rainbow's* deck, hurling death and scattering her crew. A roar shook the merchantman as her larboard cannon sent a broadside of chainshot into the warship's rigging, bringing spars and sail crashing to the deck.

Eben now spun the wheel and the *Chanticleer's* sails snapped full and pulled her behind the warship's stern, where a blast of her starboard guns crippled the *Rainbow's* rudder and ended all chance of pursuit. So sudden and ferocious was the little ship's attack that Hargrove's men were taken completely by surprise. By the time they were ready to return fire, the *Chanticleer* had done her damage and was fast fleeing the wounded warship.

Ill-prepared and outnumbered, the Navy boarders on the *Chanticleer* made for their longboat through a deadly path of sword and shot. Those who could scrambled over the side while others dove into the sea. For the wounded there was no escape. Gilchrist tried desperately to help one comrade to the rail. "Save yourself, sir," the man cried. "I'm done for. Save yourself." He fell limp and Gilchrist laid him on the deck, then turned to leap into the sea.

Suddenly there appeared in front of him a giant black man with a shaven head and tattooed cheeks. Jubilee smiled wickedly as he snapped a whip around the lieutenant's ankles and jerked his feet out from under him. Gilchrist landed on his back, the black man's dagger at his throat.

"Now I kills you, little white man," Jubilee hissed. "I throws you into the sea -- piece by piece."

"Hold there, Jubilee," said an Irish voice. "What have you got there?" Gilchrist breathed heavily as he looked up at Darcy O'Flynn. "Well, well. If 'tisn't Mister Gilchrist of the *Rainbow*."

The tattooed black face beamed with triumph. "I kills him, eh? Makes him dead."

"No, Jubilee, not this one, not now." Darcy explained. "I'm thinking the captain will want this one alive."

There was a grunt of protest from the negro who strode off to one side where he stood quietly licking the blood from his knife. Darcy hauled Gilchrist to his feet. "I thank you, sir, for my life," Gilchrist said politely. The mate grinned. Gilchrist watched the *Rainbow* growing smaller in the afternoon light. "I am your prisoner."

"Aye, lad, that you are," Darcy replied. "Sam! Rolf!" Two youths looked up from the pile of fallen Navy men. "Any other prisoners?"

"None as will last the night," Sam answered.

Darcy nodded. "I'll take care of them. Take this one below and lock him up." Gilchrist was seized by the shoulders and propelled across the bloodstained deck to the forward hatch. Out of the corner of his eye he saw Jubilee, still licking his knife and smiling.

On the dimly lit lower deck, lined with still warm guns and the strewn possessions of the crew, Gilchrist was shoved into a small cell at the bow. The cell had a rough sturdy wooden wall and a heavy wooden door with a small barred window set into it. The floor was covered with molding straw onto which Gilchrist was thrown. The door banged shut, the lock clicked and he was alone.

Through the little window he watched the crew swab out the cannon and sort their belongings. Others brought down the wounded. He recognized Doctor Hartley who now moved among them, binding the few wounds and pouring out doses of laudanum, but from the pitiful cries coming from above, Gilchrist feared his own men did not fare so well.

Hours passed. From the shouts above, Gilchrist knew that another ship had been sighted, the *Bold Cockerel.* There was renewed scurry as supplies were lowered through to the hold. The big frigate that the *Rainbow* had chased for the last three days was nothing more than a cargo ship for this little merchantman.

It was dark night when, in the midst of the celebration on the main deck, Darcy and another man opened the cell. "Well now, lad," Darcy said grandly, "what think you of your quarters."

Gilchrist looked up. "My men?"

"All dead," Darcy answered. "'Twas necessary. Their wounds were mortal and they would have suffered more. Count it as the only mercy you're like to see here." Gilchrist turned away in disgust.

"Cap'n says 'e's to be searched thorough," called a voice from the hatch. "Every stitch of 'im." A bundle was tossed down. "'Ere's some clothes for 'im once you get those off."

"Aye, we'll see to it," Darcy called. He gathered up the bundle and a pair of manacles and returned to the cell. "On your feet, lad." Gilchrist stood slowly. "Now come here." Gilchrist did not move. "I said come here, boy," the mate ordered.

"I am an officer in His Majesty's Navy and no boy -- not to you nor to any other pirate mongrel." His voice was resolute despite the slight tremor in his hands and knees.

"You were an officer in His Majesty's Navy -- boy," the mate said as he pulled Gilchrist from the cell. "Now you're a prisoner aboard this ship and bound for service in the plantations -- if ye live. Do as I tell you. Now strip."

Gilchrist picked himself up and slowly pulled off his shoes and stockings and his uniform coat. He untied his cravat and the laces of his shirt, and then added them to the pile at his feet. "Is that enough, Mister O'Flynn?" he asked, his fair skin very white in the lantern light.

"My orders are that you're to be searched down to the skin," Darcy said. "Get your breeches off."

"No," Gilchrist answered boldly.

"Fool," Darcy said. He gave a slight nod to the other man, then suddenly slammed the prisoner against a pillar where the other man was waiting with a length of rope. He bound Gilchrist's neck to the pillar and held his wrists. Darcy looked the young man in the eye as he reached down to unfasten his breeches. Gilchrist twisted wildly, hot blood of humiliation rising in his face, even as the rope tightened about his throat, strangling him.

"Hold him fast there, Eli," Darcy laughed, "for he fears we mean to bugger him." Moments later the rope was loosened and the bundle of clothes tossed at him. "Dress in these, lad. 'Tisn't our intention you should catch your death lying naked in your cell."

Darcy gathered up the fallen articles of uniform and handed them to the other man. "Run these up to the captain. I'll finish with him." The sailor left as Gilchrist pulled on the frayed sail cloth slops and tightened the drawstring at his waist. "I want no more trouble from you," Darcy warned sternly. "Your passage with us doesn't have to be unpleasant unless you make it so."

"'Tis much what the captain said to us when we boarded that foul prison ship," Jamie said as he stepped up behind Darcy.

"And if I had my way, you might still be on it," Gilchrist replied tartly. "I might have known that I would get less than honorable treatment on any vessel that would rescue a traitor like you, James Hawkwood."

"Hold your tongue, Gilchrist," Darcy ordered, "and Master James, you belong elsewhere I warrant."

"I came to see this royal monkey," Jamie said. "I have a question or two for him."

Eben swung down through the hatch. "As have I. Jamie, get aft with you now. We have business with the prisoner and it's not for you." Jamie started to turn, but stopped when he saw the knotted rope whip that Eben was carrying.

Darcy looked sharply at Eben. "You overstep your authority, Mister Carr. The captain has not ordered this."

"Aye, but 'twill come in time." Eben's dark eyes glinted coldly. "Jamie, go now."

"I dinna ken why I should," he answered stubbornly.

Eben took Jamie's arm and led him to the base of the ladder. "Do as you're told, my friend. Trust me. There'll be no soft treatment for this poor bastard, I can promise you that." Jamie nodded and climbed to the deck above. Eben turned to the mate. "Hold him fast there, Mister O'Flynn, and let's see if we can flog the truth out of him."

Darcy shrugged. "Your orders then, Mister Carr, but don't be saying I didn't warn you." With that, the burly mate grabbed Gilchrist's wrists and held him tightly against the pillar while Eben struck a series of savage blows on the prisoner's bare back. Despite the whip's sting Gilchrist uttered no cry, although his contorted face and white knuckled fists spoke eloquently. He struggled against himself to give his tormentors no satisfaction and was only vaguely aware of the questions the quartermaster asked him between blows . . . something to do with Hartland Point.

There was an angry shout from above and the merciless lashing stopped abruptly. Gilchrist was barely conscious of Darcy locking the manacles to his wrists and lowering him onto the straw. A shirt was thrown over him, then the cell door scraped shut and again he was alone.

Exhaustion and pain wiped memory from him, and throughout the dark damp night even the familiar slap and roll of wave on wood seemed a distant thing. He did not hear the soft click of the lock or the creak of the door as it opened. He did not feel the gentle movement of the shirt being lifted from his welt-raw back nor the caress of small cool hands. He could not smell the sweet scent of the mint salve, did not feel the warmth of the blanket that was draped over him, did not feel the kiss that brushed his cheek.

CHAPTER ELEVEN

THE RELUCTANT PIRATE

Come listen to me, sailors to this tale I do report,
Beware of roaming pirates that will plunder any boat;
I left me lovely Nancy for to sail the ocean blue,
And I was taken prisoner by a wild and wicked crew.

folksong

In the morning Gilchrist awoke from what he hoped was a nightmare, but discovered it was all painfully true. He pushed himself up from the straw, but sank again when the sore flesh of his back overwhelmed him. He lay still for some time. Then the bolt slid in the lock and the cell door opened.

"Good morning to you, lad," Darcy said cheerfully. In his hand he held Gilchrist's shirt. "You may not want anything as ragged as that other shirt against your back, so I thought you might like your own soft linen again."

"Thank you," Gilchrist said, now forcing himself up, wincing with the movement.

"If you want to put it on, I can unlock the bracelets for you."

"Please," Gilchrist said, holding out his wrists. The key clicked open the manacles and he gingerly pulled on his shirt while Darcy watched him from the cell door.

"The captain will be wanting to see you when you're done dressing," Darcy said. "I have orders to bring you up straightway." Gilchrist nodded. "See that you mind your manners, lad, and do as you're told."

"I am ready," Gilchrist said. Darcy snapped the manacles again on the lieutenant's wrists and led him along the gun deck to the aft hatch. In the brief moments he was on the main deck, Gilchrist blinked in the bright sun and squinted at the great billow of canvas overhead full of fair wind that blew them westward. Not far off to starboard sailed the heavily armed frigate he had watched from the *Rainbow*.

The captain's cabin was a tidy chamber. Beneath the stern ports was a narrow bunk, crisply blanketed. To one side there was a table and two chairs. Behind these stood a three paneled screen that obscured the view into the inner chamber beyond.

Eben Carr entered from behind the screen, his swarthy face glowering at the prisoner. Gilchrist noted that the quartermaster's lower lip was now swollen and that his left cheek bore a deep red welt. Eben pulled out one chair and indicated that the prisoner was to sit. There was a quickly whispered conversation with Darcy, after which Darcy placed a key on the table, and left with the quartermaster.

Gilchrist could hear a soft rustling in the chamber beyond. "Feel free to unlock the manacles," a smooth low voice said. "The key is on the table." The voice betrayed little of its speaker. Puzzled, Gilchrist took the key and with some difficulty opened the manacles, placing them with the key on the table.

"My thanks to you, Captain," he said.

"'Tis little to thank me for." She stepped from behind the screen.

"Mistress Hawkwood!"

She was dressed much as he had last seen her, in a plain red skirt with no petticoats, a man's shirt and coat much too large, and a wide silk sash through which were thrust two pistols and a dagger. "I see I have startled you," she said as she sat on the opposite chair. "It should be no surprise, Lieutenant." She looked at him probingly. "If any is surprised, 'tis I. Who would have thought that Hargrove would leave his most gallant and able officer in the hands of pirates?"

"He had not much choice," Gilchrist replied.

"I suppose not," she shrugged. "And yet, after our parting in the cove that morning, I had not thought to see you again. In any case, welcome aboard the *Chanticleer*."

He shifted slightly in his chair, then winced. "'Twas a warm welcome your quartermaster gave me last night."

Anne frowned. "Mister Carr exceeded his authority and has been sternly reprimanded for it. You have my sincere apologies for the flogging you received."

"Thank you, mistress --"

"Captain here," she said unsmiling. "Duly elected by the crew -- though I admit with my late father's encouragement and full endorsement. I have sole charge of all prisoners and you will take orders from me and from my officers. I want you to remember that every minute of every day you are aboard this ship."

"Aye, Captain." The title caught in his throat.

Anne rose and disappeared for a moment into the side chamber, returning with his uniform coat. She sat again, spreading the coat on the table. "Do you recall the papers you carried?"

He looked confused. "Papers? 'Twas my commission only. What of that?"

"Nothing of your commission," she answered, drawing out a paper from inside his coat. "Here 'tis and there is naught to say of it. No, I meant this." She held a small crumpled paper in front of him. He shook his head. "'Tis a letter from your friend Colonel Campbell."

Gilchrist watched her warily. "Well, what of it? 'Tis no shame or secret that I worked with the man."

Anne nodded. "The letter says in part, 'You know my chief concern should you find yourself in possession of the Hawkwood vessel. I trust your honor will in no way deter you from settling the matter we discussed . . .' Would you care to explain the colonel's statements?"

"How can I, mistr -- Captain? I did not understand the reference myself." He did not look at her.

"I do not believe that such a man as Colonel Campbell is in the habit of writing letters that the recipient will not understand."

"Exactly what do you wish me to tell you?" He looked again into her face, as delicate and as cold as a marble Venus.

"The name of the spy." Her expression did not change.

Gilchrist turned his eye away. "I cannot."

"You do not deny this spy's existence," she observed.

"Nor do I confirm it," he replied, looking up at her.

To his surprise she smiled and tucked the letter inside her coat. "I think you should understand your situation here, -- Gilchrist, is it not?"

"Aye, Lieutenant Philip Gilchrist."

"Well, you are no officer no longer," she said, folding his coat as though to pack away his past with it.

"So I was informed last night."

"The *Chanticleer* is small and no passenger ship. We carry but two commodities -- crew and cargo."

"Of which I am currently the latter," he said.

"Precisely. You do have a perception of your status then. You may alter this through three courses. The first and most acceptable is to sign articles with us and go on the account."

He looked at her resolutely, his expression revealing his disgust with her suggestion. "And dishonor everything that I am or am likely to become?! Nay, Captain. I have served too long and seen too much to endorse now the very thing I went sea to fight."

Anne shrugged. "I will not dispute with you the morality of our trade. Indeed, I have had disputation enough with my arrogant young brother. The second course available to you is to give me the name of the spy aboard the *Cockerel*. For that, I could make shift to release you unharmed without incurring the anger of my crew."

"And I have already told you that I cannot give you that name." This time his eyes did not leave hers.

"So be it, Philip Gilchrist. The alternative is as you were told last night -- sale in the plantations. Jamie will no doubt be delighted."

"He that was so recently rescued from that very fate," Gilchrist said with a sad smile. "I would have thought he might have some pity."

Anne gave a chilling laugh. "On the contrary, man. He would sell you to the most cruel Spanish galley captain alive if I let him have charge of the matter -- which I do not intend to do. But if he should learn what part you played in the death of his cousin Tristan, God help you."

Gilchrist stared at her. "Tristan MacDonald is dead?"

"Aye. Murdered on the cliffs of Hartland," she answered. "At least, it seems so. His body has not been found." She noticed his stare. "You did not know?"

"Not until this instant, I swear it," he protested, shaking his head in disbelief.

Anne said nothing for a moment, then looked at him squarely. "When we reach the Indies you will be sold. 'Tis your value as a slave that will be your chief protection from my crew. Campbell's spy and your association with him is completely unknown to them. See that it remains so. Only Eben, Darcy and myself aboard this ship know aught of the spy. Only Doctor Hartley and Captain Ward know of him on t'other ship." She tapped her fingers lightly, her eyes never leaving his face. "Until we reach the Indies, you will be required to do your share of work. During the day you will have the freedom of the ship, but at night you will be returned to your cell. You are, I am sure, well aware of the action that will be taken if you attempt in any way to impede the progress of this ship or do harm to any person aboard her."

Her relentless gaze unnerved him. He looked away as a shiver raced through him. "Aye, Captain."

"You did me a kindness the night the Rookery was searched and I have not forgotten it. I would likewise protect you, but my position here is tenuous. I have this ship and am her captain, but I am also a woman and dare not let the men know of any weakness. I have their trust and confidence and will not risk that for anyone. Father taught me that there must be no favoritism beyond that of kin."

"I understand."

Anne lifted the manacles. Gilchrist patiently extended his wrists, but Anne laughed and dropped the chains into her lap. "You can hardly work with your hands bound. Until there is evidence that such restraints are necessary, you will not be required to wear them. You may go now."

He rose to leave, then stopped in the door. "You said there were three courses by which I might alter my current state. What was the third?"

"Death, my friend." She turned away.

"You are a very fortunate man," Darcy said as he settled himself beside Gilchrist on the deck that afternoon.

"I do not see how." Gilchrist tried not to notice the maggots crawling on the bread he was dipping into his stew. He turned to look at the mate, grimacing as the tender flesh of his back was pulled by the motion.

"You owe a thanks to Master James. Had it not been for him whining to his sister about being left out of last night's entertainment below, Mister Carr might have taken every inch of your hide." Darcy's deep voice dropped to a lower tone. "He wants the name of the spy, lad, and he won't be giving you a moment's peace until he gets it."

Gilchrist glanced around. No one had taken any notice of him and the mate. "I have told Mistress Hawkwood that I cannot give her the name, nor can I add anything to the truth of young MacDonald's fate."

"And does she believe you?"

"There is no reason for her to doubt me." Gilchrist swallowed another mouthful of greasy barley and salt beef. "She said she would protect me, at least until we reached the Indies."

"Then, of course, you're hoping she will go on protecting you, keeping you alive so that you might give her that name without force, because she --" Darcy broke off as Gilchrist's shy smile confirmed his suspicions. The mate's burst of laughter startled the lieutenant. "By all the saints, boy, you are a fool! Mister Carr is the real power here and causing dispute between him and the Captain will do nothing to endear you to either one. They were playmates in childhood, constant companions. He will be jealous of any attention she gives you and in a position to make you suffer for it." He lowered his voice again as several other sailors looked up. "The woman is not for you. There's nothing she loves more than power -- and that she has in her captaincy. She won't be risking that to save you -- not when you hold information that could well cost her life. And then there's Master James. For all his airs and fine ways, he has a cruel streak to him. If ever he learns of this spy and the truth of his cousin's death -- well, lad, I wouldn't wager heavily on the captain's protection then."

Gilchrist sighed. "She seemed a very different person in the great hall of the Rookery. So gentle and so elegant."

"Aye, lad," Darcy said, sopping up the last of his stew, "'tis no wonder. Like her father she is." He rose and looked down at the prisoner. "Fear the captain, Gilchrist. Above all, she has power to do you hurt." He walked away.

"And she alone has power to help me," Gilchrist whispered.

Gilchrist rarely saw Anne and when he did, Eben saw to it that there was no opportunity to talk. Gilchrist worked with spirit, frustrating every attempt to goad him into some act that would allow the healing stripes to be reopened.

"'Tis enough now, Gilchrist," Darcy called late one afternoon. "Sun's nigh gone, so get to your cell." Gilchrist gratefully left the pump and dutifully climbed up from the hold to his cell. Standing near the cell door, waiting for him, was Jamie Hawkwood.

"Why, Master Hawkwood," Gilchrist said. "Come to see that I do not stray from prison. 'Tis a ship, sir, and there is no escape save into the sea."

"I know that," Jamie snapped. "'Tis no why I came." He stepped closer. "You were with that Campbell at the Rookery."

Gilchrist glanced away quickly down the line of cannon behind Jamie. "I was with Colonel Campbell. 'Tis true and no denying it."

"And were you with him when my cousin Tristan died?" Jamie asked belligerently.

"No," Gilchrist answered, stepping back. "I know nothing of your cousin. I never saw him but that one night."

"I dinna believe you," Jamie said, stepping closer. "I will know the truth. I will tear it out of you."

"There is no more to tell."

"Liar!" Jamie's fist swung for the prisoner's face, but Gilchrist stepped back and the blow missed. Jamie flung himself forward to grapple Gilchrist, but was caught by the strong hand of Darcy O'Flynn.

"Now, Master James," Darcy said as he pulled Jamie away and slung him to one side, "haven't I told you time and again that this no place for you?"

"You dinna give me orders, O'Flynn!" Jamie shouted. "I shall go to my sister and make report of you."

"'Twould avail you nothing, brother," Anne said from above. She swung down from the ladder and marched up to Jamie. "Christ, boy, I heard you yelling all the way aft. I will not have the operation of this ship hampered by anyone. Do you understand me, James Hawkwood?"

"Aye," he grumbled.

"And if you think for an instant that I will not have you punished for insubordination, then you have a lot to learn of me," she continued. "This prisoner is valuable cargo, worth a hundred or more pieces of gold to whatever lucky planter who buys him. And I cannot be sparing my mate to keep an eye on him all the time." The questioning look in Gilchrist's eyes went unnoticed as Anne continued to berate her brother. "If you cause me another moment's worry, Jamie, I shall transfer you to the *Cockerel* and you may spend the remainder of the voyage under watchful eyes there. Is that clear?"

"Aye," was the grudging assent.

"Go to the cabin and wait for me there," she ordered. "Mister O'Flynn, confine the prisoner." She watched Jamie climb out of sight, then turned again to the cell door as Darcy locked it. "Leave us a moment, Darcy." The mate strode off. "Gilchrist," she said quietly through the barred window, "please reconsider. Give me that name. Such a man is not worth your life."

His long fingers gripped the bars as he looked earnestly into her face, shaking his head sadly. "I leave my fate in your sweet hands, Captain."

"You talk like my brother Simon," Anne said with exasperation. "Do not leave your fate in my hands. Every day Eben and Jamie grow closer and more curious. 'Twould be beyond my power -- aye, even with Darcy on my side -- to keep them from mischief should they begin talk amongst my crew." Gilchrist made no answer. "Your only other hope is to sign articles with us. Then, at least, you would not face sale in the plantations. Do you not understand? When we reach the Indies I must either sell you or explain to my men why I do not sell you. If you were one of us, then the latter explanation would not be necessary."

"And I would still be in danger from your quartermaster." His fingers were pale against the black iron bars, his fine features little more than shadows in the dimness of the cell. "I cannot sign your articles. I have thought and thought on it, but can see nothing in it for me except dishonor and the gallows. I am no pirate."

"You are no slave either," Anne mused. "'Tis a puzzle to me what you are." She started to turn away, then looked back at him. "You realize that the time will come when you or I must lose everything. And you have left the choice in my hands. That is not wise. I should give the matter more thought, if I were you. And meanwhile, be very careful, Philip Gilchrist. Very careful, indeed."

It was after a month of sailing that a convoy of Dutch flytes and merchantmen was spotted. The convoy had barely survived a storm and several vessels were damaged, amongst them a fine merchantman whose masts and rigging lay about her in chaos as she struggled behind her companions. The convoy's only well-armed ship, a frigate, made an effort to keep close to the straggler and it was against these two that the *Bold Cockerel* chose to make a strike.

The *Chanticleer* had rarely seen combat, being mostly a smuggling vessel, but Anne, Darcy O'Flynn and Eben Carr had all spent their season aboard Mad Jack's ship and knew well what to expect when Ward signaled that he meant to take a prize.

"No doubt to buy our victuals and rum in the Indies," Eben said as he watched the *Bold Cockerel* cut in front of the Dutch frigate and her damaged companion. He ordered a new course and the *Chanticleer* swerved in to the straggler's windward side.

"But these are Dutch ships," Gilchrist protested.

Eben shrugged. "We have a perfectly legitimate Letter of Marque against them. They are a prize like any other." There was a deafening roar as the Dutch frigate fired on the *Bold Cockerel*. "Bloody damn! They mean to fight!"

"Good luck to them," Gilchrist said softly.

Eben heard the remark and turned, angrily striking Gilchrist hard across the mouth. "Get below," Eben ordered. "You have cannon to man, mister."

Gilchrist rubbed his chin as he drew himself upright. "I will take no part in your piracies," he declared.

Eben drew his pistol and spanned it. "You'll do as ordered or suffer the usual penalty for desertion of duty."

"I have no duty to you," Gilchrist argued. "And you know as well as I what the captain would say of you shooting me." The two men faced each other, glaring, then a small tapered hand took the pistol from Eben.

"Mister Carr," Anne said calmly, "your command ends when battle begins. I am in sole charge now. See to boarding the Dutchman while I deal with the prisoner."

"You are too soft with him," Eben accused.

Anne took a deep breath and pressed her lips into a firm line. "His back can pay the price of insubordination later -- as can yours." She handed the pistol back to Eben and waved him away, then took Gilchrist by the arm, her nails digging in painfully. "You will go below and aid the gun crew."

"No," he replied flatly.

Anne's black brows drew together. "You are either very bold or very stupid, my friend. Your noble refusals will not save those Hollanders. But even so, whether or not you approve of the taking of this prize, the crew of yon Dutch frigate could not care less for your opinions and will blow you to hell with the rest of us should we fail. Now, get below." Without a word he wrenched himself free of her and climbed down to the gun deck.

The *Bold Cockerel* fired on the protective frigate and received her fire in return while the *Chanticleer's* guns kept an incessant barrage of chainshot and barshot spinning into the frigate's rigging. Grappling hooks were whipped around the Dutch merchant's bowsprit and railing, allowing Eben Carr and a dozen men to board the helpless victim. The trapped frigate fired on the *Chanticleer*, but found that her shots fell on the Dutch ship she was trying to protect and that to fire over her caused the shot to fall harmlessly into the sea on the *Chanticleer's* far side.

On the gun deck, Gilchrist found himself working beside an unlikely ally, Jamie Hawkwood. It was several minutes before either noticed the other, then there was a pause as Gilchrist wiped his brow and looked at his fellow gunner.

"Gone from treason to piracy, eh, Master Hawkwood?"

Jamie glanced up, then continued swabbing out a cannon. "Have I much choice? Under the circumstances, to argue the morality of my politics over my family's profession would be useless and unprofitable."

"And you will hang in either case," Gilchrist added blandly.

Jamie stopped swabbing and gave Gilchrist a stony look, then laughed grandly. "Seeing that you have been loading cannon as fast as I, then I should think 'tis a fate awaiting you as well."

The battle did not last more than an hour. The Dutch frigate lowered her colors and permitted Ward's crew to board. The merchantman had already surrendered and was being stripped of anything the pirates found of value. In the flush of triumph they had forgotten about Gilchrist and he made his way to the deck with the thought that he might escape to the prize vessel. As he approached the railing to which the Dutch ship was tied he could see Anne making her way through the chaos on the prize's deck. The Dutch crew had been lined up and Anne appeared to be inspecting them as she might livestock at a village fair. He was considering his next move when a large hand gripped his shoulder.

"You had best return to your cell, Gilchrist," Darcy said, "although you may find it crowded for a time. We have need to confine some cargo until transfer can be made to the *Cockerel*. If you make any attempt to leave this vessel or to hamper our work, I have the captain's word that she will give you o'er to Mister Carr before sunset."

"Thank you for the warning, O'Flynn," Gilchrist replied. "I shall obey, of course."

Sometime later the cell door was pulled open and two young Dutch sailors were thrown in. There was barely room for one man, let alone three, but Gilchrist did his best to be hospitable. They were only there for perhaps an hour before they were removed to the *Bold Cockerel*. He was sorry to see them go. He enjoyed the company, even if they did not speak English and there was something to be said for safety in numbers.

For all tales of piratical brutality, of tortures and murders inflicted on captive crews, Gilchrist saw a remarkable restraint amongst the Hawkwood pirates. There were few shots or cries after the Dutch ships' surrender and little evidence of mistreatment of the prisoners he saw taken. Even the sounds of revelry that continued after he was confined to his cell were restrained and subdued, broken only by an occasional cry -- though of pain or of joy was unclear.

There had been women passengers on the merchantman. He had seen them briefly on the deck before he was sent below. Much to his surprise the women were treated civilly, not as they might have been had they been taken aboard a navy ship, where only the most nobly born would have escaped rape. He had been at sea long enough to know of the navy's brutality, not only toward prisoners, but also toward the poor lads who made up the crew. He knew that in the battle with the *Rainbow* had his men been victorious, the Hawkwood crew would have been treated far worse than these Dutch had been, and Anne, what would have happened to Anne? . . .

He shuddered and pulled the blanket over him, wondering if he had believed wrongly all his life the tales of famed pirates as Bartholomew Sharp, Henry Morgan, Richard Sawkins and L'Ollonois. Perhaps their atrocities were exaggerated by writers like Esquemling to sell more sensational journals. Growing up in a country rectory, with his father preaching hellfire against the evils of such men it seemed so clear. Seeking the patronage of a wealthy squire and through him a commission he had become a model officer, dedicated to the eradication of the plague of the seas. Now he was not so certain. There might indeed by no difference between the Royal Navy and the pirates other than paper commissions and a uniform. As he fell asleep, he thought of freebooters and lovely Anne Hawkwood.

Early the following morning the cell door banged open and two men entered. Gilchrist was jerked roughly to his feet and shoved from the cell toward the hatch. They answered none of his questions as he was propelled toward the quarterdeck, but he felt his blood grow cold when he saw Eben Carr and a small group of men waiting for him. Jamie stood to one side, his pale features beaming triumphantly. There was no sign of Darcy nor of Anne.

"Bring the prisoner forward," Eben said. Gilchrist was pushed from behind until he stood near the ratlines. "You are charged with insubordination, Gilchrist -- in that I ordered you below and you refused that order. Now it is up to me to choose whether to have you flogged or keel-hauled."

A cry of protest rose in Gilchrist's throat as he dodged the hands that reached for him. "Mister Carr, your captain has --"

"My captain was wounded yesterday," Eben replied, "so it falls to me to decide your punishment."

Gilchrist stood stunned, his mind racing helplessly to think of some escape. The men pressed closer, eager eyed. Suddenly Gilchrist came to himself and cried out, "May I not speak?"

Eben stepped close to him and said quietly. "There is only one thing I want to hear you say. You know what it is." Gilchrist shook his head. "No? Well, then I'll finish what I started the night you came aboard."

There was a gasp from the men around him. Gilchrist turned from Eben and saw what had so suddenly halted the course of pirate justice.

"Can I not lie wounded in my cabin for one day but that you will disobey me, Mister Carr?" Anne was leaning against Darcy, her shirt bloody below her left arm.

"The man was insubordinate," Eben argued. There was a general chorus of agreement among the men.

"Aye, that he was," Anne replied, "but it is for me to determine his punishment."

"Very well then, Captain," Eben said, bowing graciously, "but name it."

Gilchrist watched Anne's face, her expression a mixture of physical pain and something far less distinguishable. "I would wait until I am healed to consider this matter," she answered, but there was an angry buzz of disapproval.

"You are too soft with him," Eben said. There were more shouts in Eben's favor.

"Come now, gentlemen," Gilchrist said, his manner boldly affable. "I am worth nothing at all to you dead and little more than nothing if I am too weak or scarred to fetch a good price. 'Twould be like pitching pieces of eight into the sea, and for what?"

"He speaks well, Mister Carr," Jamie admitted grudgingly. "He speaks the language of profit."

"Aye," Anne said, pressing a cloth over her bloody side, her face frighteningly pale. "Still, I would have him take some time to think on his behavior of yesterday." She turned to go, Darcy holding her as he might some fragile doll. "Tie him in the sun and let no man speak to him or touch him." Followed by her brother, Anne Hawkwood returned to her cabin.

His mouth parched from lack of water, sweat and sunburn stinging his back, Gilchrist was cut free in the afternoon and taken to the captain's cabin. It was less orderly than before, red soaked bandages strewn over the floor and dirty soup bowls littered the table.

"Sit down, Philip." Anne was propped up on the bed, several charts spread over the blankets. She had changed her shirt which hung loose over her red skirt. Her sash and weapons lay on the floor next to the bed.

He moved a basin of bloody water from one chair and sat down. "I was grieved to hear of your wound, Captain."

"One of those Dutch bastards sliced into me with a knife, just before we released the ships. 'Tis no terrible wound. Patrick assures me that I will survive." She rolled up the charts and rose slowly from the bed. "No, no, let me," she said as he moved to help her. "You sit. There's drink in the pitcher there." He poured himself a tankard of rum, watching Anne as she opened a small chest and took out a small green jar. "It is fortunate for you that Doctor Hartley left this salve with me before he transferred back to the *Cockerel*." She supported herself with one hand on his chair while the other stroked the mint ointment over Gilchrist's reddened shoulders. "He thought you might be needing it again after I told him about your little rebellion of yesterday."

"A very perceptive doctor," Gilchrist said.

"You have very fair skin," she remarked. "Far too fair to be left to the lash and the sun. You must be more careful. You were unquestionably insubordinate in refusing not only Eben's orders, but mine as well. I will not have my authority so abused." She put the cork into the jar and returned it to the chest, then drew out a long narrow bundle and set it on the table in front of him.

"Open it," she commanded, taking the chair opposite him.

Puzzled, he untied the string around it and unrolled the canvas, revealing the gold headed riding whip and the stained linen rags. "What are these?" he asked.

"You do not recognize them?"

He shook his head. "I have never seen these things before."

"Are you quite certain?" She gazed hard into his face.

"I swear it."

Anne smiled sadly as she fingered the piece linen. "'Tis all that remains of Tristan MacDonald," she said, studying his reaction. "A great pity it is that the lad should survive Glencoe and then suffer torture and death at the hands of your friend Campbell."

"Campbell is not my friend," Gilchrist answered firmly, then added, "but even so, I swear that neither he nor I took any part in this murder."

"'Twas the spy then?"

"I suppose it must have been." He looked away from her and the dark spotted rag in her hand.

"Someone you met in the Red Cock?" She leaned closer, grimacing slightly from the pain of movement. "Aye, we know you were offering bribes in the tavern. Who took your coin?" He silently shook his head. She sat back exasperated. "You would do well to name this man. Eben will tear it out of you in time."

"Upon my word of honor, lady, I cannot tell you his name."

"Can not or will not?" Her eyes narrowed when he could not meet her gaze. "My friend, were it to become common knowledge that you hold such a one's confidence, have you any idea what would happen to you?" Gilchrist lowered his eyes and shuddered. "I cannot even speak of the things of which my men and those of the *Cockerel* are capable. Please think on it."

He looked up and smiled. "I think on little else."

She started to rise, then groaned and seemed to sink into her chair, the faint color in her cheeks fading. She gestured toward the pitcher and he hurriedly poured wine for her and held it to her lips. "Thank you," she gasped. "I am more hurt than I thought."

"Should I ask Mister Carr to --"

"No," she replied. "Help me to my bed, if you please."

He took her outstretched hand and placing his arm around her he gently raised her from the chair. She stumbled and for one brief moment he held her, then he lifted her into his arms and laid her upon the bed. He paused awkwardly, uncertain of what to do next. "I should return to my cell and leave you to your rest."

She nodded weakly, then shook her head. "The things on the table," she whispered. "Put them away for me."

"Yes, Captain," he said quickly. His hands shook as he rolled the canvas around the pitiful relics and tied the string. She nodded encouragingly as he opened her sea chest and laid the bundle within, next to a rolled parchment which he guessed to be the ship's articles and a small doll made from a piece of sail, with twine hair and a worn painted face. Puzzled he started to lift the doll.

"No prying now," she said softly, then added, "My father made me that doll when I was five. It is a girlish attachment, nothing more."

"Of course, Captain." He closed the chest and stood up. "I'll leave you then."

"Say nothing to the others. It wouldn't -- it wouldn't be in your best interests."

"I understand." He paused in the door, gazing at the pale woman lying against the pillows. "One thing more," he said. "What happened to the man who stabbed you?"

"Jubilee killed him," she answered absently. "Very slowly."

The news reached London that two Dutch vessels had been attacked, stripped of cargo and some men, then left to the mercy of the sea. Their comrades in the convoy had returned to help them, although too late to catch the pirates. The convoy arrived in Amsterdam and announced that they had been robbed by Englishmen with a bewildering Letter of Marque against them.

The news reached another of their countrymen, William of Orange, King of England, and he had a number of choice things to say to the man under whose sponsorship the letter had been given. The fact that the letter was years out of date did not spare Lord Golding the King's ire that it had been issued at all, or that it had never been withdrawn.

"You were long with the King, m'lord," Hargrove observed as Golding entered the antechamber where the Navy commander sat on a richly brocaded bench with Colonel Campbell.

"Aye, long it was and no thanks to the pair of you," Golding snapped, striding up and down in front of them, his footsteps muffled by the thick carpet. "Curse the day I e'er heard of Hawkwood."

"I couldna agree with you more," Campbell replied.

"Then why did you let that damned woman steal your horse?" Golding demanded, turning on him. "You have never answered that question to any satisfaction."

Campbell leapt to his feet. "'Twas you that spared young Hawkwood," he accused.

"And I that lost him to a clever rescue," Hargrove said. "Gentlemen, these recriminations will avail us nothing and only serve to set us arguing amongst ourselves. 'Tis action we need now." He turned his sharp, sea-tanned face to the daintily powdered and frilled Golding. "What said His Majesty to my request for a fleet?"

"Three ships -- no more. And there's little powder and shot to spare, so you'll have to requisition most of your munitions from the governor of Jamaica," Golding said, adding bitterly, "And I am to pay a full third of the venture. You are to sail immediately."

"Aye, m'lord," Hargrove replied, rising to his feet and giving a formal little bow.

"And you, Colonel," Golding continued, "are to go with him."

"I dinna see why," Campbell retorted. "My duty is here in England, not on the sea."

"Your duty, Colonel," Golding said, poking a finger at the officer's chest, "is to finish what you started. I do not wish to see you again until the Hawkwoods are hanged."

"Aye, m'lord," Campbell replied, smoldering.

So it was that two sloops, the *Prince Rupert* and the *Prince of Wales*, and the huge third-rater the *Princess Royal*, set sail for the Indies -- their commission to seek out the Hawkwood vessels and sink them, to kill the pirate crew, but to bring the two captains and young James back alive to suffer the anger of an indignant and outraged law.

CHAPTER TWELVE

MAID IN BEDLAM

For if I become a swallow, I would seek him in the air,
And if I lost my labor and could not find him there
How quickly I would become a fish and search the foaming sea,
I love my love because I know my love loves me.

folksong

Anne looked unrelentingly at the four men sitting with her in the cabin of the *Bold Cockerel.* "I tell you, gentlemen, that he will say nothing," she argued. "I am not yet fully convinced he has aught to say at all." They looked at her doubtfully. "'Tis possible that he knows nothing," she protested. "Campbell need not have shared confidence of his spy's name."

"I cannot believe that," Darcy replied. "I saw them in the Red Cock and Gilchrist was as eager as the colonel to take those Jacobites. And there is that letter he was carrying."

"It need not have been a reference to the spy," Anne insisted. "But I tell you, I know this man, I know his type. He has a stubborn sense of honor and that will keep him silent."

"The man does not live that cannot be broken," Eben said. "You have not allowed me to truly test him."

"You put him to the lash," Anne replied.

"'Twas but a taste."

"Aye, Mister Carr, but from a taste you can tell the quality of the meal." Anne sat back and took a long pull from her tankard.

"The problem remains," Ward said, "that this prisoner may hold the key to finding our traitor and it is imperative that the traitor be found. Mister Carr has made fine argument that this prisoner has not been put to direct and hard questioning. Surely, Anne, the sacrifice of this one man is but a small price for the safety and protection of our ships and crew." Ward refilled his tankard with dark sweet rum. "We cannot long remain without a port. We have been a fortnight in sight of land and have not dared go ashore for more than water. Jamaica is no haven."

"Patrick, what say you?" Anne turned to the doctor, her dark eyes searching his face.

Patrick drew on his pipe thoughtfully. "I have never known Anne to be wrong in her assessment of a cargo's value -- be it pearls, chocolate, or a man. If she says that this Gilchrist is better dealt with in a less barbarous fashion, then I think we should abide by that and let her crack him in her own time."

"But we do not have time!" Eben slammed his fist down on the table, rattling the tankards. "Do you think that Hargrove is sitting in England waiting for us to come to him? Like his lieutenant, he, too, is a most dedicated man and I, for one, have no wish to tangle with him while knowing there is a spy amongst us."

"Again, an excellent point," Ward said, thoughtfully tapping his fingers together.

"Allow me to be suggesting a compromise," Darcy said as he rose and stood behind Anne's chair. She looked up at him expectantly. "'Twill be at least another fortnight or so before any fleet of Hargrove's will be reaching these islands. During that time, we can put into Tortuga --"

"With the French!" Eben exclaimed in shock.

"Aye, lad, I know they are the enemy just now," Darcy replied, "but Tortuga is filled with brother pirates and they will accept us without regard to our origin."

"'Tis a port in any case," Ward added. "Go on, O'Flynn."

"Let the lady have a fortnight more. At the end of that time the prisoner must give us the name or be put to more direct means of persuasion."

Eben looked doubtful. "I think 'tis a waste of time. The man has been in our power for some two months and shows no signs of breaking."

Anne shook her head. "You are wrong, Eben. The constant fear is working, albeit slowly. This Gilchrist is the sort who would willingly give up his life for a principle, but not if it means dying by inches. Already he is softening. Just a little more time."

Patrick nodded in agreement and all eyes turned to Ward. He scratched his beard, then nodded his assent. "We will stand by Darcy's plan," Ward said. Eben lowered his eyes and clenched his fist, but finally gave a nod of agreement. Anne said nothing more. She stared out at the night beyond the ports, and those who knew her best could not tell what thoughts lay behind her guarded expression.

The island of Tortuga lay baking in the afternoon sun, ripples of humid heat rising from the docks. "This foray ashore may not be wise, Captain," Eben said as he sat with Anne in the ship's small canoe. "Tortuga is full of French and they could take us for enemies. I like not leaving the ships so empty with the day going fast."

"There are plenty of men still aboard," Anne replied, "and 'tis long since I set foot in Cayona. Grown to a fine town, I hear."

"And I have the need of the feel of land again," Jamie said from behind his sister. "I tolerate the sea better than brother Simon, but 'tis no my home as 'tis for Anne."

On the grimy shore they met with a party from the *Bold Cockerel*, each man's purse jingling with the coin earned from the sale of the Dutch cargo. The leave to go ashore was welcomed by the men who had spent so many weeks at sea and so many days in sight of land. John Ward strode forward to greet Anne, while Patrick, Calum, Judas Jones and Luther Devlin trailed behind.

"And where is O'Flynn?" Ward asked.

"He stands the watch on the *Chanticleer*," Anne answered. "He will take his leave on the morrow."

"I left a stout watch," Ward said, "and bloody angry those lads were not to be first ashore and aboard some tavern whore."

"Too many damned French," Eben muttered.

"You did not bring the lieutenant with you," Patrick observed with a teasing smile.

Anne looked him with slitted eyes, a look she gave only to those whose questions were treading on dangerous turf. "He is manacled and confined to his cell while we are in port." She marched on ahead through the narrow muddy streets crowded with society's remnants and dregs. Grizzle faced sailors in ragged trousers and little else mingled with wealthy captains in fine, if exotic attire. Just beyond the docks was a market where the plundered riches of the Caribbean were peddled at bargain prices.

"Was it like this in Port Royal?" Anne asked in an awed whisper. "I cannot recall."

A gaggle of strumpets flounced by, their breasts barely contained in their low cut bodices. One of them cast a longing eye on Jamie whose cheeks blushed red.

"'Tis no wise," Calum said, noting the boy's sparked expression.

"Aye," Luther warned. He winked, nodding at Judas, then added, "Find yourself a clean woman. 'Tis sin still, but 'twill cost ye less."

Judas leaned in against Jamie. "Best listen to 'im, boy. 'E means to save ye from the pox, for those be poxed whores if ever there was and that is a vile fate, boy, a vile fate, but worthy of those who commit the sin of fornication."

Jamie drew away from them and took refuge at his sister's side. "Well, Jamie," she said, "what think you of this fine town?"

"It smells a bit," he replied, "but 'tis no worse than the prison or the transport ship."

"Aye," Eben agreed, "and 'tis as fine company -- if you like the French."

"Until we know what plans the Royal Navy has for us we are better off out of English waters," Anne explained to Jamie. "So, since we may not go to Jamaica, Carolina, or Virginia, we can visit with the Spanish, the French or the Dutch. The former will not have us and the latter would take ill our treatment of their countrymen. Hence, Tortuga, French and all."

After they had made a circuit of the market square the little party divided. Jamie and Eben strolled off to tour the town. Ward and Calum saw two other members of the *Bold Cockerel's* crew and vanished with them down an alley. "Belike he's after news of Hargrove," Anne said to Patrick as they stopped in front of a dingy little tavern.

Luther tapped Judas' arm. "Judas, m'friend, what do ye say to a quiet dram in a slightly more respectable establishment? I know of several young men who run a most elegant parlor." The suggestion seemed to please Judas and he departed with Luther down the narrow street.

"Well, 'tis but the two of us then," Anne said as she and Patrick stood before the tavern. "Will you drink with me, my good doctor?"

"Indeed, mistress, 'twill be a pleasure." Patrick took her arm and led her into the tavern.

The room was low-ceilinged and Patrick had to stoop to pass under the heavy black beams that supported the smoke grimed roof. As their eyes adjusted to the dim light they saw a number of men sitting at several long tables or leaning against the greasy wooden walls. The women present were of the most slatternly sort, dirty and coarse. Three of them stood to one side, raising their skirts so that the others, and anyone else who cared to, could admire their brilliantly colored drawers.

"Look there," whispered Anne, pointing to a slight pixie-faced man who stood beside a large barrel. "'Tis that Irish devil, Sean Alwell. I had wondered what waters he sailed these days." She watched for another moment as Alwell lifted up a skinny dark haired young woman and set her on the barrel where she sat picking rust and burned food from a frying pan.

Anne and Patrick sat at a table near the center of the room and called for rum. "Any luck with Mister Gilchrist?" Patrick said.

Anne looked up sharply, then saw there was no mockery in his question. She shook her head. "Patrick, I do not know what it is about the man. He is as brave as he is stubborn. I am not even certain he knows the spy, but even if he does I cannot believe that it will be forced from him."

"Perhaps you do not want to believe it can be forced from him," Patrick observed quietly. "You are too modest, Anne. I have seen the frightening power in you."

"Is it a power?" she asked, shrinking into her oversized coat. "'Tis no more than the Hawkwood rage, surely. Like Father's." She stared off, her expression clouded. "Am I mad, Patrick?" He looked at her quizzically. "I feel as though there were two Anne Hawkwoods. One is a lady who would love a man like Philip Gilchrist. The other is a bold pirate who wants to see him suffer because he dares to disobey her."

"And do you love him, Anne?" Patrick raised his reddish brows and smiled.

Anne thought for a moment. "Yes, Patrick, I do love him. But at the same time I find it damned infuriating that he should put me in so dangerous and untenable a spot by denying me the name of that spy."

"As you have said, he may not know it."

"But he has never denied knowing it," she said, "only that he cannot give me the name. There is a subtle difference."

"Perhaps he prefers to continue in that difference thinking that it will keep him alive."

"Signing articles would be a better course," she replied.

"Aye, but is not his honor the obstacle there?"

She nodded, glancing up as a slovenly woman set down two tankards of rum before them. With nothing more than a cold glance from Anne the barmaid left them. "I think he may be weakening on that point," Anne said, pausing to drink from her tankard. "Whether 'tis a fondness for me or a sense of desperate self-preservation, I cannot tell, but nevertheless, I hear far less talk against piracy from him in these last few days, and far more comparisons with the Royal Navy -- in which we come off favorably, I think. We may make a pirate of Philip Gilchrist yet."

"But he must tell you the name of Campbell's spy," Patrick warned. "Nothing less will suffice."

"Aye," she said, "and I can scarce control my fury when I think on it. To come so close to such a man, to so very nearly win him over to my way of thinking, and to risk all because he will not utter a single name. I swear I would rather beat it out of him myself." She drank deeply.

"Ah, Mademoiselle Hawkwood!" exclaimed a gratingly familiar voice from the door. Anne whirled around to see the entrance blocked by a tall man surmounted by a large plumed hat, which was whipped off in a magnificent bow.

"Damn!" she hissed as LeBoutellier swept up to her and boldly sat down beside her. Behind him came some half dozen of his crew, fully armed and positioned in a threatening ring around one end of the table.

"And who is your companion?" LeBoutellier asked.

"Doctor Patrick Hartley," Patrick answered, keeping a wary eye on the men. His fingers fluttered near the hilt of his sword.

"All over Tortuga it is known that the most lovely of all privateers is in Cayona," the Frenchman said, stroking his pristine coal black beard and staring at her intently. "The question on the lips of every man is, why?"

"Because I go where I choose to go," Anne answered bluntly.

"Mais non, cher." LeBoutellier continued his steady perusal of her. "Is there not more, eh? Perhaps some crime in your own country for which you are sought."

"We have our letters, LeBoutellier," she replied. "We are still legal privateers."

He looked up briefly at his men, then returned to his study of her. "It was a cruel trick you played on me. Oui, to leave me to my fate at the hands of your English dogs who mistook your crime for mine and fired upon me. Cher Anne, why did you not speak and tell them their mistake?"

"Because then they would have fired on me," she answered tartly. Nervously she eyed the members of *La Panache's* crew who stood between her and the door. "I owe you nothing, LeBoutellier. That you are here proves that no serious harm was done."

"And that you are here, mademoiselle, proves that you fear your countrymen in Jamaica and Carolina. 'Twas a man of value you took from the transport, eh?"

"'Twas my younger brother."

"Ah, yet another Hawkwood?"

"At least, so says his mother," she replied.

"Say what you mean, LeBoutellier," Patrick demanded.

"Very well then, monsieur. I intend to deliver this woman and all others of her crew that can be found to the governor of Jamaica. If there is a bounty, then such reward will be put to the cost of damage done to

La Panache. If there is no reward," he shrugged, "then still we will have done our duty to God and to France."

Anne applauded sarcastically. "Indeed, mon capitaine, I am flattered that you feel the need of six armed men to take one small woman. Are these the only odds with which you feel secure?"

The Frenchman twisted a thick black lock that curled from beneath his hat. "You insult me, ma cher?"

"Why do you bring so many to take so few unless you and your men are afraid?"

"You would prefer to fight one to one, as equal?"

"Aye," she said, "and if I win, I walk out of here free."

"No, Anne!" Patrick protested.

"She will not win," LeBoutellier said confidently. "If she did, I would call her the greatest of flibustiers and would feel obliged upon my honor to give her aid. This cannot happen, of course." The sign between LeBoutellier and his crew was imperceptible, but seconds later one of the men seized Anne and hauled her to her feet.

"You do not fight me yourself, you poxy coward!" she thundered.

"I am a French gentleman of great chivalry, mademoiselle," LeBoutellier answered grandly. "I do not fight women."

Patrick leapt up, drawing his sword, but LeBoutellier's sword was out and at the doctor's throat. "She and I have a bargain, monsieur. Do not attempt to aid her or I shall kill you." Two of LeBoutellier's men stood behind Patrick as he stood drawn but helpless.

Anne twisted free of her attacker, knocking the bench and her trailing red skirt out of the way. Suddenly the man grabbed up a tankard of rum and flung the sweet stinging liquor in her face. Momentarily blinded she could not dodge his hand as he seized her by the hair. She bit down hard on his wrist and he jerked away in pain. He struck her across the face, knocking her to the floor. Her side ached as she lay panting at his feet. The man stood back and laughed.

"This woman has not the mettle of our Tortuga ladies, eh?" LeBoutellier said as he patted his crewman on the back and acknowledged a salute from the Irish pirate by the barrel. He started to turn away from the fallen woman when there was a sharp gasp as Anne rose, drawing from her boot a gleaming dagger.

"Laugh for me again, you great Gallic goose," she hissed through clenched teeth.

"Aye, laugh again!" boomed a powerful voice from the door. LeBoutellier spun around to see John Ward push into the room with four men, swords and pistols drawn.

The pistols blazed and one of LeBoutellier's men fell. Patrick engaged the French captain as Ward's men cut a path through the sailors. Anne rose to her feet and renewed the attack against her opponent. Soon other men pressed into the tavern, some to fight on a particular side, others to fight anyone who might be available. On the barrel by the wall the skinny wench wielded her frying pan, hitting anyone who came within range while her Irish companion stood placidly drinking and occasionally putting his boot to those who fell against him.

"'Tis a fine brawl you have started here, mistress," Ward said between parries.

"'Twas so dull before LeBoutellier came," Anne gasped. Her opponent had lost his weapon, but as she drove her knife down at him, he took her by the wrist and wrenched the dagger free. She dodged his strike and waited breathlessly for him to lunge again. Behind them the battle was easing as the French pirates sank into defeat. LeBoutellier himself was pinned against a pillar with Patrick's sword at his throat. He made no move to escape, preferring to direct his attention to the only fight that mattered.

Ward shoved back his wounded opponent, then stepped in to help Anne. "Nay, John," she panted, squaring off with the sailor, "'tis my affair."

"Anne has a wager with this French fop," Patrick explained, gently pressing the tip of his sword into LeBoutellier's throat. At that moment Anne's opponent lunged at her again. Although surprised she quickly caught his hand, and with one dainty foot behind his leg, she pushed him over backwards. The knife clattered to the floor behind him. He started to rise, but Anne drove her knee against his jaw and he fell back unconscious.

"Tres bon, cher Anne," LeBoutellier said. "Now if monsieur will release me."

"Why should I?" Patrick growled.

"It was not part of our wager," LeBoutellier said, seeming unperturbed by the sword denting his flesh.

"I don't believe we discussed what should become of you should our fortunes be reversed," Anne said. "Still, this is a French town and you are a Frenchman. I would not wish to seem a churlish guest." She waved her hand and Patrick reluctantly released the French captain. The crew of *La Panache* were helping their wounded from the tavern. One of their men was dead, another dying.

"As you will see, mademoiselle, I am a man of my word." LeBoutellier bowed deeply. "You are indeed a great flibustier."

"The greatest?" She glared at him.

"You had this help," LeBoutellier said, gesturing to Ward and his men.

"I won my fight and that is all I said I would do," she argued.

"You are free to go, cher Anne," LeBoutellier replied. "And you have my respect. Do not ask for more."

"I could have had your life but a moment past," she declared angrily. "You have a debt to me, Frenchman." She turned on her heel and marched from the tavern, Patrick, Ward and his men following.

"I shall not forget," LeBoutellier said softly as he watched her go.

Anne sat brooding in her cabin for a long time. The fight in the tavern had stirred that violent other self within her and she could feel control slipping from her. She pulled her big coat closer around her despite the tropical heat in the cabin, and huddled against the raging frustration that threatened to burst her. Drowning her feelings with brandy had failed.

The *Chanticleer* was very quiet. Many of her men were still ashore, while others had sought comradery aboard the *Bold Cockerel*, riding at anchor a short distance away. There were only three men keeping watch over the merchantman and one of them was chained up below.

The very thought of Philip Gilchrist was enough to flush her face with anger. "How dare he!" she hissed to herself. "How dare he put me in this situation!" She pounded the table with her fist, nearly overturning her liquor, but even she could sense the falseness of her rage and she felt a tinge of fear that she was about to lose a battle with herself.

"Mister O'Flynn!" she called suddenly. A moment later the hulking mate poked his head through the door of his small side cabin.

"Aye, Captain?"

"Fetch the prisoner up here." The coldness of her tone startled the mate. "And be quick about it, man!"

"Aye, Captain." He ducked out of the cabin and hurried below. When he opened the cell he found Gilchrist sitting in the dark, gently turning his wrists in the manacles. "Up, lad," Darcy ordered.

"Why?"

"This is no time to be difficult, lad," Darcy said as he took him by the arm and hauled him to his feet. "Our sweet captain is in a bloody minded mood. Take the hide off both our backs if she be thwarted in such a foul humor."

"What does she want with me?" Gilchrist asked as he was led to the ladder.

"Don't be a fool, mo bhuachaill. You know as well as I." Darcy pulled him across the empty deck. "There was a tavern fight earlier and she's been working on a rage ever since she came back aboard. I think she means to settle all with you. If you're lucky, then 'twill be no more than hard talk. If you're not lucky, well --"

Gilchrist entered the cabin and stood tensely just inside the door. One look at her glowering face affirmed that he was not to be lucky. The canvas bundle lay unrolled in front of her, the gold headed riding whip gleaming in the flickering lantern light.

"Give me the key, Mister O'Flynn," she said, "then leave us." The mate handed her the manacle key, then turned to go. "We are not to be disturbed," she added. Darcy gave Gilchrist a pitying look as he left.

Anne poured another glass of brandy. It was evident that it was not her first. Without a word, she unlocked the manacles and watched as Gilchrist massaged his chaffed wrists.

"Thank you," he said quietly.

"You have nothing for which to thank me," she said sharply as she resumed her seat.

"I am not yet handed over to Mister Carr. That is something for which I am very thankful."

"'Tis not to last. You have but a few days more, then I must honor my agreement with Eben. The lash will be the least of your torments and there will be no protection."

"Then you have my thanks for your kindness so far." He watched her every move, every trace of emotion that pass over her face like clouds scudding before the wind.

"I have not tried to be kind." Anne knew it was a lie, but his noble manner and conciliatory speech only aggravated her.

"May I sit?" he asked, coming to the edge of the table.

"You may not," she said icily. She took a deep drink. "Captain Ward and Eben -- they think I am too soft with you."

"Because you are too gracious and gentle to yield a hapless prisoner over to torture? 'Tis surely no more than Christian goodness, but not softness." The spark of anger in her shadowed eyes warned him that such remarks only made matters worse. "Darcy said you were in a fight earlier."

"Aye," she grumbled, "an old rivalry with LeBoutellier."

"And you won."

"Aye," she nodded, then her cheeks flushed hot. "Do not attempt to change the subject!" she thundered at him.

"I only meant to inquire --"

"By God, sir, have you always been such a mooncalf, such a dolt!?" she railed, leaping to his feet. "You do not know me, man."

"I know you better than you think, mistress," he answered.

"Do you indeed?" She glared at him, allowing the powerful beast of her rage to rise, overwhelming her. "Take off your shirt," she ordered.

He looked her steadily in the eye. "May I ask why?"

"Because I order it," she snapped.

Gilchrist bit his lip thoughtfully then complied, pulling off his shirt and letting it fall to the floor. Slowly her fingers closed around the riding whip. "I want the name of that spy, even if I must beat it out of you myself."

"Your threats mean nothing," he retorted, standing unmoved. "I made a promise to that man and I will keep it. 'Tis sheer stubbornness that keeps me silent and there is naught you can do about it. I have been whipped and starved and abused and have born all as meekly as a man might, so that my presence does not jeopardize your position, but I will not tolerate abuse by you as well. If that angers you then so be it. I know that you have not the will to do me hurt, Anne Hawkwood. I look at you and see only a young woman in her father's coat. You cannot wear power like a garment." He regretted the words as soon as he spoke them, but her rage was like a thing contagious.

As she brought the whip down across his shoulder, he seized her wrist and twisted it. The whip fell to the floor. They struggled for a moment in the warm silence of the cabin. She uttered no cry as she fought against his tight hold, but he pinned her arms against her sides and kissed her forcefully, passionately. He could feel her protest as he wrapped his arms around her, his lips never leaving hers. She continued to struggle as he pushed her backwards and shoved her down on the bed, but still she did not cry out.

"I could take you here and now," he whispered. "Your men will kill me anyway, but I could have my pleasure before Darcy and old Eli could get in here to stop me." Then he smiled and relaxed his hold. "But I would not want to if you were not willing." He released her and sat on the edge of the bed. "I suppose I am done for now, eh, Captain?"

Anne lay very still while behind her brooding features the mad web became further entangled with the new feelings that she could not fully comprehend. "The last man to attack me thus was put to death by my father," she whispered in a tiny voice. "I can still hear his screams," she shuddered.

"My death would not make you happy," he said, stroking her soft black hair and white shoulders. "What would, Anne?"

She looked up, startled by the use of her name, then shrugged slightly. "I suppose what I want most is some peaceful resolution to the quandary of this spy's identity. I do not want to see you harmed nor to see you sold. . . . Because I -- I love you." Her words sounded very small against the steamy quiet of the ship. "And," she admitted hesitantly, "I am afraid."

"Of loving an enemy?" His fingers delicately touched her breasts through her shirt. It had been a long time since he had been with a woman and never with one such as Anne Hawkwood.

"Aye, and of what it will mean -- to my crew, to Eben and my other brothers, to John Ward . . . and to the spy you are concealing. I had hoped to prove that you did not know the man's name, but now you have admitted that you do. How can I in good conscience give myself to you while knowing that a man you are shielding could end my livelihood and my life?"

"He was acting out of loyalty to his king and his only intention was to betray your traitor brother."

"Then why did he set the soldiers on Simon and Patrick in the Plymouth Theatre?" she asked. "You didn't know that?" He shook his head. She sat up and took Gilchrist by the shoulders. "Both my brothers! Why shouldn't I fear to be next?"

"I will protect you, Anne. That's something I've wanted to do ever since I said nothing of your muddy boots that night we trapped the smugglers."

"Then if you care for me so much, why not name the spy?"

"Because I don't know his name," he admitted.

"What?" she said, half rising from the bed.

"I don't know his name," he repeated.

"Describe him then."

"I can't. I won't. I only saw him that once and it was dark. He was Campbell's man, not mine." He lowered his eyes from hers, his hand moving boldly along her thigh. "I made a promise upon my honor and that is a hard thing for me to break. Do not ask that of me, Anne. Perhaps I can find a way within myself -- and I have yet a few days more, eh?" Again he pressed his lips to hers and she was caught in his hungry embrace. "Let it be tonight, Anne," he whispered against her ear. "Then even the loss of my life may seem a worthy price for this one night with you." He pushed back her bulky coat and gracefully, like a cat stretching, she slipped her arms free of it.

"Am I such solace to a man so doomed?" she asked wonderingly as he caressed her neck. Pausing, she listened to the silence of the ship. There was no sound other than that of the water lapping against the hull. With a sudden burst of brazen boldness she cast aside her father's shirt and pressed into Gilchrist's arms. "Aye," she said, "let it be tonight."

"And tomorrow?" He gazed longingly into her eyes.

She lay back on the bed. “Tomorrow must take care of itself.”

They lay together that night and like two children they gave no thought to the consequences. For Gilchrist it was the culmination of the fantasy that had sustained him through the weeks of abuse and uncertainty. For Anne it was a willing surrender after years of protective paternal custody and careful gamesmanship.

“You are my first lover who is neither my inferior,” she explained, “nor a business associate -- as yet.”

“Do you think that is likely?” he asked, his fingers idly tracing over her bare breasts and along the puffy new scar beneath her left arm.

She turned to look him in the eye. “Much as it pains me to mention it, there is still the matter of your situation. You must chose between your honor and me. If you choose your honor, then somehow I must beat down my affection for you and hand you over. If you would escape torture and slavery, and have both my love and your life, then it must be at the cost of your honor. There is no other way.”

“Unless,” he mused, “I can find honor in piracy.”

“If you would but read our articles, you might see that there is little difference between our trade and that of the Royal Navy. We fight the same foes often as not, and are as committed to the defense of England as you are.” He started to protest, but she raised her hand, silencing him. “I know you would say that we attack England’s allies as well as her enemies, but that is only when absolutely necessary. Most of our strikes are against French, Spanish and Portuguese shipping, rarely Dutch, German or English. We must take the occasional friendly vessel to pay our keep, but we take only what we need and kill as few as possible.”

“I will read your articles and I will think on what my honor will permit,” he said, adding with a wry smile, “I have no wish to die.”

Anne climbed from the bed, modestly pulling on her shirt before going to the chest. She lifted the tattered roll of parchment and handed it to him, then adjusted the lantern so that its yellow light fell on the sheet as he unrolled it. She left him to read it while she cleared away Tristan’s relics, hiding them again in the chest, and dressed herself.

“These are most civilized articles,” Gilchrist commented. “I had expected nothing so much like the Navy -- to obey officers, to keep no portion of a prize for oneself, to take no woman or child aboard for personal use, and no drinking on duty or gambling. And the compensations for the wounded are generous."

"'Tis well we compare favorably with the Navy," Anne said, "for it is from the Navy that we gain most of our recruits."

"The punishments listed are much the same," he added. "I suppose that it is only to be expected, the sea being the sea, no matter the vessel."

"Can you sign these articles?" she asked, studying his face.

"I think so, Anne," he answered, "but it is a great change for me and if I have a few days more, I should like to give the matter some thought."

Disappointed, she sighed, "Very well, Philip. What time is left you may have for reflection, but in the end I must have your signature and the identity of the spy. On that there can be no compromise and my love cannot protect you." She glanced out of the stern port where a faint glimmer of light tipped the water. "You must dress yourself and go back to your cell. Until the spy is hanged and you are under articles, this night did not happen nor can any of my men know of it." As soon as he had pulled on his shirt, she snapped the manacles around his wrists. "I will do what I can to gain you time."

CHAPTER THIRTEEN

HERE'S A HEALTH

Here's a health to the company and one to my lass,
We'll drink and be merry all out of one glass,
We'll drink and be merry, from grief we'll refrain,
For we know not when we will all meet again.

folksong

Thin fingers of light cut through the dusty humid air of the barn where Eben struggled to consciousness. Above him, backlit from the tiny window, loomed Darcy.

"Why the hurry to careen?" Eben asked as he blinked sleepily up at Darcy.

"Captain's orders and she is in no mood to be questioned," Darcy answered. "Nearly took my head off when I crossed her on it." Eben sank back. "Rouse yourself, Eben lad, and help me to round up the others." He peered out of the tiny loft window. "Iosa! They'll be everywhere in Cayona and with no wish to be left behind after yesterday's brawl."

Eben kissed the drowsy girl next to him. "Duty calls, Lucy my sweet."

She snuggled closer, her brown curls mingling with the straight black hair that tumbled from the red silk handkerchief around his head. "And could you not answer later?" she murmured.

"Aye, I could," Eben said, pulling away from her and gathering his clothes from the straw covered floor, "but the captain would have my hide."

"Will you come again?" she asked saucily.

He kissed her once more and dressed. "Aye, Lucy, if ever again we make Tortuga, so will I make you." She giggled and watched him follow Darcy down the ladder, then fell back to sleep.

It was a slow process to find all the *Chanticleer's* crew. Those who had gone to the *Bold Cockerel* were quickly retrieved, but those who had found refuge in the arms of Cayona's women were not much in evidence in the thin light of dawn.

The last to be found was Jamie Hawkwood. He was in a hay pile, curled in the arms of a girl scarcely as old as he. "Rogering children," Darcy muttered as he watched Jamie kiss his honey haired Alice farewell.

"We only slept," Jamie said, then added, "Well, mostly." Eben and Darcy exchanged winks as Jamie climbed out of the straw.

"Most likely the last virgin on the island," Eben grinned. Jamie smiled and said nothing.

It was late morning when the *Chanticleer's* sails billowed with the wind and she slipped from the harbor, leaving her companion frigate shining richly in the tropical sun. Had the *Chanticleer* left port a few hours later her lookout would have seen the crisp full sails of a man-of-war and two sloops bearing down on Tortuga from the east.

On the bridge of the *Bold Cockerel* Ward raised his glass, then slammed it shut. "Damn!"

"'Tis Hargrove?" Patrick stood beside the captain and squinted into the afternoon sun.

"Aye, as sure as I am an Englishman," Ward answered. "While we dallied here and there in these islands, Hargrove has had time to put together a fine little fleet and to catch us up."

"Surely they'll no attack us here?" Calum asked.

Ward shook his head. "With Tortuga full of pirates and filibusters? Ah, don't you know that Irish fox Alwell would like to have a go at Hargrove?" The men around him laughed. "'Tis no danger as long as we stay put."

"But that means we dare not leave," Patrick observed, "and the *Chanticleer* is not where we can protect her."

The arrival of the three English ships sent an uneasy tremor throughout Tortuga. One of the sloops veered off on a course for Jamaica, but the other two ships remained. They made no attempt to pass the harbor's mouth, but neither did they show any sign of sailing away.

"That *Princess Royal* is a mighty ship," Sean Alwell commented as he and LeBoutellier watched from a cliff. "Too large for these waters, so surely they mean for the sloops to fight the battle and the big third-rater to scare bloody damn out of the prey. But is it wee Annie Hawkwood they want so much?"

LeBoutellier frowned. "I should think that I am worthy of such pursuit, but this female? Non." He shrugged. "Still, if the English wish to chase pretty girls around the Indies, I am content to let them -- eh, mon amie?" Alwell grinned. "And to watch."

After dark a longboat was lowered from the *Princess Royal* and a half dozen men were put ashore. Ward saw them, then sent a gig of his own to follow them.

"And see if you can find Devlin and Jones," Ward ordered Calum. "There has been no word of them since afore the *Chanticleer* sailed and 'tis time to assemble the crew lest we be caught unprepared for action. The French may no longer tolerate us considering the company we bring."

It was nearly dawn when the gig scraped the frigate's side and the men climbed aboard, Luther and Judas among them. Calum rapped on the captain's door, which opened to admit him and then closed behind him.

Several minutes later he opened it again. "Keep an eye on those ships," Ward ordered. "If either one of them sails, we follow."

"And about that other matter?" Calum asked.

"If we sail from Tortuga today, that man will swing before nightfall."

It was not the *Princess Royal* that sought the open water that morning, but the remaining sloop *Prince Rupert*. The warship weighed anchor at the same time, but sailed only as far as the neighboring island of Hispaniola, disappearing behind it.

"I get the distinct feeling we are being invited out," Patrick said.

"Aye," Ward agreed, "but there is no help for it. Perhaps this sloop will follow the other to Jamaica and we can rest easy."

Two hours later there was no doubt as to the sloop's destination. She was heading for the island where the *Chanticleer* lay helplessly careened. Ward merely grunted when Calum pointed this out, then said, "Call the men. We will settle the matter now."

Except for the helmsman and the lookout, the entire crew, including those who might have preferred to sleep, were summoned to the deck. John Ward looked tense and tired as he stood to address them. "Men, as you are aware, we are chasing that sloop and it seems clear that she is sent to take the *Chanticleer*. Now, no one in Tortuga could have given them her whereabouts, and yet, that sloop knows where she lies. This crew alone had that knowledge, and so it is that one of you must have provided the information to the Navy.

An angry murmur ran through the men. "'Twas learned last night," Ward continued, "that an English sailor, and God knows he'd be easy to spot in French Tortuga, sat and talked with two royal officers in a tavern. The officers were from the *Princess Royal* and carried safe conduct from the French governor. The man they found was from this ship."

There was a general cry of "Who!?" Ward raised his hands and the clamor died. "I do not know who it was, but I do know who it was not. It was not any man who was aboard this ship last night. It had to be one of those already ashore." Ward began a lawyerly pace, his hands clasped behind his back. "It was not Calum for 'twas he that brought me the news. There were some twenty men in the town last night and all but two spent the time in the same brothel. We know from the many tired whores that the men never left until Calum called for them this morning."

"And the two others?" Estey asked.

"Luther Devlin and Judas Jones," Calum answered. "I was a long time in finding them -- long after I had learned of the talk in the tavern. Jones was so caught up in his preaching that at first he refused to come with me and so slow was he to reach the gig that I nigh left him behind."

All eyes turned on the old carpenter. He looked up and shook his head. "Those lads needed to 'ear the word of God and I saw no reason to 'urry back 'ere. God's work must come first."

"Aye, so it must," Ward said, his fingers stroking his beard as he considered the shipwright. "And would that commitment to preaching include putting down all papists?" Jones started to nod, then Ward added, "Even young James Hawkwood and his Jacobite friends?"

"I ne'er made secret that I thought they were doing evil in the sight of the Lord and were justly punished for it," Jones declared.

"Then you might well be he who betrayed young Hawkwood's vessel to the Navy and with him Captain Anne and her crew," Ward accused.

Jones shook his head. "I ne'er went near the tavern."

"Then where did you go?" Luther asked, pressing forward, his dark features shining in the tropical sun.

"You were not together the entire time?" Ward asked sharply.

Luther looked up with well tempered innocence. "'E told me 'e wanted to walk alone and 'e did so several times, both last night and before. The lads 'e was preaching to didn't mind." Several of the crew laughed and Judas glowered at them.

"Laugh, ye minions of Satan," he cried, "but on that day of final judgment the Lord God Almighty will see your filth and corruption, your murders, thefts and sodomies, and 'e will cast ye down into the fiery pit, yea, even into the flames of 'ell!" Unmindful of his peril, the old man mounted a small keg to continue his oration, but he was cut short in his speech by Ward on the quarterdeck above.

"Mister Devlin, did Jones tell you where he went when he left you?"

"No, Cap'n," Luther answered, "but I ne'er thought 'e'd go betray the *Chanticleer*."

"I did not," Judas protested. "Luther, tell 'em!"

"'Ow can I, Judas?" Luther replied. "I weren't with you."

"This man is your friend, Devlin," Ward said. "Do you accuse him?"

"No, sir, I do not," Luther answered stoutly, then added, "but I ain't defending 'im neither."

Ward looked out over his crew. "Men, for months I have known that there was a traitor amongst you. Ever since James Hawkwood was captured I have waited for this traitor to strike again. Judas Jones, I am grieved, deeply grieved that you have allowed your religious convictions to influence your judgment that you would betray your mates to their enemies. I hope that God sees fit to have mercy on you, for indeed, I cannot."

"Will no one listen to me?" Judas cried desperately. "Will no one 'ear the truth, that I am innocent? 'Tis true that I 'ate all papists, but I ne'er betrayed anyone. I don't even know where the *Chanticleer* lies."

"All the others knew," Calum said. "'Twas no secret amongst ourselves."

"One of the lads talked to Luther, but I was not listening. I was on God's work," Judas argued. "I walked and prayed, but ne'er entered a tavern. Go find this woman who told ye of this, and unless she will bear false witness she will say 'twas not I."

Ward shook his head. "No, Jones, there will be no stay of sentence. What say you, men?"

"Death!"

"Hang him!"

The men pressed around Judas and pulled him from the keg. "I didn't do it!" he screamed.

Luther's eyes filled with hurt. "'Tis no good, Judas. Even I don't believe you."

Ward his hand for silence. "I have heard enough. Judas Jones, you are a treacherous dog and as such you die. Hang him."

Ward turned away as the roar of the mob swept over the deck. The only man to hang back from hauling the bound, struggling victim to the yardarm was Luther Devlin, his dark and beautiful face betraying nothing.

It had been a fearsome night on the lonely little island where the *Chanticleer* lay half careened. A raging tropical storm had swept by, smashing trees and whipping the sea to an angry boil. The *Chanticleer* lay helpless on the sand during the wild battering of the storm while her crew huddled in the makeshift shelter they had built on the shore.

In the morning the men crawled from the wreckage of their hut and surveyed the storm's devastation. Their supplies lay scattered across the sand and bobbed in the water of the cove. The ship itself seemed undamaged except for a mass of tangled rigging and a broken main mast.

"That was a rare roaring gale, Captain," Darcy observed grimly. "'Twill take time to repair."

"We may not have time," Anne answered as she joined him beside the beached vessel. She looked exceptionally small and thin, her wet clothes clinging tightly around her. "I have just had word from the cliff. There is a ship approaching."

"What manner of ship?" Eben asked, looking up from his study of the disordered lines.

"'Tis not the *Bold Cockerel*," she answered. "'Tis a sloop."

"Perhaps our prisoner can identify her, if she be Navy or no," Darcy suggested.

Anne gestured to two other men and they trotted across the sand to the tumbled hut. Moments later they reappeared with Gilchrist, wet and manacled. "Thank you," Anne said to the men, "you may go. I will see to the prisoner." She took Gilchrist by the arm and led him up the slope to the cliff overlooking the narrow mouth to the little inlet. On this cliff, as on the one opposite, were the *Chanticleer's* guns, guarding the mouth against intruders.

"'Tis lucky we were in this place last night," Gilchrist said as he looked out over the wide warm water. "'Twas nigh a hurricane."

"Aye," she muttered, handing him the telescope. "Know you that vessel?"

Gilchrist studied the ship in the distance, then shook his head. "A Navy sloop, but I can tell you no more than that." He closed the telescope and returned it to her.

"She seems headed straight for us," Anne said.

"Aye," he agreed, taking her hand in spite of the manacles.

"And could it be that she knows we are here and seeks us?"

"I do not see how," he answered.

"Damnation, Philip!" she shot back, pulling her hand away. "'Tis no accident to my mind. Surely this sloop has our position from Campbell's man on the *Cockerel*."

"Then would not the *Cockerel* be in pursuit?" Gilchrist asked. "And would not a spy be a fool to make such revelations that might put him in a sea battle between the Navy and the vessel in which he sails?"

"Aye," she said slowly, then added, "but if he were threatened with exposure or death -- and the one would surely lead to the other -- aye, then he might take the chance."

"But we know none of this for certain," he said. "If this sloop is sent to destroy us -- and we do not know that it is -- then the first concern is safety. As soon as the mouth is blockaded it is only a matter of time before we are taken."

"And so you will have your freedom and your honor," she said dryly.

He took her chin in his hands. "If it means I shall lose you, then of what worth would it be?"

"A sweet thought, Philip." She took his arm as they slid down the slope to the sand below. "Mister Carr!" she called. "Mister O'Flynn! Jamie! We must talk. Come." She led them off to one side, gesturing for them to sit. Only Darcy seemed unsurprised by Gilchrist's presence beside Anne. "We have established that yon sloop is of the Royal Navy, and that she heads for us here. Soon she will block the mouth and keep us from escape, even if we had a vessel."

"'Twill be another day at least before the *Chanticleer* might be ready to put to sea," Darcy said. "And even so, she will only be fit for some short journey to a port where she can be repaired properly."

"We have shot enough to keep the devils from entering," Eben said.

"And what if another ship follows this one?" Gilchrist replied.

"Who has given you leave to speak?" Jamie demanded.

"I have," Anne answered. "This man is well versed in the methods of the Royal Navy and his expertise could prove useful in this situation. I would have his opinion respected."

"Aye, but can it be trusted?" Eben asked coldly.

"Mister O'Flynn, release the prisoner's hands," Anne commanded. Over her brother's protests, she said, "Those are my orders!" Eben and Jamie exchanged amazed looks as Darcy unlocked the manacles.

Eben took Anne by the arm, asking softly, "Captain, is this wise?"

Anne looked him in the eyes, then said quietly, "Eben, for once, trust my judgment and ask no questions." Eben sat back in silence, studying the lieutenant.

"Now, Mister Gilchrist," Anne said briskly, "you think that another ship may follow this one."

"There is no way to be certain," he replied, "but if, as I suspect, this ship is part of a fleet under Hargrove's command, then he wouldn't send such a sloop alone to chase the likes of you."

"A fine compliment, sir," Anne said. "Perhaps the other vessels were lost or scattered by the storm."

"'Tis possible," Gilchrist agreed.

"And perhaps the *Bold Cockerel* was lost as well." Eben's suggestion was one that no one wished to consider.

"Pray God no," was all Anne would say, shuddering. "No, we must hope that the *Cockerel* follows and soon. Until then we must either hold the mouth or contrive some means of escape."

"There'll be no escaping in the *Chanticleer*," Darcy said. "She'd be no match for that sloop even if she weren't crippled."

"Will the Navy lads no try to take the guns first, then enter as they wish?" Jamie asked.

"Aye," Gilchrist answered. "They'll fire from the ship, and if the glass tells them that the ship within cannot escape, they could well send men ashore to take the guns that way."

"'Twould be a goodly number then," Jamie said, idly scratching with a stick in the sand.

"Aye," Gilchrist agreed, "most of the crew I would think."

"What are you coming to, Jamie?" Anne asked.

"Before the storm," Eben said, "Jamie and I scouted the island. 'Tis all coral along its backbone, save for a marsh in the middle. 'Tis low there. Low enough to ford, low enough to haul a gig over to the sea beyond."

"And you plan to put to sea in the gig and one small canoe," Gilchrist challenged. "How far do you think to go?"

"Oh, only as far as a virtually unmanned, heavily armed Navy sloop," Eben answered with cold nonchalance. He then shot Jamie a congratulatory grin.

"Clever," Anne said. "My compliments." Gilchrist was silent.

"We could put up a bit of resistance on the cliffs," Jamie suggested. "To keep them occupied while the sloop is taken."

"We would have to spike our own guns," Anne warned, "or see them used against us. And the men manning our cannon would be taking the risk of being taken or killed by the lads we maroon."

"Even so," Darcy said, "'tis the best we have got."

All morning the crew of the *Chanticleer* scurried about the sand, preparing for the escape. The *Chanticleer* was neither righted nor repaired, but left where she lay. Her lines and sails were stripped away and hidden in the marsh. Her broken mast and spars were buried in the tangled undergrowth with many of her supplies. Her gig and canoe were rowed to the marsh, and left with the crew's personal possessions, waiting until dark to be dragged over the narrow neck to the open water. The men who remained to man the cannon were chosen by lot and armed with all they would need, including the spikes to render the cannon useless just before they were to abandon their post.

The sloop reached her range in the early afternoon and began to fire on the cliffs. The pirates answered with shots carefully aimed to fall short of their target. Puzzled, the sloop's captain examined the small stretch of shore visible through the cove mouth. The glass revealed the beached merchantman and her crew striking a bold stance around her.

"'Tis no great hurry," Captain Yeager said to his mate. "She's aground and her crew is small in number. We'll send the lads ashore after dark. 'Twill all be done by morning, eh?"

As the warm tropical darkness descended, the sloop's boats were lowered and her crew pulled for the base of the cliffs, unaware that on the other side of the island the pirate crew were manning their small craft.

"Philip," Anne said softly as she stood beside him on the sand, "I have come to a decision."

"As have I, Anne."

Her eyes never leaving the filling boats, she said quickly, her voice cracking, "You are free to go. I will take responsibility for your escape and we will find the spy some other way. If all goes as planned, then you can rejoin your Navy comrades and we'll away without you."

"Generous Anne, such a plan would cost you much -- perhaps your very life. I cannot allow that." She could barely see the twinkle in his eye as he added, "Besides, who says I wish to escape?"

"What?"

"Rather than see you forced to choose or to give up aught for me, I would sign your articles and go on the account with you." She was about to object when he took her by the shoulders and gazed into the darkness of her face, lit only by the hooded lantern she carried. "I want you, Anne, and that is the price. If someday I hang for it, then I will still say it was worth every moment with you."

"And the spy's name?" she asked breathlessly.

"I honestly do not know it," he said, "but when next we meet the *Bold Cockerel*, I will find the man -- or he will find me. Either way, you will have him."

"Captain," Eben called in the darkness over the booming guns on the other side of the island, "the boats are ready and wanting you."

Anne looked earnestly into Gilchrist's face. "Are you certain?"

"Never more so in my life," he answered. "Now let's away and get on with cheating the king out of his sloop."

The two little boats rowed quietly around the island, the slap of their oars inaudible over the guns. The sloop's starboard cannon were firing at the cliffs, her lee side was still. Only a handful of men could be seen on her deck and they were intent on the cannon, never seeing the invaders climb aboard. There were a few sharp cries, then the splashes of bodies. The *Prince Rupert* was taken.

The rest of the sloop's crew, scaling the cliff, understood what had happened when the sloop's guns fired again, smashing their boats and leaving them with no escape but the stripped *Chanticleer.* The pirates on the cliffs hurriedly spiked their guns and scrambled down the slopes in a mad race for the back of the island where the sloop met them, taking them and the stowed supplies aboard.

Anne settled into the captain's cabin, neatly arranging her few possessions and rummaging through those of the previous owner. "Are all aboard?" she asked as Darcy entered with her little seachest.

"Aye," he said, "alive and well -- but for Travis who is but a trifle wounded. A broken finger, I'm thinkin'."

"Excellent," she said, then looked about her. "'Tis not as spacious as the *Chanticleer.* Dear God, how I shall miss her!"

"Perhaps we can retake her," Darcy ventured. "We'll be needing the *Cockerel* to do it, but stripped as she is, 'twill be a long time afore those Navy boys get any use of her."

"Perhaps," Anne said. "Are we on course for Tortuga?"

"Aye, and mayhap we will overtake the *Cockerel*. This ship carries no great magazine."

Anne opened the chest and drew out the battered roll of paper. "Where is Gilchrist?"

"Chained up below," Darcy answered, nodding at the paper. "He will sign?"

"Aye," Anne said, "and there is a part of me that is sorry for it." She sighed, then brightened. "Still, it spares me much. I thank you, Darcy, for your aid in this."

Eben scowled when he saw Gilchrist's signature at the bottom of the articles under the tidy writing of James Hawkwood. "There is still the matter of a spy unnamed," he said.

"'Tis taken care of, Mister Carr," Anne replied. "Philip and I have made an agreement on that."

"Well, I want to hear it," Eben demanded.

"I swear I do not know his name," Gilchrist explained, looking at Eben levelly, "but when we meet with the *Bold Cockerel* again, I will go among the crew and find him for you -- or allow him to find me, since surely he will fear my presence." Eben looked doubtful. "Mister Carr, I like my life as much as the next man."

As dawn approached and the *Prince Rupert* made her way across the water toward Tortuga, the crew celebrated with drinking and wild dancing. Gilchrist, so late an abused prisoner, was treated as an honored guest, as a heretic might be welcomed back into the fold after recantation. Only Jamie Hawkwood seemed less than happy.

"Ah, don't be so gloomy, Jamie lad," Eben said, giving his friend a drunken poke in the ribs. "If he keeps his word -- and he has to, understand, or I shall have him -- then we'll have that spy hanged as soon as we meet the *Cockerel*. And we have this fine ship taken and not a man lost. 'Tis cause to celebrate, I tell you."

Jamie stared at him. "What spy?" he demanded.

Eben looked perplexed, then realized his mistake. “I’m sorry. You were not to know.”

“What spy?” Jamie demanded again, taking Eben by the sleeve.

Eben pulled free. “Someone on the other ship -- told the soldiers about your bit of treason.”

“And killed Tristan?”

Eben lowered his eyes and nodded. “Aye, ’twould seem so. Your cousin’s body was never found.” Jamie turned away. “Please, Jamie, understand -- ’twas on your sister’s orders that you were told nothing. She thought to protect you.”

“She thought to protect him,” Jamie said bitterly. “Her lover.”

“Aye, but there is more, I’m thinkin’.” The two youths looked up to find Darcy O’Flynn looming over them, weaving slightly as he clutched the ratlines with one hand, a flagon with the other. “Jamie m’bhuachail, the captain is a rare judge of men, a skill she has of her father. She plays us all like a fine instrument.” He dizzily punctuated his sentence with another swig. “Eben here could be depended upon never to be letting the man have a moment’s ease, a moment when there was nothing to fear. And I would be the one to see that no serious harm came to him.” He tapped Jamie’s chest with a long calloused finger. “If you had been in on the secret, you just might have upset the balance.”

“And in the midst of all this scheming she fell in love with him,” Jamie replied with disgust.

Darcy grinned. “No, lad. That came long before. I saw it in her eyes when we rescued her from the sand the morning you were taken. She didn’t know it herself then, y’see, but I could tell. Take it in good grace. You could do worse for a brother-in-law.” Jamie stalked off. “I think the lad’s jealous,” Darcy commented.

“Aren’t we all?” Eben replied, helping himself to Darcy’s flagon.

CHAPTER FOURTEEN

CAPTAIN WARD

Go home, go home, ye tinkers
and tell the king for me;
That though he be king upon good dry land
I be king on sea. folksong

The raucous party might have lasted all the way to Tortuga had not the lookout spotted sails on the horizon. "Why 'tis the *Cockerel* come to greet us," Darcy laughed blearily.

"Aye, indeed," Anne said coming up beside the mate, Gilchrist a step behind her, "but pray, good Darcy, tell me what vessel is that following her?"

Aboard the *Bold Cockerel* the approaching sloop had been sighted. When there was no sign of the *Chanticleer*, Ward swore wrathfully and ordered his men to prepare for vengeance on the Navy vessel.

The *Princess Royal* had also been seen. Like the *Bold Cockerel* she had survived the storm, but had been blown far from her course and had lost time in catching up to the pirate frigate. The other sloop had not been seen since her departure for Jamaica.

In the cabin of the *Prince Rupert*, Anne and her officers assessed their situation. "There is no way to tell Captain Ward that we are here without also informing the third-rater," Anne said. "If we let the *Cockerel* within range she will fire on us thinking we are Navy. If we go too nigh that man-of-war, they will blow us out of the water once they see that we are not Navy."

Eben studied the chart spread out before them. "We lie close to Puerto Rico. 'Tis water too shallow for a big warship."

"You are thinking like a smuggler, Mister Carr," Gilchrist said. "'Tis something that the Navy will not understand."

"Aye," Eben replied, "but John Ward will."

"Set a new course then," Anne said with a confident smile, "and give her full sail."

The *Prince Rupert's* peculiar behavior caused a stir on both the pursuing ships. The sloop veered from her course for Tortuga and now sailed for Puerto Rico. Being the fastest of the three ships she kept her distance so that any clue to her strange action could not be discerned through the spyglass.

Puzzled though Hargrove was, he did not seem displeased. He ordered his men to remain at the ready, but made no effort to close the gap between his ship and the *Bold Cockerel.*

"Why do we tarry behind?" Campbell asked. "With the sloop afore and no sign of the other Hawkwood ship, we stand two to one. We could pin the pirates between us and finish with them."

"Aye," Hargrove agreed, "but where is the *Prince of Wales*? 'Tis a great store of powder and shot she was sent to fetch -- powder the *Rupert* will need if the pirates choose to give battle."

"Against this great ship?" Campbell looked amazed. "Surely they'd no be so foolish?"

"I thought the same when I sailed the *Rainbow* against them," Hargrove said, turning his glass back upon the sea.

"They come no closer," Ward wondered as he watched the huge warship through his glass. "Why do they lag so?"

"A trap, perhaps," Calum said, his eyes cunning and cold as steel. "We have no seen that other sloop since Tortuga."

"Lost in the storm likely," Ward answered.

"Aye, but if she didna sink then she could be in these waters waiting for us." Calum thoughtfully fingered the hilt of his cutlass. "We stand two to one and little chance to win, but if that other sloop were to come then we might as well be dead and done with it now."

Ward shook his head. "But there is something strange about this sloop. Why should a small ship with such a fearsome companion make a run for land? Surely they realize that Hargrove will be hard pressed to maneuver so close to the island."

The gunner shrugged. "I didna suspect the Navy commanders to be overburdened with intelligence."

Ward laughed sourly. "But 'tis a fool who underestimates his opponent. This man Hargrove is no fool, and I hope to Heaven neither am I."

As the shoreline of Puerto Rico grew larger in the afternoon sun, the *Prince Rupert* began to lag, allowing the *Bold Cockerel* to come closer.

"Now what does this mean?" Ward raised his glass and scanned the sloop's deck. He froze when he saw the skirted figure near the helm. "By damn, 'tis Anne!" He laughed loudly as Patrick grabbed the glass and studied the sloop.

"And you can be sure that aboard the warship they dinna ken it," Calum said.

"Devlin! Estey! Morgan!" Ward shouted. "Look lively, lads. Pull away from the sloop. Let the warship come between us and we'll smash her with broadsides."

Hargrove could sense the inevitability of the coming confrontation. There was still no sign of either the *Chanticleer* or the missing sloop, and rather than wait for what could be an unfavorable change in the odds, he ordered a shot fired across the frigate's bow. The frigate made no move to flee or to reply. Instead, she slowed and waited for the *Princess Royal* to come broadside. The *Prince Rupert* slipped back and, upon seeing no fire was offered from either vessel, moved easily to the warship's larboard side.

When the *Bold Cockerel* fired it came as a shock to Hargrove. He had not anticipated an easy surrender, but neither had he envisioned anything as seemingly foolhardy as a direct attack on two ships of the Royal Navy. He returned Ward's fire and waited for the sloop to slip from his lee, but the sloop remained where she was. The pirates' next blast brought down the topgallants, but before the *Princess Royal* returned that volley, there was another surprise for Commander Hargrove. The English flag was lowered on the sloop's masthead and replaced by a red flag with a leering skull on it.

"Sweet Jesus!" one sailor cried. "The *Rupert* is gone pirate!"

Hargrove now took a closer look at the sloop's deck. The crew were wearing a motley assortment of borrowed and ill fitting uniform coats and near the capstan stood a dark haired woman who snapped a playful salute. "Fire!" Hargrove bellowed at his gunners. "Fire on the *Rupert*!"

But the sloop's guns answered first, sending chainshot into the warship's rigging and raking the deck with grapeshot. Now the *Bold Cockerel's* heavy starboard guns sent balls crashing against the *Princess Royal's* hull. The warship rocked with the impact, then answered with all her forty cannon in a deafening roar. Ward lost his mizzenmast and fire burst with the hotshot in his topsails, but the warship's guns were aimed too high to hurt the sloop.

The *Bold Cockerel* now turned and cut in front of the warship, firing on her in passing. The huge *Princess Royal* took no major damage, but was helpless in the light wind and shallow water of the nearby island. "Can we no sail back to our own depth?" Campbell demanded as Hargrove attempted to explain the situation.

"'Tis not like a cart, Colonel," Hargrove answered with exasperation. "We cannot simply back up."

"Then we must remain here till they sink us?"

"Nay, man," Hargrove answered. "Our hull is built to take such fire. They'll never hole her, but they can cripple us even so."

The *Bold Cockerel* fired again. Hargrove watched in dismay as his foremast toppled into the sea, tangled with the remains of his bowsprit. He ordered his forward guns to spray the frigate with grapeshot and was gratified to see several pirates fall.

"Bring her about!" Hargrove yelled to his helmsman. The sailor twisted the great wheel, and slowly the warship turned to starboard as her larboard guns readied to strike the pirate frigate with another broadside.

Then the *Prince Rupert* fired. The spinning deadly chainshot whirled through rigging and men, felling all in its path. The helmsman beside Hargrove collapsed, headless, to the deck and the wheel spun free, lurching the warship back into the path of another blast from the *Bold Cockerel.* Hargrove grabbed the wheel and attempted to bring his ship back to course, but the broadside from the frigate shook the ship and knocked the commander off balance.

"Take the helm," Hargrove shouted to the sailor who ran to help him to his feet. "Increase fire on the *Rupert*!" he bellowed. "Fire on the frigate only as necessary."

"Is this wise, Commander?" Campbell asked.

"One ship at a time, Colonel," Hargrove said as he pushed past him. "We'll destroy the sloop, then bring all we have to sink the frigate."

Campbell scowled at the brusque treatment. "Tell me, Hargrove," he demanded, "how did Mistress Hawkwood come to hold your sloop?"

Hargrove turned and smiled. "Perhaps the same way she took your horse, Colonel."

The *Princess Royal* turned and passed between the frigate and the sloop, exchanging shot with each. The frigate's foremast crashed down amid a mass of shattered spars and ripped, burning canvas. The volley against the sloop brought a rousing cheer from the men of the *Princess Royal.* A ball sank into the sloop's bow, leaving a hole through which the warm seawater poured.

"Get men on the pumps," Anne commanded as soon as Eben told her of the damage, "and see what can be done to patch it."

Hargrove watched the struggling sloop. "She cannot last long," he said to Campbell. "Even if they can keep her from sinking, they have no escape."

"Aye," Campbell said, his seamed face dirty with smoke. "They canna fight and do double duty at pump and cannon. Now do we take the frigate?"

"Aye, Colonel," Hargrove said.

The warship threw all her considerable power against the *Bold Cockerel*, but the disparity between their sizes was not to the warship's advantage. She was too big a target to miss and slow to maneuver, although heavy enough to withstand most of the shots that slammed against her.

"Clear her decks!" Ward bellowed. "Hot shot and chain for them. I want that great water pig to have no peace." After a frightening carnage on the *Princess Royal's* deck, Ward watched with satisfaction as Hargrove ordered every man below. "Now, strip her masts and bring them down." The cannon thundered.

"How does the sloop?" Patrick asked.

Ward turned his glass toward the *Prince Rupert*. "She lies low. I think we must get to her and take the crew aboard or stand to watch them drown." He yelled to the helm, "To the lee, man! We'll go by their stern!" Lighter and faster than her opponent, the frigate gained enough momentum to sail past the lumbering warship, even with only tattered smoking remnants of sails hanging from makeshift yards on jury-rigged masts.

"Fire!" The warship's blast brought down the pirates' mainmast and, in the frantic effort to fire a second broadside before the frigate was angled away behind the stern, the haste became a deadly foe. One sailor failed to soak his swab and when the powder charge touched the remaining embers in the hot cannon, there was a roaring explosion. The cannon burst, killing the men nearest and blowing a hole in the warship's side.

"'Tis above their waterline," Ward grumbled. His own guns fired and the *Princess Royal's* stern took the full impact of the fifteen shots as they passed.

"I think we have holed her," Calum reported proudly. Ward drew out his glass and examined the spot to which the gunner pointed. "'Tis another arsehole for Hargrove, eh?" There was indeed a deep indentation at the warship's waterline.

"Aye, and with all the chaos on their gundeck 'twill take them time to realize it," Ward commented. "Well done. Try for another."

Repairs, born of necessity, went rapidly aboard the sloop. Gilchrist's knowledge of the sloop's construction and fittings made the work more precise. He arrived dirty, wet, but smiling in the cabin where Anne waited with Jamie. "The hull is patched," he reported, "but 'twill not hold forever. We have some sail rigged and could try for an escape around the reef."

"Not without the *Cockerel*," Anne answered.

"She sails to us now," Gilchrist replied. "She's damaged, but under sail, so that --"

"Anne, look!" Jamie pointed through the stern port. There were shouts from the deck as Anne leapt to Jamie's side and paled as she saw another sloop bearing down on them, storm bedraggled but fit to fight.

"Hargrove has a third ship and she's here to kill us." Anne ran from the cabin, Jamie and Gilchrist following on her heels.

On the *Prince of Wales* the surprising defection of her sister sloop caused a rapid reassessment of the plan to transfer the powder commandeered in Jamaica. The sailors scurried to return the kegs and canisters to the safety of the magazine, then to load and prime the cannon to destroy the *Prince Rupert*.

One sailor hoisted a keg to his shoulder, but it slipped on his sweaty palms and crashed to the deck near the hatch, scattering powder on the deck and below.

"Clear that away, Turner!" the bo'sun shouted. "This is no time to be careless."

"No time to be tidy neither," the sailor muttered as he kicked the loose powder through the open hatch.

Darcy swung down from the splintered quarterdeck, his broad bare chest streaked with smoke, sweat and blood. "'Tis low on powder we are, Captain," he reported.

"Yon sloop has plenty," Anne observed bitterly. "'Twas meant for us, one way or another."

"Aye," Darcy replied, "though perhaps they meant to deliver it over the side rather than through the muzzle of cannon."

Anne looked ruefully at the tattered red flag fluttering above. "'Tis as Simon might say -- a short life and a merry one," she sighed. Shots from the warship whizzed by. Gilchrist pulled her behind the capstan.

"'Twould seem my life as a pirate is to be very short," he said, kissing her.

"If our articles are lost, no one need know you signed," she answered. "There is no reason for you to hang."

"Dearest Anne, I truly regret nothing," he said earnestly. "There is no other way it could be done. My honor is satisfied and I do not fear the rope."

"I only regret that I did not allow myself to love you sooner," she whispered. As she leaned into his embrace again, over the joyful shouts from the *Princess Royal* could be heard a wild cry.

"Look!" Eben was pointing at a bony ridge thrust from the island into the sea. Beyond the reef could be seen another sail of another frigate.

"'Tis crowded in these waters today," Anne sighed. "Would that it were less so." She left the shelter of the capstan and squinted at the frigate. It was close enough to see her deck and gaudy decoration. Anne gave a sharp gasp. "*La Panache*!"

Before there was time to assess the French ship's motives, *La Panache* swept down on the *Prince of Wales*, then veered off her lee, firing all her larboard cannon pointblank as she passed. There was a shattering explosion as the Navy sloop disintegrated in a ball of fire.

Anne stared as the remains of the sloop showered down across the green water. "I had never thought LeBoutellier to be such an excellent shot," she said with wonder. "I must remember to have more care of him in future."

La Panache sailed on, coming close by the helpless *Prince Rupert*. On the frigate's deck stood the elegant figure of her captain, resplendent in velvet and plumes. As the Frenchman passed he gave one sweeping bow to the lady on the stricken sloop. Anne, deeply moved, dropped a courtly curtsey, then watched the Frenchman sail on.

From the deck of the *Bold Cockerel* John Ward viewed the exchange in wondering admiration, while Hargrove's spirits sank with the loss of the sloop. The *Princess Royal* began to show her list, her crew strewn about the deck like broken dolls, but still Commander Hargrove would not yield. He ordered the men into action again.

But if the warship lay in danger of sinking, that fate also awaited the *Prince Rupert*. The patch burst with the first ball to hit her and the sloop took on water faster than her diminished crew could pump it out. "She cannot hold much longer," Eben reported. "And we're down by ten men -- six sore wounded and the other four dead."

Anne looked grim. "We must get to the *Cockerel.* 'Tis our only hope."

"And Hargrove's," Gilchrist said. "That warship may not sink for a time yet, but if Hargrove means to sail back to Jamaica with our heads he'll have to do it in your frigate."

"I ne'er thought I'd hear myself say it," Darcy chuckled, "but 'tis a pity that LeBoutellier did not stay. We could use an ally."

"He kept his word. 'Tis enough," Anne said.

"The *Cockerel* must come to us," Eben said. "We lie too low now to make sail."

Ward watched as the red flag on the sloop dipped and rose. "They are going down. We must get past this wallowing pig of a warship." He snapped the spyglass shut. "Come, lads! 'Tis no time to lie about."

"We 'ave a jurymast fore and some fresh sail," Luther reported. "If it ain't blown down we'll make 'er fine."

"Good man, Devlin," Ward said. "Bring her about!" The *Bold Cockerel* creakingly turned away from the warship in an attempt to circle her to reach the foundering sloop beyond.

It was just the moment for which Hargrove had been waiting. With the remnant of his rudder he ordered the helm to bring the *Princess Royal* bow to bow with the *Prince Rupert.* As the two ships met, their shattered bows grinding together, the sailors flung grappling hooks onto the sloop and held her fast. The men poured down from the warship to the sloop and there was a sharp crack of pistols and muskets, then the ringing clash of swords. Campbell and Hargrove drove fearlessly into the thick of battle, cutting down the survivors of Anne Hawkwood's weary men.

The *Bold Cockerel* loomed over the sloop's starboard side. "Are we going to board her?" Estey asked.

Ward shook his head. "That is exactly what Hargrove wants. Then his men can board us as well. We must bide out of reach for a time."

"We cannot stand here and do nothing!" Patrick protested.

"Aye," Ward nodded. "Get Luther and Calum up here. They are our best shots. We'll pick off Hargrove's men one by one if we must."

The sloop's crew fought hard. Those who fell into the sea alive swam for the *Bold Cockerel* where they were pulled aboard. Darcy and Jubilee, like two great giants, one very red, the other very black, slowed the tide of boarders at the bow. "I have good magic with me," Jubilee laughed as he threw a sailor bodily into the sea. Darcy was about to reply when a ball struck the big black man and pitched him into the sea where he vanished.

Anne stood on the quarterdeck, laying about her with a sword. Jamie fought beside her. "You fight well for a woman," he commented as she spitted another man and pushed him back.

"Thank you, brother," Anne gasped. "Father taught me well." Jamie's opponent fell and there was a moment of respite. "Taught me what to spy in his offspring -- of which there are many." She smiled. "Whatever doubts I had about Mad Jack fathering you, there are gone now. You are, indeed, his son and proud I am of it."

Jamie started to reply gratefully when he saw the jury-rig snap free. "Anne!" He turned to shove her out of the way, but a pistol ball struck his chest. The falling spar knocked Anne to the deck, leaving her unconscious beneath it. Jamie lay a few feet away while aboard the *Bold Cockerel* Luther Devlin calmly loaded another ball into his musket.

Colonel Campbell reached Anne's side and jerked her limp body up. "I have Anne Hawkwood and will kill her if ye dinna surrender immediately!" he yelled over the din. Darcy and Eben, charging toward him, stopped abruptly.

"Let her go, Campbell," Darcy growled. "You'll ne'er get out of here alive unless you do."

"Surrender," Campbell ordered. "Tell your men to put down their weapons." There was a long pause, then suddenly there was a crack as a whip caught Campbell around the neck. Wet, bloody and grinning wildly, Jubilee finished his climb over the stern.

"I got good magic, eh?" he said as he pulled Campbell back. Anne crumpled like a stringless puppet. Darcy pushed her into Eben's arms, then smashed a huge fist against the colonel's jaw, leaving him unconscious amongst the ruins of the deck.

"Take her to the *Cockerel*, Eben," Darcy said. "I'll be seeing to Master James." Eben had barely reached the side when Commander

Hargrove took aim. The pistol fired, there was a crash and a cry, and Eben fell, Anne toppling with him into the sea.

Ward could stand it no longer. After sending two men into the water to rescue Eben and Anne, he ordered the grappling hooks brought out. Minutes later the pirates stormed aboard the sinking sloop, while the sloop's few men gave way and fled over the rails to the frigate. Leaping to the sloop's deck Ward pressed through the fight to find Hargrove. The commander was shouting brave orders to his dispirited men while fighting his way toward the sloop's stern where he had last seen all that remained of Anne Hawkwood's officers.

Darcy was kneeling beside Jamie, his back open to Hargrove's raised sword, but before the commander could strike the mate down, Gilchrist's sword struck it from his hand. Hargrove stared at his long lost lieutenant, then smiled grimly. "Gone pirate, have you? If you had fought harder against these ruffians before, you would not now fight for them, I'll wager."

"'Tis over, sir," Gilchrist said. "They have bested you. Surrender -- for the sake of your men."

"Little you care for them, traitor," Hargrove replied harshly. "Be done with it, boy. Kill me and be a pirate."

"I will not kill you, sir. You know that."

"Well, I will." Ward stepped up behind Hargrove. "Darcy, take Jamie to the *Cockerel.* And you, Gilchrist -- I take it that you have signed articles with Anne. In her stead, you will take orders from me and I order you to leave this man to me."

Gilchrist looked from Hargrove to Ward. "Aye, Captain," he said as he turned away. Hargrove whipped out his other pistol. There was a flash and Gilchrist staggered to the deck. Ward spun to face the commander.

"I think you had better surrender to me, Hargrove," Ward said, pressing his cutlass against Hargrove's chest and forcing him back against the remains of the sloop's mainmast.

"Your terms?" Hargrove breathed shallowly, his eyes on the steel pointed at his heart. The fighting around them quieted.

"You will be treated honorably," Ward answered. "We are still loyal Englishmen here. You and your crew will be set upon safe soil. Puerto Rico is nigh enough."

"No further reprisals?"

"None, upon my word as a gentleman."

Hargrove laughed. "A gentleman pirate, eh? And my ship? What of her?"

"If she stays afloat we will patch her and take her for a prize. If she sinks, she's yours." Ward chuckled and was relieved to see Hargrove smile and relax. "Have we a bargain then?"

"Aye, Captain," Hargrove said.

The fighting was over. The bloody decks were quiet except for the cries of the wounded. The sea lay calm around them, littered with the remains of ships and men.

CHAPTER FIFTEEN

SHULE AGRA

King James was routed in the fray,
The wild geese went with him away;
My boy went too that dreary day;
Go thee, thu mavourneen slaun. folksong

When Anne opened her eyes she could dimly see the dark cabin walls around the bunk in which she lay. What little light there was came from the main cabin which hummed with low voices. She swung her legs over the bunk and stood weakly, reeling as she stumbled toward the light.

"Anne!" Gilchrist stepped swiftly to her side and helped her to a chair. Blinking in the lantern light, she saw John Ward and Darcy O'Flynn seated across from her.

"What happened?" she asked dazedly.

"They surrendered," Ward answered.

"So I gathered," she replied, looking around dizzily. "The damage?"

"The sloop is gone. Sank two hours ago," Ward replied. "The *Princess Royal* is holed, but I sent some of her crew back under guard to patch her and pump her out."

"And the men?" she asked.

"Some half of Hargrove's men lie killed or wounded," Gilchrist answered.

"And of our own?" She fought to focus her eyes as she looked from Ward to Gilchrist to Darcy. "How many did we lose?"

The men were very quiet, then Ward said, "Of the *Chanticleer's* crew some fifteen dead and another dozen wounded, though of those some five are not expected to live. I have myself lost some thirty slain and as many wounded."

"Aye, but to be fighting a third-rater and to best her, 'tis fine work to be sure," Darcy added.

Anne turned to Gilchrist and saw the bloody rag tied around his left shoulder and neck. "You are wounded, Philip," she said, her voice filled with concern.

He grinned. "Aye, 'tis a parting gift from Hargrove. A mere scratch across my collar."

"And what else to tell?" Anne asked.

"The traitor is caught and hanged," Ward said. "We found him out on our way from Tortuga."

Anne was lost in thought for a moment. "What is it that you are not telling me?" she asked. A strange silence settled over them. Anne looked from face to face, but each man averted his eyes. "Where's Eben?" she asked in panic.

"Amongst the wounded," Ward answered. "We fished the two of you from the water, then gave Eben o'er to Doctor Hartley."

"How wounded?" Her fingers curled tightly around the arm of her chair.

"A ball shattered his knee," Darcy said. "He will lose the leg, but not his life."

Her fingers relaxed. "Patrick is, after all, a most skilled surgeon," Anne said. "Yet I am sorry for the loss of Eben's leg. He will receive the best compensation as befits any member of my father's crew." The silence came again. "Yet there is more to tell?"

Gilchrist rose and took her arm, lifting her carefully to her feet. Supporting her swaying body, he said, "Come with me, Anne." He led her from the main cabin to the mate's cabin, pausing in front of the closed door. "Do you remember aught of what happened to you on the deck?"

Anne shook her head slightly. "I was fighting beside my brother, then there was blackness." Slowly she understood. "Jamie?"

Gilchrist opened the door. "In here."

Anne looked in. Lying on the bunk, his face but little darker than the sheets in the lantern's glow, was Jamie. "Is he dead?" she whispered. Gilchrist shook his head. Jamie lay very still, his hair curling around his head like a silken halo. His eyes were closed, his lips a bloodless blue. "Will he live?" she asked. Again Gilchrist shook his head.

Anne entered the tiny chamber, taking a seat on the edge of the narrow bunk. Gently she stroked his hair, her fingers straying over his chilled brow. Suddenly the blue eyes opened. "Did we win?" he asked feebly.

"Aye, Jamie, indeed we did," she answered, looking around desperately for Gilchrist who had left, closing the door. "We fought side by side, brother. Father would have been pleased."

"Then you meant what you said?"

"I did." Anne looked away, blinking back unfamiliar tears.

"Tell Simon," Jamie whispered hoarsely, then groaned as the pain brought him ever closer to death. "I am dying, Anne."

"Aye." The word caught in her throat.

"The shot ... it came from the *Cockerel*," he gasped. "The spy."

"Is hanged, brother," Anne said, taking his hand and holding it tightly. "I am sorry that I did not tell you -- about Campbell's man, about Tristan. I thought it -- well, it doesn't matter now."

"'Twas an accident of battle then." He smiled wanly.

"Aye, Jamie."

"Tell Mother -- tell her I love her -- but I had to -- to do what ... Do you forgive me, sister?"

"For what?"

"For treason, for the Rookery . . . for . . ." His voice trailed off.

"'Tis nothing to forgive," Anne answered, gently smoothing his hair. "It was something you believed in -- no different from our grandfather and uncles who died for King Charles."

"What would Father have said?"

"That you were every inch a Hawkwood and a man, no matter your beliefs." Her words had their desired effect. Jamie smiled and peacefully closed his eyes.

"Thank you, sister. Pray for me," he muttered. He drifted into unconsciousness with Anne sitting next to him, holding his cool dry hand and stroking his placid pale brow. Quietly she rose and left the cabin.

"John," she said as she entered the captain's cabin, "how far out are we from Puerto Rico?"

"Nigh upon its rocks," Ward answered. "Why?"

"I want you to send a boat ashore and find me a Romish priest from amongst those Spaniards," she announced. Ward looked like a man shot. Gilchrist and Darcy exchanged smiles.

"You? Call a priest?" Ward spluttered. "Not on my ship, mistress. We'll have no papist priest here. The men will not stand for it."

"They must -- this once," she argued wearily. "My brother is dying and I will not deprive him of those rites that he holds such dear comfort. Now, fetch a priest and hurry. 'Tis late and no man other than those in the boat need know."

Anne sat beside Jamie all that night, watching the young life ebb, then flow, then ebb again from him like a tide what would be neither stemmed nor turned. It was nearly dawn with there was a gentle tapping on the door. Anne opened it to find Gilchrist outside with a tall, black robed and cowled monk.

"Your priest, madam," Gilchrist said indicating the sleepy eyed clergyman who nodded confusedly. "This is Father Christopher."

"Gracias, amigo," Anne stammered. "I speak no Latin nor Spanish."

"It is no trouble," the tall friar said. "I speak some little English. Where is this man who dies?"

"In here, reverend, uh, father." Anne stepped back and allowed the priest to stoop past her into the room. Nervously she waited beside Gilchrist in the narrow passage.

A short time later, the priest emerged. "Go to him, daughter. He will not live longer. You have done a fine thing. In nomine Patri . . ."

Anne ducked past him and the hand raised in blessing. She sat beside her brother as Gilchrist led the priest away. "Thank you," Jamie said, his voice barely audible. He gave a faint gasp and was gone. Anne fought back tears as she drew the sheet over his head and stumbled back to the captain's cabin.

Patrick sat at the table, his face showing the strain of long hours of work. Anne sank into the chair next to him and accepted the glass offered to her. "Jamie's dead," she said numbly.

Patrick nodded. "The ball lodged near his heart. 'Twas a wonder that he lived as long as he did."

"There was nothing you could do?"

Patrick shook his head. "Nay, not a thing that would not have killed him faster. I thought it best to concentrate on Eben." He smiled sadly and added, "Jamie thought so, too."

"Eben's leg?"

"Is off. He says he understands, but I think 'twill take time."

"I want Jamie buried on land," Anne said. "Near Father. With a proper stone."

"It can be arranged," Patrick replied. "Allow me to attend to those details. You need to rest, Anne. As for Eben, in a few weeks I can fit him with a wooden leg, but I think he might fare better if he were to leave the sea for a time."

"Do you think I should send him back to England?"

"Aye," Patrick nodded. "Hugo and Simon can see to him, perhaps find him work among the counting houses."

"Safer for a one-legged man than the sea," Anne commented, the exhaustion etching her drawn face. "And you will go with him?"

"Aye, that I will," Patrick replied. "This has been a great adventure, but my home is in England. I fear that my love for the pirate life is more equal to Simon's love of the sea."

"And so you will ride the roads again," Anne laughed softly.

"'Til wealth or death take me."

"And yet I wish you would stay," Anne said. "I feel so -- so cut off from all that I knew. Father's dead, Jamie's dead. Soon you and Eben will go again to the country that I might never see again. And Simon's there. It's as though I had lost all my brothers." She snapped free of her line of thought. "I should go to Eben," she said, starting to rise.

"No, Anne." Patrick laid a restraining hand on her arm. "He is resting comfortably and should be left so. And you must rest as well." He grinned. "Besides, there is a gallant young pirate waiting for you."

Anne fell asleep after crawling in beside Gilchrist and feeling the safety of his arms, as when she was a child and had slept in the security of her father's embrace. Her dreams were fitful, filled with images of Jamie and scores of pale shades. Then her father appeared and bowed to her with great flourish. He led Jamie away, leaving her alone in the middle of a swamp.

When she awoke the sun was high in the morning sky and there was a great bustling on the decks as the pirates repaired the rigging and cleared away the debris. In the main cabin there was a breakfast awaiting her. Ward, Darcy and Gilchrist chatted amiably around her. Her quiet melancholy was not mentioned, nor was its cause.

"We must be giving some thought to the prisoners," Darcy said. "Are they to be sold or executed?"

"Neither," Ward answered. "I gave Hargrove my word that all would be released unharmed." The others stared at him. "We will keep his ship as a prize. We'll decide later whether to refit her for ourselves or to sell her."

"You intend to release all the prisoners?" Anne asked. "Even that rascal Campbell?"

"Aye," Ward answered. "'Tis upon my word."

She sighed. "Then none can ask you to break it, John."

After she had eaten, Gilchrist escorted her to the fo'c'sle where many of the wounded lay, among them Eben Carr. Anne sat down by Eben and took his hand. "Well, Mister Carr, how is it with you?"

"That of me which is still here is well enough," he answered. "That of me which is no longer here is fine as well, though I know not where." His gaze wandered randomly, his face pale against his sweat soaked black hair. "'Tis some rare drink friend Hartley gives for pain. Now, that would be a fine cargo to take."

"We be in the wrong seas for the opium trade, lad," Anne said, forcing a laugh as she ran her fingers through the thick locks that lay across his pillow.

"Jamie's dead?"

Anne looked startled, then nodded. "Aye, at dawn this morning."

Eben smiled weakly. "I thought he might be. The ball took him in the chest. I saw him fall. We had agreed not to mourn the other, but I fear -- I may break the bargain."

"He died at peace, Eben," Anne said. "We even fetched a Spanish priest from bed to give him the Romish rites."

Eben closed his eyes. "I wonder who was more amazed," he muttered, "the priest or Jamie." He drifted off to sleep.

Anne left the fo'c'sle. On the deck the prisoners were being ferried ashore in a battered and patched longboat. On the sand beyond, the first arrivals stood huddled together over the few belongings and supplies they were allowed to carry with them. The pirates scowled and cursed at the Navy men, shoving them roughly whenever the opportunity presented itself.

The last of the prisoners were brought to the deck, among them Commander Hargrove and Colonel Campbell. "You see, Commander," Ward said, "I have kept my word."

"Aye, Captain, and I thank you for being a man of honor," Hargrove replied, "but still I should have preferred to be set on friendlier ground. I have no trust in the Spanish."

"We will get word to the garrison in Jamaica to send ships to fetch you," Ward promised. "We are still loyal Englishmen and wish no harm to our own countrymen, save what is necessary to keep us alive. Meanwhile, there is one man you can trust on Puerto Rico. There is a priest, Father Christopher. We have told him to expect stranded English sailors. He will act as interpreter and emissary for you."

"You make friends with a papist priest and ask us to trust him as well," Campbell retorted. "They are all with the Jacobites, I tell you, Hargrove, and as such they should hang for treason as well as piracy."

Ward pressed closer to tower over the squat colonel, his face red with anger. "You'll take back those words, Colonel, or you'll swim to land and my men shall use you for a target exercise."

"Gentlemen, please!" Gilchrist said, stepping forward. "Colonel, 'twas for Jamie Hawkwood only that the priest was called, and that by his sister. The boy is dead now and there are no other Jacobites here." He put a protective arm around Anne's shoulders.

"Well, Mister Gilchrist, you have gone on the account with these brigands," Campbell growled. "I wouldna have thought it of a man in Hargrove's service."

"You are a fool, boy," Hargrove said contemptuously. "Even as a forced man there is doubt that you could escape hanging now. Not if you take up with this woman."

"And hang you will," Campbell added belligerently. "Upon my word of honor, if I ever have the chance to hang you both, that I will."

"I think that unlikely." Ward stepped in to end the debate and to speed the officers' departure. Behind him the men murmured restlessly.

Campbell rubbed his swollen bruised jaw. "Well, Captain, I'll warn you that this Gilchrist often fails his orders, but 'tis just as well. Now one of your own will lead ye to me."

Ward gave an uneasy glance at the yardarm. "Don't think to cause distrust among my crew, Campbell. That man is hanged already."

"Is he indeed?" Campbell replied. "Then surely --" There was a thud as a knife struck the colonel's chest and he dropped to the deck. The crew was in an uproar. Some cheered while others stood amazed. Darcy strode to the fo'c'sle and met the doctor as he came to the deck to investigate the noise.

"I want the man who threw that found!" Ward ordered over the din. "Find him!"

"Don't ye dare think to punish 'im," shouted one pirate.

"Aye, or we'll make him captain in your stead," added another.

Gilchrist hurriedly pushed his former commander and the remaining six men to the side where they climbed down into the longboat. Gilchrist cast them off, saying, "Get you gone, sir, and good luck to you all." As he watched the boat pull away he saw Hargrove bestow a grudging smile.

Anne stood over Patrick as he examined the fallen colonel. "Is he dead?" she asked.

"Aye, as dead as any cod." Patrick rose.

"Who has done this against my orders?" Ward demanded, turning to the crew. Again there was an angry murmur through the crew.

"'Twas Luther what done it," yelled one man, "and a good thing, too!"

Jubilee came forward with Luther, dragging him by the arm and dropping him in front of Captain Ward and Anne. "I finds him in the sail locker," the African said. "Him hide."

"So, men," Ward said, "if it be such a good thing Luther has done, then why does he hide himself like a guilty dog?" This brought some thought to the men and they looked at Luther expectantly. "Luther Devlin," Ward said, "did you not hear me when I said that no prisoner was to be harmed?"

"I was all night below at the pumps," Luther explained as he rose to his feet.

"Even so," Anne said, "you know that our articles give all prisoners to the captain's care. You have heard my father give that order. You have heard John Ward give that order. You have heard me give that order."

"I don't take orders from no woman," Luther grinned as the crew laughed.

"Well, you do take orders from me," Ward said hotly, "or at least you had better!" He struck Luther a mighty blow across the face, knocking him to the deck.

"There is no call for that," Jonathan said sharply. "Luther did naught but kill a royal swine."

"Silence!" Ward's deep eyes flashed in his lined face as he looked at the men around him. "Now, I do not give a damn for the life of the colonel and would rather see him in hell -- the sooner the better -- but I'll be blasted if I will see my orders go unheeded." Ward drew his sword. "Now, by Christ, if ye want to mutiny ye must deal with me first." The men nearest him stepped back respectfully. He turned again to Luther who had not risen from the deck. "What prompted you to kill a prisoner to whom I had given safe conduct?"

"'Twas for Judas," Luther declared getting to his feet. "'E was my friend and because of this man Campbell, poor Judas was tempted and turned spy. 'E was never so strong for all 'is prayers." There were sympathetic mutterings from the men and many understanding nods. Even Ward seemed persuaded.

"Strange that I do not recall this man Judas," Gilchrist said, stepping forward.

"Campbell was --" Suddenly Luther caught sight of the young officer, a man he had not seen since a night in Bideford. "You swore to secrecy! Upon your honor!"

"And I have kept my word, at great cost, I might add," Gilchrist replied. "But you have as much as admitted knowing me."

Luther shook his head. "I don't know you. Ne'er seen you before in my life."

"Now that is a lie," Darcy said. "You know well enough that you were with me and poor Jones when this man and the colonel approached us in the Red Cock with gold and said they were looking for some rebels."

"Perhaps that once," Luther admitted, "but I 'ave ne'er seen this man since."

"Your memory fails you," Gilchrist said.

"'Ow shall I remember every royal lackey that crosses my path?" There was sporadic applause.

"Well, I recall rightly enough," Gilchrist said. "You came to the colonel's lodgings the night following."

"'Tis lies, I say," Luther pleaded. "All lies!"

"I cannot say who betrayed Simon Hawkwood and Doctor Hartley in Plymouth, nor who told the fleet where the *Chanticleer* lay careened, but," Gilchrist looked at Anne, "I was there when Jamie was sold and this is the merchant here."

There was considerable outcry amongst the crew. Some still supported the popular bo'sun, but others bellowed for blood. Anne and Ward stared intently at Luther.

"But your brother was a traitor himself," argued Jonathan. "Forgive me for saying so, Cap'n Anne, but what is Jamie Hawkwood to us?"

"Because if Luther can sell one man, he can sell another," Ward retorted.

"And I say this royal popinjay lies!" Luther rasped, pointing at Gilchrist. Anger and hatred marred his features, causing the cross-shaped scar to burn with livid prominence. "'E'll say most anything to save 'is skin and win the wench."

Gilchrist turned to Anne. "I wish now I had spoken sooner. If I had perhaps your brother would still be alive and many others besides, including those of my old comrades."

"That is true," Anne said sadly. "In time I will forget, I suppose. As Simon might say, 'twas a bad draw of cards."

"I did not know this man Judas," Gilchrist continued, "so I cannot say what part, if any, he played in Devlin's actions. Nor can I say aught of Tristan MacDonald. Devlin did not say where he came by his information."

"I want a full confession, Devlin," Ward said. "Perhaps if I had taken time to get one from Jones, he might have proven himself innocent."

Struggling and still protesting his innocence, Luther was taken to the bow. Not far behind came two men bearing the stocky corpse of Colonel Campbell. A rope was tied around the corpse. The other end was tied around Luther, binding his arms to his sides. "What are you doing?" Luther whined as he was pushed to the foremost point of the bow.

"Fishing." Jubilee grinned as he drew his dagger and slit open the legs, wrists and belly of the dead colonel. Upon Captain Ward's command both the corpse and Luther were tossed over the bowrail so that Luther dangled on one side of the bowsprit and the corpse on the other, their feet a scant half yard above the water. Luther stared in horror at the body hanging nose to nose against his own, blood and entrails dripping into the water.

"Please," Luther begged. "'Twas Judas what done it! He hated papes." A fin appeared in the water below, then another and another. Luther danced in frantic fear. Around and around the fins swirled, inches below his feet. A huge toothy jaw opened and caught the foot of the bleeding corpse, tugging at it hungrily. "Pull me up!" Luther screamed. "I'll -- I'll confess. I did it!"

"What did you do?" Anne called down.

"I took that young Scot," Luther gasped, his eyes bulging. "I beat the truth out of 'im and told the colonel."

"And then you murdered him." Anne's voice was passionless.

"I 'ad to. 'E would've talked." Luther jerked his feet up and away as another jaw opened beneath him. "'E was a pape and no kin. 'E didn't matter."

"You betrayed Simon Hawkwood and Doctor Hartley in Plymouth," Ward accused.

"Aye!" Luther howled. "Golding promised me some papers and I -- pull me up! I swear 'twill ne'er 'appen again!"

"If ever you spoke truth, the last statement was," Ward said.

"And the *Chanticleer*?" Anne's voice was strangely predatory and those who knew her best could see the rise of the old beast in her dark circled eyes.

"Campbell said 'e'd kill me if I didn't tell 'im where ye was careening. I 'ad to, don't ye see?!"

Anne leaned further over the bow to view the macabre spectacle. "And the shot that killed my brother came from this ship." She seemed in a trance as she gazed down on the two bodies, marionettes dancing above a sea of sharks drawn by the fresh kill. Slowly her hand closed around a smooth wooden haft. Soundlessly she lifted the axe. "And I was to be next," she whispered.

Luther screamed. "I am your brother--" There was a sharp snap as the axe blade severed the rope and a strangled cry as both living and dead plummeted into the sea, vanishing in a frenzy of fins and foam.

"You 'ave no right to execute on this ship, mistress," said a blunt voice behind her. There was chorus of agreement.

She did not turn to face the crew who stared at her in horrified amazement. "Forgive me for being so bold," she said so softly that only John Ward heard her. He nodded and took her arm. "Of my blood, for my blood," she muttered as Ward escorted her from the bow. As Gilchrist came to her side, Anne said to Ward, "I should warn the men not to bathe in these waters for a time. I understand there are sharks here."

Even as the men laughed Anne sank into Gilchrist's arms, unconscious.

Anne awoke in the cabin, Gilchrist sitting beside her. Patrick was laying a cold cloth on her forehead. "What happened?"

"You fainted," Patrick answered. "You must rest, Anne. That was a heavy blow you took yesterday and there has been so much excitement as well."

The gentle creak and roll of the ship surprised her. "Under sail? Tortuga?"

"Not yet," Gilchrist said. "Captain Ward though we might retake the *Chanticleer*." She nodded, pressing the cloth against her brow as she sat up.

"Ah, no you don't, Anne Hawkwood," Patrick scolded, pushing her back against the pillows. "I want you to rest -- at least until the time comes to take the *Chanticleer*. I know there will be no way to keep you abed once there is action to be had."

They stood on the Jamaican hillside and looked down at the fresh grave. The crudely carved stone bore a representation of a bird of prey and the name Hawkwood. An older grave lay nearby.

"I had thought Father's grave lost in the earthquake last year," Anne said soberly. Gilchrist put his arm around her. "Here the Hawkwoods lie."

"Such melancholy does not become you, love," Gilchrist replied. He glanced down at the water where the *Chanticleer* rode at anchor beside the *Bold Cockerel*. "We daren't stay long, Anne. Soon word will reach the governor to take us on sight."

"I know," Anne sighed. "'Of my blood, for my blood.' I had never given those words much thought until this week past. Here lie my father and one brother. Simon is so caught up in thoughts of his own death that I fear he seeks it and I will never see him again. Eben is most likely another brother. We could be twins but for our different mothers. But he must return to England, where I might never go again." She looked out over the sea.

"I do not think that young man will ever truly like me, so I cannot say that I grieve to see him go," Gilchrist admitted, "but I do understand how you will miss him."

"Like losing a part of myself," Anne replied, turning away from the graves.

Gilchrist hesitated, then asked, "Anne, was Luther Devlin a Hawkwood?"

"He believed so," she answered. "He might well have been. Father never denied bedding Devlin's mother. I should have foreseen the consequences of Devlin's fantasy, his envy of those Father favored." Seeing the question in her lover's eyes, she explained, "Oh, Father was good to him, although not as with me and Simon or even Eben. Luther came to light too late for schooling and such refinements. But Father gave him preferment among the crew and he was very popular. Then came that business with a man called Richards. Luther's affection for him put Mad Jack in a foul humor, said he'd never acknowledge a sodomite as kin. I could never see that it mattered one way or t'other, but Father set different standards for kin and for crew. Then Richards took a notion to have me and Father had him killed." She paused and looked shyly at her hands. "That is why I did not cry out when you first seized me in the cabin. I didn't want that to happen again."

"My thanks," Gilchrist replied, with a grateful smile.

"I suppose Luther waited all these years for his revenge on us all. If anything I should be surprised that he waited so long." She shuddered, then laughed. "Do you realize that I must go the rest of my life looking in each port for my father's possible progeny? There was always some brothel, some merchant's wife or daughter -- and I dare say, some convents -- that have seen the planting of my father's seed. It could well be a world full of Hawkwoods." She stared out over the sparkling water. "'And other seed fell upon good ground, and did yield fruit that sprang and increased; and brought forth, some thirty, and some sixty, and some an hundred'."

"If it isn't a world full of Hawkwoods, then we shall make it one." Gilchrist gave her a loving hug as they walked down the hill toward the harbor.

EPILOGUE

AN EPITAPH

Cover his head with turf or stone,
'Tis all one, 'tis all one,
With turf or stone, 'tis all one. a round

March 1710

"Health and long life to our sovereign Queen Anne, and confusion to the French," toasted the lawyer grandly as he raised his glass of wine in salute.

The youth opposite him followed, smiling shyly as he drank. From below could be heard the laughter and songs in the Red Cock's common room, but the upper chamber was quiet and empty except for the two men. The lawyer was dressed in a dark suit of fashionable cut, his laces and ribbons neatly pressed and tied. His wig of cascading white powdered curls were an odd contrast to his dark eyes and swarthy complexion, just as his velvet kneebreeches appeared strange tied over his wooden left leg.

"We have been a long time seeking you," the lawyer said.

"I do not see why, Mister Carr," the youth answered, his eyes following the lawyer's every move. "I have never left Bideford in all my years."

"Then you know something of the Hawkwood family."

"Who in these parts does not?" The youth pushed back a straying titian curl. "Famous criminals some of them."

"Some of them," Carr answered noncommittally sipping his wine.

"I know that the Widow Hawkwood lives on at that big house and is never seen," the youth went on with growing relish. "There is talk about her."

"She is a harmless old woman, a bit mad with loneliness and grief, 'tis all," Carr responded, shifting in his chair. "But 'twas she who asked that you be found. Ever since her solicitor, the late Hugo Stone, took me for a partner, she has asked that we look for you. And here you are, under our very noses the entire time."

"I think you had best explain all this, Mister Carr," the youth said impatiently. "Who am I that the great and infamous Hawkwood family would take such interest?"

He rose, drawing out his pipe, and limped heavily to the fire. "Who are you indeed?" Carr smiled.

"The bastard son of a long dead tavern maid," the boy answered. "Brought up by a blind woman who begs by her harp and a shoemaker. Am I still of such importance?"

"What do you remember of your mother?" Carr asked, lighting his pipe.

The boy looked wistful and sighed. "But little. She died of drink when I was five. Her name was Jenny and she was very beautiful."

"And your father?" Carr looked at him probingly.

The boy stiffened, his deep eyes narrowing. "Why do you ask about him?"

"He is of importance to you, is he not?" Carr asked. "What did your mother say of him?"

"She never mentioned him, and she beat me whenever I spoke of him or dared to ask about him."

Carr nodded thoughtfully, smoke wreathing his dark features. "Yes, that is quite understandable." He stood by the window and looked out over the streets of Bideford. "It all began here in this room of this tavern."

"Will you kindly speak plain, Mister Carr," the boy pleaded.

"My apologies," Carr answered absently. "A bad habit acquired during my apprenticeship with Lawyer Stone. Very well then, to begin -- you are Benjamin O'Hara, son of Jenny O'Hara, deceased."

Carr returned to the table and sat, drawing several yellowed papers from inside his coat. "This," he said, selecting one, "is the last will and testament of John Hawkwood, commonly known as 'Mad Jack.' This," he held up another paper, "is the last will of his eldest son, Simon Hawkwood, who was hanged as a highwayman but a few weeks after your birth. Simon Hawkwood died a pauper, having been disinherited in favor of his sister Anne upon his arrest. His father had made a later will, leaving all the property to his daughter and it was only upon Simon's arrest that this will came to light. Still, Simon Hawkwood felt that he did have something to pass on to his only heir."

"And what has this to do with me?"

"Because, my boy, you are Simon Hawkwood's true and legitimate son." Carr noted the stunned look on the youth's face. "He married your mother shortly after she discovered she was pregnant by him. Later she changed your surname to hers and told you nothing of your father, but 'twas not from shame of his robberies. No, I would wager 'twas from shame over her part in his death."

"How so?" Benjamin's voice was barely a whisper.

"I shall speak the plain truth to you, Benjamin." Carr's face tightened, revealing remains of his renegade sparkle under the lines of maturity. "Your mother thought that Simon fancied another woman, and so for a pocketful of coin, she sold him to the soldiers."

"No," Benjamin protested, "I don't believe you."

"She was mad with jealousy and once it was done it could not be undone." Carr paused as memory overtook him. "I was but newly back from the Indies where I had lost my leg. The doctor who accompanied me was a great friend of your father's. He was with Simon when the soldiers came. Doctor Hartley managed to escape, but your father was taken. 'Twas a year before he was hanged."

"And did he -- did he die well?" Benjamin asked.

"Very well and with much dignity," Carr answered. "I was there, being then but a few years older than you are now. Crippled as I was, I sat in the carriage with Lawyer Stone who had tried every legal -- and some not so legal -- means to win your father's life. Unfortunately, a similar effort had been made once before to save your Uncle Jamie and the law has a long memory." Carr paused and looked into the youth's sober face. "Small comfort though it is, lad, I have never seen any condemned man conduct himself better. 'Twas as if he were well practiced in the art."

Benjamin sat back and thought for a moment. "Well, I can hardly mourn a man fifteen years dead. But how is it that you could not find me?"

"Your mother left Bideford for a time right after Simon's arrest and did not return until long after he was hanged. We knew of you, of course, but thought only to look for a dark haired child. For some reason we never thought you might take after your pretty mother. 'Twas Blind Kate who broke the secret a few weeks ago, coming to the Rookery to tell us that you had not perished as we had thought, but were alive and apprenticed to the shoemaker. She wanted to better your lot. We made the appropriate inquiries and verified that you are indeed the son of Simon Hawkwood."

"And this will of my father's?"

"He died penniless, as I have said," Carr explained. "The widow who currently holds the property does so as a matter of courtesy. Our researches have proved that her marriage to the late captain, your grandfather, was of the irregular Scots variety -- perfectly acceptable in Scotland, but of dubious legality here in England. The true heir is Anne Hawkwood, your aunt, but she is quite happy with her life in Carolina and has no desire to manage the family trade here in Devon. I have taken over that management, but I am nigh to forty and have but the one peg. 'Tis time a legitimate Hawkwood worthy of the name was found to take charge of the Rookery."

"And the will?" Benjamin asked impatiently.

"Aye, of course." Carr opened the tattered paper. "'To my child by Jenny O'Hara, I leave all my worldly possessions such as they are, to wit: the name of Hawkwood, being all that I have left after my wild ways and women have stripped me of my very life. Do not mourn the father you never knew, but look for the good in all your kin, and your kin in everyone. Done this sixth day of January, 1695 in Newgate Prison'."

There was a long silence as Benjamin stared at the paper, then at the lawyer, and finally out to the streets. At last the boy said, "What exactly is this family trade?"

Carr smiled warmly, feeling an exuberant glow all the way down to his wooden leg. "Your Aunt Anne and Uncle Philip will doubtless explain it in greater detail when they arrive in the summer, their first visit here in some fifteen years and all to see you." His eyes glinted slyly. "Suffice it to say that it is the merchant trade -- the import, export and transfer of foreign and domestic goods."

"It sounds very respectable," Benjamin said, refilling his glass.

"Oh, it is, lad, it is. Very respectable indeed."

Printed in the United States
By Bookmasters